Praise for *A Doomful of Sugar*

"A likable protagonist and a sweet-as-maple-syrup setting are just part of the appeal. *A Doomful of Sugar* is more than a mystery, it's an engaging tale about family and the twisted paths that lead us home."

—Julie Mulhern, *USA Today* bestselling author of the Country Club Murders

"Filled with food, family, and murder, first in series *A Doomful of Sugar* by Catherine Bruns is a Vermont-set winner."

—Lynn Cahoon, *New York Times* bestselling author of *Secrets in the Stacks*, a Survivors' Book Club mystery

"*A Doomful of Sugar* is a delightfully decadent maple-infused mystery to die for! Bruns pens a smart multilayered puzzler in this first in a series that is sure to become a reader favorite!"

—Jenn McKinlay, *New York Times* bestselling author

Also by Catherine Bruns

A DOOMFUL OF SUGAR

A Maple Syrup Mystery

CATHERINE BRUNS

Poisoned Pen
PRESS

Published by Poisoned Pen Press, an imprint of Sourcebooks
P.O. Box 4410, Naperville, Illinois 60567-4410
(630) 961-3900
sourcebooks.com

Printed and bound in the United States of America.
KP 10 9 8 7 6 5 4 3 2 1

For my grandfather

CHAPTER ONE

THE YELLOW AND ORANGE LEAVES swirled around in a light breeze as if they were dancing, then slowly fluttered to the ground for their finale. As I sat by the window watching them, I couldn't help thinking what a shame it was that Florida had no change in seasons. How I'd missed autumn and my hometown.

Sugar Ridge, Vermont, was situated on a mountain near the New York border with a population of about five thousand people. The main attraction in our small town was Sugar Lake, a large body of water that adjoined the park and beach and was constantly bustling with tourists during the summer. Swimming and boating were in season then, while ice fishing and skiing were enjoyed during winter months.

"Nature at work" was what my father called the beautiful fall foliage. I smiled as an image of him came to mind. He'd always had a story or a thoughtful musing about every subject under the sun. For a man who hadn't even graduated from high school, he was the wisest person I'd ever known.

The first real memory I had of Dad was from twenty-four years ago. I had recently turned four and was playing in the sandbox with my younger brother, Simon. We'd been given strict orders to stay clean, since my aunt and uncle were coming for Sunday dinner. I was wearing a new pink and white gingham dress that I'd loathed. I almost laughed out loud, recalling how much I'd hated that dress. Too many frills for my taste, plus it had itched.

Maybe I'd been feeling the injustice of the world that day, even at the tender age of four. More than likely, I'd been envious that Simon had been allowed to sample the *maamoul* cookies our mother had baked for dessert, while I'd been told to wait. Whatever the reason, my little blue pail full of sand somehow wound up on Simon's head.

Simon had screamed so loud that the neighbors must have thought I'd been performing some unique type of torture. After my mother had grounded me from television and sandboxes for an entire week, she took Simon upstairs to clean him up, and I'd been left alone with my father. I wasn't worried about him yelling. My father never yelled. He was the only one who understood me.

Once Mom and Simon were out of sight, my father had reached down and scooped me up in his strong arms. He was a big man—not overweight, but solid and over six feet tall, with prematurely graying hair at the temple and large dark eyes that twinkled constantly. My father had carried me out to his work shed and sat me down on the bench. He'd reached into one of the drawers and turned around to face me, both hands balled into fists.

"Pick one, *habibi*," he said. The word meant "my love" in his native Arabic language.

I always picked his right hand and was never disappointed. My father uncurled his fingers to reveal a piece of maple candy in a plastic wrapper and smiled while I squealed in delight. He knew how much I loved them and always brought home pieces for Simon and me to sample, while my mother watched with disapproval. She complained that it made us bounce off the walls.

The maple candy pieces were thick and creamy—and deliciously sweet. It was the cure to my distress that day. My father always knew the remedy to make me feel better. The candy was made at Dad's farm, Sappy Endings, which he had bought that same year, consisting of over 300 acres with approximately 5,000 maple trees. Dad had decided not only to make and sell his own syrup but to feature a café and a gift shop with other homemade gifts such as candles, maple sugar, and, of course, my favorite, the candy.

Back then, I'd had no idea of the blood, sweat, and tears that had gone into the farm. My parents were no strangers to hard work. It wasn't until I was in my twenties that I'd discovered Mom and Dad had spent the first two years in business working around the clock just to keep their heads above water. Their hard work had finally paid off, and Sappy Endings had become one of the top producers of maple syrup in the entire state.

"I want to go to work with you," I'd told him that day. "It's boring here. Mommy makes me help her in the kitchen and I hate it." It was always a treat to go to Sappy Endings and watch him work, especially during sap gathering season in late winter.

He'd given me a kiss on the forehead. "When you are bigger, Leila, I promise." He spread his arms out wide. "Then you will run the entire business, like me."

"Yes, I want to be boss!"

My father had laughed as he picked me up and hugged me tightly against him. His arms were my safe place. I'd always known I was his pet and reveled in it, in much the same way that Simon was my mother's.

"There are great things in store for you, my little one," my father had told me that day. "Remember that you can do anything you want. Never let anyone take away your dreams."

At the time, I hadn't fully understood what he'd meant, but now, as I looked back, it was apparent that he'd had a plan for me. My mother did, too, but hers was much different. After they could afford to hire help, my mother had taken a step back from the business and stopped managing the café. She still did some of the baking but always from her house because she wanted to devote more time to her children and home.

As a teenager, I'd worked summers at Sappy Endings by waiting on customers in the café or ringing up purchases in the gift shop. It had been a relief to be away from my mother, as we'd fought constantly. She had realized early on that I had no desire to be her mini-me. I preferred to have my nose in a book instead of baking baklava or maple doughnuts and crocheting in the evenings. Perhaps it was best that I'd left, but now I regretted the lost time with my father even more.

"Leila, did you hear what I said?"

"Huh?" I turned away from the window with a start.

My best friend, Heather, was standing at the edge of the leather sofa, watching me intently. She pushed her ash blond hair back from her face and sipped her coffee. Heather and I had been friends since the first grade and were kindred spirits. We'd always stuck together like maple syrup and butter, but she was my total opposite where looks were concerned. While I had ebony-colored hair, dark eyes, and a Mediterranean complexion, Heather had been blessed with peaches and cream skin and eyes the color of a cloudless sky.

She frowned. "I said maybe I should wait outside. This is only for family, after all."

"You're family to me," I insisted. "Besides, my mother won't mind." Then again, Theo Martin, my father's attorney, probably would. We were sitting in his office waiting for him and my mother and brother to arrive. Theo was an affable guy, but everything was by the book with him. It was likely he'd refuse to let Heather stay for the reading of my father's will.

She flopped down on the sofa next to me. "When are you going back to Florida?"

"I don't know. In a couple of days, I guess." As much as I loved my family and Vermont, I couldn't wait to return to

Florida. This had been the most difficult week of my life, and I needed some type of normalcy, especially after the shocking news I'd received.

Ten days earlier, my brother, Simon, had called me with the horrifying news that our father's lifeless body had been found inside his office at Sappy Endings. He'd been shot and left for dead.

After the initial trauma had worn off, I became convinced that Dad had been killed for the money in the safe and registers. A robbery gone wrong. It wasn't clear how much they'd gotten away with, but it couldn't have been much. Most of my father's customers paid by credit card. There probably wasn't more than a few hundred dollars in the till. The mere thought made me physically ill.

This type of crime didn't happen in my hometown. I knew these people. They were kind and considerate, like my father. They helped one another and cared about their neighbors. If my students had asked me to name one of the safest towns in the United States, I would have answered Sugar Ridge, Vermont, without hesitation.

Now the joke was on me.

Heather eyed the box of chocolate chip cookies Theo's secretary had placed on the coffee table. She reached for one, then pulled her hand away. After a second thought, she grabbed two and stuffed one whole in her mouth. "I've got to stop eating or I'll never fit into my wedding dress."

"You've still got six months to go. Besides, you don't need to lose any weight." Heather's figure was curvy in all the right places, and she looked like a million bucks.

She let out a groan. "Easy for you to say. I'd kill to be your size." As the words left her lips, she winced. "Oh, Leila, I'm sorry. Dumb things have a way of flying out of my mouth."

"It's okay." I placed my head in my hands. "I just can't seem to wrap my head around this."

Heather put an arm around my shoulders. "Do the police have any idea who might have done it? Has Simon heard any rumors at the newspaper?"

I shook my head. "No, but the police have been great about keeping us informed. They think only one person was involved, and it may have been someone who knew the layout of the building well, since Dad was there after hours—alone. And they knew where he kept the—" I broke off and shuddered. "Why would they kill such a wonderful man? For a few lousy hundreds?"

Heather pursed her lips together tightly. "People kill for far less these days, Lei. Maybe your father gave them a hard time about handing the money over."

"Maybe." No matter what we surmised might have happened, the end result remained the same. Victor Khoury, a well-loved and respected citizen of Sugar Ridge, was gone. He had been a selfless person who had worked hard his entire life and come to this country from Lebanon as a teenager. He'd had next to nothing back then but still would have given you the shirt off his back.

A powerfully built man with sandy colored hair opened the door and smiled warmly at us, sweeping into the room. He set his leather briefcase on top of the walnut desk. "How are we doing, ladies?"

"Heather, do you know Theo Martin?" I asked. "Theo, this is my best friend, Heather Turcot."

Heather studied him for a moment and held out her hand. "No, not personally but I know your name, of course."

"Nice to meet you," Theo said politely. He'd been my father's tax and estate planning attorney since Sappy Endings had opened. Although Theo was several years younger than my father, they'd struck up an immediate friendship a few years after my dad had opened the farm. Theo was an avid golf and tennis player who enjoyed the social scene—all things that my father had detested. They didn't have much in common, but, as the old saying went, opposites did attract.

"Would you like me to leave?" Heather asked.

Theo's face grew stern. "I hate to ask, Heather, but I'm a stickler about these kinds of things. Only family is allowed for the reading, I'm afraid. Once Selma and Simon arrive, I'll have to ask you to go."

To be honest, I hadn't even thought about the will's contents. I assumed everything would go to my mother, as it should. Of course I wanted some keepsakes of my father's, some photos and perhaps the trumpet he often played, if Mom was okay with it. I didn't know what would happen to Sappy Endings and assumed she'd sell.

Heather squeezed my hand and rose to her feet. "No worries. I totally understand. I was just keeping Leila company until you showed up." She turned back to me. "Do you want me to wait in the car or meet you at the house?"

I glanced at my watch. "I'd rather ride back with you if that's okay. Then we can join my family for dinner. Mom's been cooking up a storm all day."

She gave me a wistful smile. "Every occasion in your family calls for a huge Lebanese dinner. Nothing made your father happier than to see everyone eating in his house."

A laugh bubbled near the surface. "You did know him well." Neither one of us would ever forget the time my father insisted that she dine with us at Thanksgiving, even though Heather had already eaten dinner at her own house. The thought of my father heaping spiced rice with almonds and pine nuts onto her plate with game chicken and kibbe still made me smile.

"The reading will only take a few minutes," Theo assured her.

Heather slung her purse over her shoulder. "No worries. I've got my friend Instagram to keep me company." She nodded to Theo. "Nice meeting you."

"Take care." Theo waited until Heather had shut the door behind her, then settled onto the couch next to me. His dark blue suit was perfectly pressed without a wrinkle and suited his professional demeanor. "How are you holding up, Leila?"

I wiggled my hand back and forth. "To be honest, I'm numb. It still feels like a bad dream."

Theo's expression was grim. "Shock, most likely. I've been there myself. Your mother's doing better than I expected, though. Everyone knows how much your parents loved each other."

"She's a tough cookie." At the age of fifty-eight, Selma Khoury looked as fragile as a China doll but was built of sturdier material. Somehow, someway, she'd get through this.

Theo rose to his feet and extracted a folder from his briefcase. "She rarely works at the farm anymore, correct?"

"Yes, not at all. She still bakes for the café but prefers to do it from home." Years ago, my mother had also handled the books for Sappy Endings but made no effort to disguise the fact that she didn't care for it. Mom was much happier at home as the perfect wife and mother. She'd raised two polite children, kept her house spotlessly clean, and always had dinner waiting on the table for my father. She was the Donna Reed of the twenty-first century, minus the pearls.

"I don't know what's going to happen to the farm." The words fell out of my mouth before I could stop them. "Mom needs the money it brings in, but, with no one to run things, I suppose we'll have to sell."

Theo stroked his chin thoughtfully. "There are people to run the farm, Leila; it's just that no one in your family cares to. It will all work out. Your father was a planner, remember? One of the things I admired most about him."

A tap sounded on the door, and Theo opened it for my mother, followed by Simon. Mom looked like she'd aged ten years in as many days. Her ebony-colored hair was tinged with streaks of gray that I didn't remember seeing before. Mom's dark eyes, always her most striking feature, were large and round in her peaked face.

Simon was tall like our father, with the same broad shoulders. At twenty-six, he was handsome in a dark and brooding manner, with the same ebony-colored hair as mine, piercing dark eyes, and an adorable dimple on the left side of his mouth. He lowered himself into a plush armchair across from me while Mom joined me on the sofa.

I immediately covered her hand with mine. "Would you like anything, Mom? Some water, maybe?"

She twisted a lace handkerchief between her fingers that my father had given her years ago and smiled at me. "No, thank you, Leila." She then stared up at Theo, who moved toward the center of the room, envelope in hand. "We're ready whenever you are."

I marveled at her self-control, but, then again, she'd been raised with that trait. Her parents had been strict, from the old country, and conservative. She and my father had loved each other, but public displays of affection were few and far between. It was simply the way they were raised.

My mother and I had never had a warm and fuzzy relationship, but things had taken a turn for the worse after my engagement to Mark Salem had fallen apart, and it still held some of those scars.

My parents had known the Salem family in Lebanon. They'd encouraged the Salems to settle in Vermont, and it wasn't long before my mother was arranging a marriage between their son and me. Mark was handsome, respectful, and on his way to becoming a successful attorney. I had no desire to have my life dictated by mother, but before I knew it, I'd fallen in love with Mark, and him with me. Or so I'd thought. A month before our wedding, he broke off the engagement. My heart had been crushed into tiny pieces, and the only logical solution to me was to leave Vermont.

My father had begged me to stay, but I told him I wanted to start over elsewhere. On the other hand, my mother had been furious, certain that the breakup was my fault. She'd wanted details of why the engagement had ended, and I'd refused to tell her anything. After I left Vermont, we didn't speak until I returned home for Christmas several months later, and, even then, only when necessary. Over the next three years, we learned to tolerate each other.

Theo unfolded the piece of paper in his hands and coughed. "I'll admit that I was surprised to learn that Victor had made a new will, Selma. He never breathed a word of it to me."

Simon leaned forward in his seat. "Whoa. Dad made a new will?"

My mother nodded. "Only last month. He didn't want anyone else to know, so he had a lawyer from New York draw it up. The attorney's wife and I were the only witnesses." She glanced sheepishly at Theo. "I think it was a spur-of-the-moment thing."

Theo looked none too pleased. "Well, Victor certainly was known for doing spur-of-the-moment things, and, of course, it was well within his right. But I do wish that he'd consulted me first. That's what I get paid for. Anyhow, let's proceed." He paused for a few seconds. "'I, Victor Khoury, being of sound mind and body, hereby direct my Executor to pay all of my debts and funeral expenses as soon as practical after my death.'"

We all knew that my father had selected Theo as executor of his estate, and my mother was more than happy to leave the matter to him. The will was straightforward. My mother had been left the house, which was already paid off, along with Dad's personal possessions. There was also a stipulation that the Maronite Catholic Church, which he and my mother had faithfully attended for years, receive a substantial donation in his memory.

Then it was my turn.

"To my beloved daughter, Leila Maya Khoury, I leave my farm, Sappy Endings, for her to run as she sees fit."

Three sets of eyes fixed on me, waiting for my reaction. I blinked—once, then twice. I must have heard Theo wrong. For the first time since learning the news about my father, I began to laugh, while everyone continued to stare at me with blank expressions.

"He wasn't serious," I protested.

My mother watched me anxiously. "Yes, it's true, Leila. Your father left the business to you. He wants you to be in charge of Sappy Endings. It was his greatest wish."

No. There had to be some mistake. My heart sank into the pit of my stomach. This simply couldn't be happening to me.

CHAPTER TWO

"WHY?" I FINALLY MANAGED TO say.

Everyone remained silent, and I was forced to speak again. "I can't do this. I already have a job in Florida. Fifteen hundred miles away. I teach high school, remember?"

My mother spoke in her usual demure tone. "Yes, Leila. We all know how much you enjoy teaching." Her eyes gazed into mine until my face began to heat like the burners on a stove top. Mom's perception never ceased to amaze me. How did she know? I'd never said anything to my parents about being unhappy with my job.

She continued. "Your father always thought that you were making a huge mistake by leaving here."

"Yes, I know," I said wearily. "He told me so, several times."

Simon spoke up. "Personally, I think you should sell the farm. How can you possibly handle all that?"

"Jessica takes great care of the café, so that's one less thing for me to worry about." Jessica Fowler was about my mother's age, a warm and kind woman whom we considered family. She did all the food preparation for the café, and, even though there weren't endless menu items, she still had enough to keep her busy.

"Yeah, but Dad's shoes will be hard to fill. He stepped in wherever he was needed, remember. Plus, there's the finances, ordering supplies, and about a half a million other jobs. It's a lot for anyone to take on," Simon explained. "I'm sorry that you can't count on me. Remember, I already have a full-time job."

The words might have sounded harsh, but my brother didn't beat around the bush. Like my mother and me, Simon and Dad had never seen eye to eye on anything. Simon had been the one to suffer the brunt of Dad's expectations. When he'd dared to profess his distaste for the business as a teenager, it had not gone over well. My father had hoped that both of us would follow in his footsteps one day. Dad and Simon argued incessantly, which my mother often said was the result of the stubborn gene that rooted itself in all Lebanese men.

As for me, I was also headstrong, but being Daddy's little girl, I'd received more leniency. I'd actually enjoyed working summers at Sappy Endings. Simon had once bitterly told me after a heated argument with our father that, "Daddy's princess could do no wrong." The words had stung.

When Simon announced his plans to become a journalist, Dad hadn't been pleased. He couldn't understand

Simon's love of the written word any more than Simon could appreciate Dad's love for the farm. With his son out of the picture, my father had started to rely more heavily on me each summer. When I'd accepted the job in Florida, he'd tried to talk me out of it. My father claimed it was too dangerous to work in public schools these days. Come back to the store and he'd make it worthwhile. Working there would be much safer, he'd insisted.

Oh, the horrible irony.

Theo's face took on a neutral expression. "There's another clause included in this will that stipulates you only have to run the business for one year. At that time, if you no longer feel it's a good fit, you can choose to sell and split the profit with the rest of your family." He looked up at me. "A year isn't a long time, Leila."

Forget the year. Who said I was a good fit at all? Sure, I'd spent summers working here and watched my father carry out his business daily, but that didn't mean I could do it alone, or that I even wanted to. In fact, the thought of running Sappy Endings by myself was downright terrifying. *Dad, how could you do this to me?* I wanted to scream in frustration. Why did Father always think he knew best? I also didn't like being forced into anything, and my father had known that as well.

"I—I need to digest this," I said honestly. "What happens if I say no?" *Was that even an option?*

The silence in the room was so loud that you could have heard one of my mother's hairpins drop. She patted my hand stiffly. "Of course, you have your own life to

consider. Perhaps we could ask Noah if he's still interested in buying the place. He's been running things since
Daddy's death. But it's only him and Jessica there now to
take care of everything. Once sugaring season starts, the
place will need more help."

Noah Rivers was a complete stranger to me. He'd
been employed at Sappy Ending since sometime last
spring. I knew nothing about him, save the fact that Dad
had raved he was a wonderful worker and a fellow sugar
maker. "I don't remember seeing him at the wake," I said.
"Did he show up?"

Simon nodded, his deep voice reverberating through
the thin walls. "He was there, but only for a few minutes.
I think you were in the back room with Heather at the
time. He didn't come to the funeral. The farm's been busy,
plus he's taken over the candle making, so he told Mom he
figured he'd be more use there."

"Wait a second. If Dad liked Noah, why didn't he sell
the farm to him?" I asked.

"Your father wanted it to stay in the family," Mom
explained. "He was very clear about that, Leila. But it
wouldn't be practical when you have another career already."

She spoke the words stiffly, and I knew what she
wouldn't say out loud. My mother wasn't thrilled about me
being in charge of Sappy Endings. She must have tried to
talk my father out of it. She preferred to see me married
with a minivan full of kids rather than running a business.

What exactly *had* my father been thinking? I thought
he understood that I wanted to live my own life. Didn't

parents encourage their children to follow their dreams? Of course things hadn't worked out the way I'd expected, but I needed to be patient. I loved working with kids, especially younger ones. Unfortunately, the kindergarten teaching job I'd initially applied for had been filled before I'd even arrived for my interview in Orlando. Instead, I'd been offered a position teaching ninth graders at a private school.

I hadn't particularly wanted the job but was too embarrassed to return home. To me it would have been like admitting failure. The children were mouthy, disrespectful, and way overprivileged for my taste. I found myself filling in for a teacher on maternity leave, and once she'd returned, I was delegated to monitoring two study halls and instructing a history class. It wasn't what I'd anticipated.

"Is there any more to the will?" Simon asked, his face hopeful.

"Yes," Theo said. "I'm sorry that I got sidetracked. Your father left you a collection of baseball cards and his trumpet."

Simon said nothing, but it was obvious he'd been anticipating more.

Theo placed the document back in its envelope. "We're finished here. I know that you're anxious to get home. Selma, we can talk later. Feel free to call me whenever you like. It shouldn't take long to get this through probate."

"Thank you for everything, Theo," my mother said gratefully. "You've been very good to us. Why don't you join us for dinner? We'd love to have Laura and the boys as well."

Theo bussed her cheek. "Thanks, but Laura's out of town. And the boys are so busy with school and sports that I hardly see them myself." His face shone with pride. "Teddy's receiving a great deal of interest from some of the top colleges in the Northeast for next year."

Theo's son was a senior at the local high school. "Congratulations. Is he going to follow in his father's footsteps and go to Columbia Law School?" I asked.

Theo's chest puffed up faster than a loaf of freshly baked bread. "I'm not sure, but I'm certainly going to try my best to persuade him."

"He's a wonderful young man," my mother gushed. "Please give Laura and the boys my best when you see them."

"Will do. And Laura wanted me to tell you that, if you need anything, anything at all, we're both at your disposal, day or night." Theo's gaze shifted over to me. "Leila, take a couple of days to make your decision. The business is in good hands for now."

There was a tap on the door, and then a burly-looking man with a head of thick silver hair peered in at us. "Okay if I come in?"

Theo nodded. "Sure, Alan. We're finished now."

Police Chief Alan Crosby was the first one to arrive at the crime scene after Noah had found my father's body. He'd been my father's dearest friend for over thirty years. Chief Crosby could have long since retired from the force, but he loved his job too much. Like the rest of us, my father's death had hit him hard.

He looked around the room at all of us, his expression grim. "Sorry for the intrusion, Theo, but when I spoke to Selma earlier, she mentioned the family would be here. And this isn't something that can wait."

A chill ran through me. "What's wrong?" I asked, unsure of how many more potential shocks I could deal with today.

Chief Crosby gestured toward my mother. "Selma, maybe you'd better sit down."

Her dark eyes regarded him solemnly as she shook her head. "I'm all right, Alan. Please tell us what's happened."

Crosby blew out a breath. "One of my detectives has been going over the evidence that he found in Victor's office again. He doesn't think Victor was shot in a random holdup. He feels strongly that it was premeditated murder."

Murder. Like a Ferris wheel, the word spun around in my head. This simply couldn't be happening. I stared mutely at my mother and brother, hoping it was some type of sick joke.

"I don't understand. Why didn't you tell us about this sooner? Dad's been gone for over a week now," Simon said, anger reverberating in his tone.

Chief Crosby tugged at his whiskers. "Detective Anderson failed to write it in his initial report. He got married the next day and left on his honeymoon. When he got back yesterday, he came to my office to tell me about his screwup. I'm sorry, Selma. There's no excuse for this."

"Why does your detective think that it was premeditated, Alan?" my mother asked.

"For one thing, the registers in the gift shop and café still had money inside them," Chief Crosby explained. "Your father hadn't emptied them yet."

A chill crept up my spine. "Why would someone do that to him? No one disliked Dad." Tears started to sting my eyes. Everyone had the greatest respect for my father. He'd given to every charity imaginable, even extended credit to those in need. He was generous, kind, and had worked hard all his life, building a successful business with his own two hands. How had this been his reward?

My mother sank back down on the couch, her face pale and unreadable. Fine wrinkles had gathered around the corners of her eyes. I'd never noticed them before. They certainly hadn't been there when I'd visited last spring. Little had I known back then that it would be the last time I'd ever see my father alive.

"I had a feeling something bad might happen." My mother folded her hands primly in her lap. "Victor was acting strange for the last couple of weeks. Whenever I asked him what was wrong, he would brush it off." She tapped a finger to the side of her coiffed dark hair. "But I knew he was upset. I could always tell when he was hiding something. That's what happens when you've been married as long as we were."

Thirty-six years, to be exact. "Do you think it had to do with the farm?" I asked.

"I'm not sure," she admitted. "The night before he died, I woke up about two in the morning and saw that he hadn't come to bed yet, so I went downstairs looking for him. He was in his study, looking at something online but shut the computer down when I came in. I asked him what was wrong, but he refused to tell me."

Mom's hands began to tremble as she continued. "Victor got angry. He never acted like that. He told me to go back to bed, so I did. When I woke up in the morning, he'd already left for work." She bit her lower lip. "That was the last time I ever spoke to him. We didn't even talk on the phone that day."

My mind was racing with ideas, none that I was particularly fond of voicing, but I did so anyway. "Wasn't Noah the one to find Dad?"

"That's right." Simon furrowed his brow. "What are you getting at?"

"Noah wanted to buy Sappy Endings, and Dad refused him," I explained. "To me, that sounds like a good motive to kill someone."

My mother gasped. "Noah is a good man, Leila. He would never have done such a thing. Why, he thought the world of your father."

"We don't have any proof that it's Noah," Chief Crosby put in. "He came back to the store that night because he'd left his phone behind in the sugar shack. He noticed your father's car was still there and went to see if everything was all right. Then he called 9-1-1."

It sounded a bit too convenient to me. "Maybe he came back to confront Dad about not selling the business to him, and things turned ugly."

"So, he shot him?" My mother asked in disbelief.

"The gun wasn't found, right?" I asked Chief Crosby. "Were the entire building and the farm searched? What about the sugar shack? Noah keeps his personal items in there, right? Did you go through the place?"

Crosby almost smiled. "Leila, he'd have to be pretty stupid to hide it there. But, yes, in answer to your question, every inch of Sappy Endings was searched. The gun wasn't found. Chances are the killer took it with him."

"Why are you all defending Noah?" I asked angrily.

"Leila, please stop this," my mother begged.

"I'm not defending him." Chief Crosby spoke in his usual gruff voice. "I know this is hard for you, and it is for me, too. But you simply can't put people in jail without some type of evidence, and you can't blame the first person you think of. Everyone who was at Sappy Endings that day has been questioned—Noah, the customers, and Jessica. Trust me, okay? If it's the last thing I do, I'm going to find this son of a—"

My mother rose to her feet, clutching her purse tightly. "I think that we should go back to the house. I don't want to discuss this any further."

Chief Crosby's face sobered as he looked at her. "I'm sorry, Selma. It hurts me to be the one to tell you. Victor was like a brother to me."

She clasped his hand and smiled. "I know. He felt the same way about you."

"I'll be in touch," Chief Crosby said. "Please let me know if you need anything." He nodded to me and Simon and then let himself out.

Theo took my mother by the arm. "I'll walk you out, Selma."

She looked over at me. "Leila, are you coming with me and Simon?"

"No, Heather's waiting outside for me. I'll see you back at the house. I just need to ask Simon something about the newspaper first."

As soon as the door closed behind them, I squared off against my brother. "I want to know who did this. Maybe taking over Sappy Endings for now is a good idea. It will give me a chance to take a closer look at everyone, including that so-called prized employee of Dad's."

Simon put his hands on my shoulders. "Easy, sis. I want to find this guy as much as you do. He was my father, too, you know. Everyone seems to forget that."

"I'm sorry. Still, I don't think it would do any harm to ask customers questions and—"

"No," Simon barked. "That's the worst possible thing you could do. Do you want to alienate all the clientele? People will stop coming in for maple syrup, coffee, or souvenirs. They'll take their business elsewhere. Trust Crosby and his department. They'll find the person responsible." He paused. "I have a lot of regrets about how I left things with Dad. More than you know. Now it's too late to make them right."

The sadness in his voice devastated me. Simon was the quiet one in our family who put down on paper what he couldn't manage to say out loud.

"Come here." I was five-foot-five to his six-foot-two, so my brother stooped down to let me put my arms around him. His shoulders shook underneath my grip. After taking a few seconds to compose himself, he released me. I stood on tiptoe to kiss his cheek. "Don't blame yourself. Dad loved you. Always remember that."

"Yeah," he said gruffly, "but we all know that you were his favorite, Lei. And I'm okay with that. I just wish I hadn't been so pigheaded all the time."

"I think it runs in the family," I said gently.

Simon smiled and blinked back tears. "No doubt. Look, maybe it's not a good idea for you to become involved with the farm right now. I don't want to see something happen to you as well."

I placed my hands on my hips. "What's that supposed to mean?"

"It means that I know you and that inquisitive nature of yours. You're like me running around town trying to get a juicy story." He winked. "Forget Dad's crazy idea and sell the business. It's safer that way. Besides, Mom can use the money."

Apparently, Simon didn't know me as well as he thought. Whenever a person told me I couldn't do something, it only made me more determined to prove them wrong. "I wonder if it could have been a customer or employee who killed Dad." He'd been running Sappy Endings for twenty-four years. That was a lot of customers to consider.

Simon stared at me in amazement. "What are you saying—a customer killed Dad because he overcharged them for maple syrup? That's ridiculous."

"I don't know," I said earnestly, "but Dad must have made some enemies over the years. What about fellow competitors? You know as well as I do that there's several syrup producers in Vermont, and not all of them have had the success our father did. Problems can escalate fast, and into something else."

"There's got to be more to it," Simon insisted. "I can't believe someone wanted him dead because he was successful."

Whatever the reason, I was determined to find out. I planned to go through every sheet of paper in my father's offices, both at work and home to see if it might lead to a killer's trail.

Simon rolled his eyes at the ceiling. "Come on, Leila. I know how your mind works. Like Crosby said, let the police handle it. Maybe it's not a bad idea to have Noah continue to run Sappy Endings until Dad's killer is caught."

"No. It's settled. Dad wanted me to take over, and that's what I intend to do. All I have to do is stick it out for a year." *And find his killer.* "Don't worry. I'll be watching Noah's every move."

"Look," Simon muttered. "I know you're ready to hang this guy, but don't come right out and accuse him of anything, okay? Give him a chance to slip up on his own."

The thought of my father dying alone and helpless filled me with anger. It also made me sad, especially for my mother. Dad had talked about selling the farm in the past, but I'd never thought the day would come. He'd dreamed about buying an RV and traveling around in it with my mother, seeing the world. That would never happen now. My parents had both been robbed of their futures. In light of the new developments, I wasn't going anywhere, or at least, not until Dad's killer was found.

Simon sighed. "Guess there's no talking you out of this, huh? You're really going to do it. What about teaching? I know how much you love it."

I crossed my fingers behind my back. "Yes, but this is more important. I'll call the principal tonight and ask for a leave of absence for a year. I don't think it will be a problem. Then, bright and early Monday morning, I'll be at Sappy Endings to carry on Dad's legacy."

As for Mr. Noah Rivers, he was about to find out that the Khoury family would be sticking around at Sappy Endings, and that was no pun intended.

CHAPTER THREE

"NERVOUS?" HEATHER ASKED AS THE light turned green and she moved the car forward.

"Not a bit." It was seven thirty in the morning, and we were on our way to Sappy Endings. *My farm. My business.* A café, gift shop, and sugar shack with maple syrup production to supervise. This was a lot for me to take in, and I worried that I couldn't handle it all.

Heather had graciously offered to drive me back and forth until I got a vehicle and even mentioned us going car shopping tonight. She worked as a hairdresser, and her schedule was flexible.

Sappy Endings was only two miles from my parents' house on a private road. My father had wanted to build a house on the farm for us many years ago, but my mother had refused to consider it. She wanted to keep the business separate from our family life and was afraid

Dad might have difficulty doing so if they were next to each other.

With a sigh, I stared out at the dusky blue sky above. It was already shaping up to be a beautiful fall day, a bit on the warm side for early November, but snow and Santa were right around the corner.

We passed the town square, where the Jolly Green Grocer and Sugar Ridge Post Office stood at opposite corners from each other. I smiled when I spotted Paige Turner going into the grocery store. She always stopped there first, every morning. Some things around here never changed. In addition to being the town crier, Paige had been the town's librarian for as long as I could remember. Despite her stern nature when it came to overdue library books, she had a heart bigger than the entire state. Paige had broken down in tears at my father's wake. Sugar Ridge wouldn't be the same without Victor Khoury, she'd said sadly.

I swallowed the painful lump in my throat as Sappy Endings came into view. The red and white brick facade of the combined café and gift store building was welcoming along with the giant front windows that Jessica decorated during every changing season. A wooden sign hung from the porch, depicting a maple syrup jug and plate of pancakes with *Sappy Endings, Est. 1998* inscribed underneath. The wraparound white porch still held the summer's rocking chairs and a few wicker tables for customers to sit and enjoy their coffee and maple treats outside.

Heather placed her SUV in park and reached for her coffee that we'd grabbed earlier from The Busy Bean. I took a long sip from mine and cupped my hands around the cup, savoring its warmth. "Okay, I lied. I'm terrified."

She grinned. "You think that I don't know? Come on, girl. You'll be fine."

"I'm used to dealing with kids, Heather. This is a big change for me."

"But you've helped out here lots of times," Heather protested. "You can handle it."

"It's been four years since I last worked here. Things are different now. And what about the employees? Jessica won't give me any trouble, but Noah—who's to say that we can trust him?"

She rolled her eyes. "You haven't even met him yet."

"Have you?"

"Not personally," she admitted. Her blue eyes gleamed in the sunlight. "But I will say that he's a popular topic among the women in Sugar Ridge. I went to Paint and Sip last week, and his name was mentioned in passing. There are several eligible women in our town who'd like to get to know him better, if you catch my drift."

"He's not married?" I asked curiously.

Heather shrugged. "I don't think so. No one really knows much about him, except that he bought a little cottage over on Sweet Hollow Road a couple of months back. Now, forget about him and remember who's boss, okay? Do he and Jessica even know that you'll be here today?"

I opened the car door. "No idea. My mother told Jessica I'd be in sometime this week. It's none of their business, anyway."

"Hey, don't get so defensive." She regarded me solemnly. "I'm worried about you, Lei, that's all."

I let out a deep breath that felt like I'd been holding it in for a week. "Sorry, I didn't mean to be such a jerk. Everything's going to be fine."

"What about your mother?" Heather wanted to know. "Is she all alone at the house today? I can drop in on her before my first appointment."

My mother, along with everyone else in Sugar Ridge, adored Heather. It was impossible not to. She was a girly girl who loved my mother's cooking and marveled at her sewing skills. She'd knitted her fiancé a sweater for Christmas with my mother's help. She had more in common with Mom than I did.

"That's totally up to you. Simon said he'd stop by to see her before he goes to work this afternoon." He was all my mother needed, anyway. Even though I was nervous about going to the farm today, I knew it was the right thing to do. I couldn't sit around anymore. It gave me too much time to think about my father.

"What time should I pick you up?" she asked.

"The store and café close at five, but don't come until five-thirty. I might have some last-minute things to do, and I don't want to keep you waiting."

Heather waved a hand in dismissal. "No worries. I've reserved the entire night for my bestie. We'll grab a quick dinner, go car shopping, and you can fill me in on all the demanding orders you give everyone today." She winked. "Good luck, boss."

I waved as she drove away. After another deep breath, I unlocked the front door of the building, turned on the lights and entered the code into the panel on the wall for the alarm system. A sharp pang of grief shot through me and sadness bloomed in my chest as I looked around. My father would never again walk through this building. I vividly pictured him in my mind everywhere. To the left, I saw him behind Sappy Hour Café's counter handing a maple latte to a customer while he joked with them. On the right, he was explaining the differences between two kinds of maple syrup to an elderly woman, who'd ended up purchasing both.

I stopped to marvel at the shelves of the gift shop, which held rows of maple syrup products available for purchase in glass bottles and plastic jugs, all different shapes and sizes. The prized maple sugar candy that I loved sat next to them. As I ran my hand over the boxes, I remembered with great fondness all the times that Simon and I had called my father on the phone, begging him to bring some home with him, and the first bite of the creamy sweet taste.

In addition to syrup and candy, the gift shop also sold greeting cards, puzzles, and homemade candles. The candles were our most popular item besides syrup and were available in both maple and cinnamon scents.

A walkway area separated the gift shop from the Sappy Hour Café. I moved into the small dining area, which consisted of a handful of wooden tables and chairs arranged on the speckled linoleum floor for people to sit at, although most people took their orders to go. The front counter was where people placed orders, and there was a small display case next to it. A workstation area behind it contained a fridge, stove, and sink. Two people could stand in the area—three for a tight fit. We sold house blend coffee, decaf, and maple lattes. Desserts in the café varied daily, from my mother's baklava to maple shortbread cookies.

I moved back to the walkway area that led to a corridor and the restrooms. A separate room off the corridor was used for storage, and another smaller room was used as a break room for staff. At the very end of the corridor and situated near the back door was my father's office, a door simply marked *Private*. I unlocked it and placed my coffee cup and purse on top of the L-shaped wooden desk. I tried not to think about the fact that my father had spent his last moments in this room, but it was difficult. A shiver ran down my spine, and I quickly left the room. I unlocked the back door and walked over the grass to the sugar shack while keeping my eyes peeled for any sign of Noah.

Warm sunshine cascaded down on my face as I inhaled the sweet scent of hay and freshly mown grass. I'd forgotten how much I'd missed living in Vermont and always taken the crisp, clean air and country living for granted.

In front of me stood the sugar shack, a wooden cabin where the maple syrup processing took place. It was divided into two parts, with a workstation and packaging area on one side. The other side consisted primarily of a walkway that led to a 6,000-gallon evaporator on the next level that was used for boiling sap. Stacked against the walls were steel drums used to store the syrup after it passed through the evaporator.

There was no sign of Noah. I assumed that, like Jessica, he started at eight o'clock. Back in the packaging area was a large wooden desk he used as his own. It was littered with bags of soy wax, glass jars, gold ribbon, and labels. During the off season between May and January, there was no sap to gather but many other tasks to keep things going. My father had helped out in the café or gift store when necessary and sent shipments of his syrup out daily. He also made sure that the tap lines were ready for the upcoming sap gathering season, which began in late February or March. About three years ago, he'd started making candles for the gift shop. They were enormously popular, especially around Christmas time.

"Looking for something?"

I emitted a small squeak. Clutching my chest, I whirled around and found myself staring into a pair of ice blue eyes. They were striking, surrounded by long, dark lashes that any woman would envy. The man's perfectly chiseled features looked like they'd been carved out of stone, and I could find no fault with them. I opened my mouth to say something—anything—but no words came out.

He was about six feet tall and lean, wearing dark jeans and a gray flannel shirt. The shirt was open down the front and a white T-shirt stretched tightly across his muscular chest in all the right places. Dark wavy hair was slightly mussed as if he'd just run his fingers through it. Now I understood why Noah Rivers had all the women's tongues in town wagging. He was good looking enough to grace the cover of *Esquire* magazine.

My mouth was as dry as an unbuttered piece of toast. Finally, I managed a cough and said, "You must be Noah, I presume?"

He nodded, his mouth turning slightly up at the corners, as if amused. "Yes, ma'am, I must be. Nice to meet you, Miss Khoury."

"How did you know—" I stopped myself. What a dumb thing to say. My father only had about a dozen pictures of Simon, Mom, and me decorating the walls of his office. Of course, Noah knew who I was.

His lips parted, revealing perfect white teeth, but his smile reeked of arrogance. Noah extended a hand for me to shake, and I brushed a couple of fingers across it. His palm was like sandpaper, and his fingers hard and rigid as steel. I noticed several calluses and remembered my father once telling my mother that you could always tell a good worker by the condition of his hands.

"You're much prettier in person," he drawled, and I detected a faint Southern accent in his tone.

"Thank you." He'd instantly managed to fluster me with the comment.

Noah rocked back on his heels. "So, what would you like to be called?"

Heat crept up my neck. "Excuse me?"

He leaned against the wall. "Should I refer to you as Boss, Miss Khoury, or The Chosen One?"

"My name is Leila. *That's* what I'd like to be called."

So far, I wasn't impressed with the new stud that women around here couldn't seem to stop talking about. "And what exactly do you mean by 'The Chosen One'?"

"Your father picked you to run Sappy Endings," he said smoothly. "I'm sure you're aware that I wanted to buy the farm, but Victor refused me."

"I'm sorry that you seem to have a problem with that."

He cocked an eyebrow at me and chuckled. "No, ma'am. I don't have a problem. I thought maybe he'd change his mind when he retired, that's all." He paused, and an awkward silence enveloped us. "But family always gets first preference. It's clear that your father thought the world of you. If you change your mind about selling, I'm still interested."

I clenched my fists at my sides. "That's not going to happen."

Noah shrugged and rubbed a hand over his clean-shaven chin. "Whatever you say, ma'am."

I decided to talk to him like he was one of my students, with a calm, cool, and professional demeanor. "All right, let's get down to business. What do you have planned for today?"

Noah seemed amused by my question. "Well, rest assured, I won't be sitting around on my laurels. I'll be making candles for the holiday rush, and I have people coming in for tours today. I'll also be helping out Jessica in the café if she needs me and running the gift shop, unless you plan to. In my spare time, I need to package up a few shipments of syrup as well."

"Jack-of-all-trades, aren't you? How can you keep an eye on the gift shop from here?"

He chose to ignore my smart-aleck remark. "We have a bell on the counter that tells people to ring for service. Jessica will buzz me on the intercom, or, if I'm not here, they can always take the products over to Jessica and she can ring them out."

Before I could respond, he continued. "Just so we understand each other, Miss Khoury, I like to work alone. As for the syrup, I'd prefer to take charge of the sap gathering plus all the packaging and distribution. No offense intended, but it will be better for everyone if you leave that to someone who knows what they're doing—until you catch on."

What a pompous jerk. "Excuse me, Mr. Rivers, but I happen to know quite a bit about the maple syrup business." Okay, that was stretching the truth a bit. Even though I'd watched my father make syrup before, I'd never done it myself. My only experience with syrup consisted of liberally pouring it over french toast and pancakes.

He barked out a laugh. "Let's be honest, ma'am. You're only running the farm because your father wanted you to be in charge. Your mother told Jessica about the contents of your father's will. I figured that you'd be here today."

I gritted my teeth together in annoyance. I adored Jessica, who'd worked here for over ten years, but she couldn't keep a secret if her life depended on it. The thought of my employees discussing me behind my back was too much for me. "I'm here because it's my farm. Isn't that enough reason?"

He ignored my snide comment. "You want to prove to everyone, including yourself, that you can do the job. There's nothing wrong with that."

"Well, you're wrong. I don't have anything to prove, especially to you." Jeez, why was I so defensive and letting this guy get under my skin? "I have no intention of leaving my father's business in the hands of someone who, for all I know, might even be—"

The smile faded from Noah's face. His unrelenting eyes waited for me to continue. "Ah, I get it now. Why don't you come out and say it? You think I killed your father."

"No. I never said that."

"You didn't have to. It's written all over your face." The smell of his spicy aftershave wafted through the air and managed to distract me for a moment.

Instead of giving me a chance to respond, Noah turned his back on me and sat down at the desk. He typed a password into the laptop. "No worries. I understand that you're grieving."

I lifted my chin in defiance. "You don't know anything about how I feel." *Ugh*. I was doing it again.

Noah looked up until our eyes met. "I know more than you think."

His expression had grown somber, almost sympathetic. For a moment, I stared back at him in silence, wondering what he'd meant. Noah was a complete stranger to me. Sure, he might be a good worker, but what if he did kill my father? He'd had both means and motive. Simon's words of caution came back to me. I needed to let Noah slip up on his own, but instead, I'd practically come right out and accused him of being a murderer.

"Maybe you do." I smiled brightly. "Look, since we'll be seeing each other every day, let's make an effort to get along, okay?"

"Whatever you say, ma'am." Noah studied me like I was a bug under a microscope, then picked up a glass jar from his desktop. "If you'll excuse me, Miss Khoury, err—Boss." His voice had turned cold and brimmed with sarcasm. "I have work to do."

CHAPTER FOUR

FUMING, I MARCHED BACK TO the main building, mumbling under my breath. Who the heck did this Noah Rivers think he was, anyway?

A liar for starters.

The man obviously resented the fact that my father had chosen me to run the business over him. He wanted Sappy Endings, there was no denying that. But how badly had he wanted it, though? Enough to kill for it?

Perhaps Noah figured that, if my father was out of the picture, his grief-stricken widow might decide to sell the farm to him. He hadn't counted on me entering the picture.

As I hurried toward my office, I noticed the lights were on in the Sappy Hour Café, which only meant one thing—Jessica had arrived. I walked over to the counter, my boots tapping against the linoleum. Jessica peered out from storage room behind the tiny work area. Her face lit up when she saw me. "Good morning, Leila, honey. Ready to take the reins today?"

Her face was the breath of fresh air I sorely needed, especially after my heated conversation with Mr. Perfect. Jessica Fowler's life hadn't been an easy one, but she was one of the most positive people that I knew. She'd lost her husband to an accident at the manufacturing plant where he worked, shortly after she'd started working at Sappy Endings. Her two sons were grown and married but visited her often. Jessica didn't need to work because of the substantial death settlement she'd received from her husband's employer, but she loved baking and chatting with the customers. I suspected that the job kept her busy and from becoming lonely. My father had always praised her work, saying that she was a faithful and dependable employee.

"It's going to take me some time to get used to all of this," I said honestly.

Jessica was in her late fifties, with grayish blond hair that she wore back in a neat bun at the nape of her neck. Her face was well rounded and pleasant, and her amber eyes always shone as if she had a fun secret to tell. She was tiny, and I felt like a giant next to her. Despite her size, she was tough as nails and had a deep sensitive side. Her eyes misted over at my statement, and she reached for a napkin.

"It's been so strange without your father here." Her voice caught and caused that familiar lump to rise in my throat again. "But I'm so glad that he picked you to run the place." She reached over to squeeze my hand. "You remind me so much of him."

Coming from Jessica, I knew that was quite a compliment.

"How about a breakfast sandwich, hon?" she asked. "I remember how much you love them."

Jessica made the best all-day breakfast sandwiches in town, a perfectly toasted English muffin with scrambled eggs, sausage, and Vermont cheddar cheese, topped with a generous spoonful of maple syrup. My stomach growled at the mention of food, even though I'd had a bowl of cereal before leaving the house. "No thanks. I can already tell that it's going to be a problem for me to work here full-time. You know that I can't resist your breakfast sandwiches."

Jessica beamed. "Well, they can't compare to your mama's cooking, but most of the people who come in seem to like my food just fine." She busied herself lining a muffin tray with paper inserts for the maple cornbread muffins she was making. "Did she send in any baklava with you today?"

My mother's baklava was similar to the traditional Greek kind, except that she made hers with rose water. The sweet dessert consisted of thin layers of phyllo dough that were buttered with nuts in between each. She substituted the rose water with maple syrup if she planned on sending the dessert to the farm. Every food in the café contained my father's rich maple syrup, which was more prominent in some than others.

"Not today, but I'm sure she'll send some in tomorrow." I glanced around the spotless work area. "Do you need me to help you in here this morning?"

Jessica waved a hand dismissively. "Honey, you have more important things to do. Besides, Noah will stop by later if I need a hand." She filled a napkin dispenser for one of the tables.

"Do you like working with Noah?" I asked curiously.

She looked surprised by the question. "Of course! He's a fine young man. And so knowledgeable about the farm. Why, in the short time that he's been here, Noah's made quite a difference." She glanced around the café, as if afraid he might somehow hear. "I suppose you know that he wanted to buy the place."

"Yes, I heard."

Jessica checked on the muffins in the double wall oven. "Noah lived in New York State before relocating to Vermont. I guess he worked on a farm there for a time, tapping trees. The man knows what he's doing." A smile tugged at the corners of her mouth. "And he's not too difficult to look at, if you get my drift."

Heat rose in my cheeks. "Jessica!"

She giggled like a school girl. "I know, I know. He's probably the same age as my oldest son. Don't worry, darling. I don't rob cradles. I'm more interested in men my own age. Like your father—of course, I don't mean I was interested in him, only that I like men who are around that age."

It seemed like an odd remark to make, but I chose to ignore it. Jessica wouldn't intentionally disrespect anyone. "Did you ever hear Noah arguing with my father?"

Jessica opened the oven door and removed one of the

muffin trays. The sweet warm smell was already filling the small space around us. "Never. Why, they were like father and son. More so than—"

She stopped suddenly, an embarrassed look on her face. It didn't matter, for I knew what she was going to say. Jessica was thinking about my father and Simon. The two of them were like opposing lawyers in a courtroom, always battling it out, with each one trying to have the last word.

"I'm sorry, Leila," she said quietly. "You know that I adore your brother, but Victor used to get so upset after they argued, especially the day that he died."

An uneasy chill crept down my spine. "What happened that day between them?"

Jessica hesitated for a moment, and bit into her lower lip. "Simon stopped in late that afternoon to see your father. I watched them go into his office together. They weren't inside for more than five minutes when I heard them shouting at one another."

Simon hadn't mentioned this to me. "Do you know what they were arguing about?"

She cast her eyes down toward the floor, as if afraid to look at me. "It was about money. I overheard Simon asking your father for a loan. I—I think that Victor turned him down."

I fought the urge to ask Jessica if she'd had her body pressed up against the office door, or perhaps she'd been blessed with golden ears. Still, it was obvious that the conversation was making Jessica uncomfortable, and me as well, so I tried another tactic. "Do you remember my father having an argument with anyone else besides Simon recently?"

Jessica seemed amazed by the question. "Why, what a thing to say. Everyone loved your father, Leila. He was one of the kindest, sweetest men that I've ever known. It was only a couple of weeks ago he donated twenty-five gallons of maple syrup for the raffle at the town library. They're hoping to build a new one next spring and—"

"Doesn't it seem strange to you that someone would have killed him"—it hurt every time I said the words—"in such a manner? If it wasn't for the money, why did they make it look like a robbery?"

Jessica offered me a muffin, which I gratefully accepted. It was warm and sweet and completely satisfying, like eating a piece of french toast, which was my favorite breakfast food. Like my mother, Jessica was always happiest when she could feed someone.

"That's a good point," she said as I chewed, "I hadn't thought about that when Chief Crosby came by to question me and Noah. But all you have to do is read the papers, honey. There's crazy people out there who would kill for a measly twenty bucks." Her voice quivered. "It's a horrible shame that something like that happened to such a wonderful man."

The front door closed, announcing a customer. A middle-aged couple walked over to the café and stared at the chalkboard on the easel where Jessica had printed today's special treats. Her face creased into a generous smile. "Morning, Chet, Donna. The usual?"

"I'll be in the office. Let me know if you need any help," I said.

"No worries, honey. I can call Noah through the inter-com," Jessica said as she filled a coffee cup.

My skin prickled at the mention of his name. Mr. Noah Rivers, jerk of all trades. "No, Jessica. Please call me instead."

Jessica's eyebrows rose slightly. "Of course, honey. Whatever you say."

My tone was sharper than I'd intended, and I wanted to apologize. But another customer came in, and it seemed like a good time to retreat with my tail between my legs. The day wasn't starting out as I'd planned. With a sigh, I went to my office. I sipped my coffee thoughtfully as I stared around the quiet room with an empty, nostalgic feeling.

Memories of being in here with my father as a child swept over me like a cool breeze. Why had my father wanted me to run the farm? And what had inspired him to make a new will at the last minute?

The office was too warm, so I opened the window behind the desk and gazed out at the beautiful scenery. There were rolling hills in the distance and a cluster of maple trees was only a few feet away on the sprawling lawn. I remembered my father once mentioning that there was a beautiful view of the sunset from his office window.

With a sigh, I turned back to the desk. Dad had been a wonderful man, but organization was not his specialty. He never threw anything away. The desk was littered with papers, receipts, and manila folders, plus an ancient desktop computer that he'd refused to update.

"It still works," he'd told me when I'd been home and complained about its slowness. "Why waste money if you don't have to?"

I'd worried that being in the office would bring me to tears again, but instead, I found it strangely comforting. My father had spent so many hours in this chair that it felt as if he was with me. "Help me, Dad," I whispered. "Help me find out who did this to you."

The cream-colored walls were filled with framed photographs—a black and white portrait of his parents from their wedding day and, next to it, one of my mother and father posing in front of their own wedding cake. Another photo showed my father cutting a yellow ribbon in front of Sappy Endings on the day that it had opened. There were several photographs of my mother and a few of me, mostly school pictures. There was only one picture of Dad and Simon together, which had been taken on his graduation day from college. They both stood stiffly in the photo, side by side, attempting to smile, with neither one successful.

Why had Simon wanted to borrow money from my father? As a reporter for the *Maple Messenger*, he didn't earn top dollar, but he seemed to be getting by all right. He had an apartment near the newspaper office that he shared with an old high school buddy of his. Simon had mentioned to me in a text last month that he had a new girlfriend, but I hadn't met her yet.

I brought up the History tab on the computer. To my surprise, there was nothing listed. Someone had cleaned out the entire history. Dad wasn't fond of technology, so I doubted he would have taken the time. Maybe the police? No, that wouldn't make any sense. Perhaps the killer had done it, but why? What were they trying to hide?

I opened the main drawer to the desk and started rummaging through its contents. A pile of newspaper articles was held together by a paper clip. I started to flip through them. They were in no particular order. One showed Dad holding up a trophy from the time his syrup had garnered first prize at the state fair. There was another article about Dad and his dedication to syrup making. He was standing by one of the maples, examining the tap. There was even an article about me winning a spelling bee in fifth grade. It brought a smile to my lips. He'd been so proud of me that day and we'd gone out for ice cream afterward. "You can do anything, *habibi*," he'd told me that day. "Don't let anyone ever tell you differently."

An obituary fell out from behind the spelling bee article. The man's name was listed as Dennis A. Browning, but it didn't seem familiar to me. I studied the brief paragraph in hopes that it might strike a note of recognition.

Dennis A. Browning, age 40, died suddenly Tuesday evening. Dennis was born and raised in Bennington, Vermont. After he graduated from Maple View High School, he worked as a mechanic and was one of the original proprietors of Sappy Endings Farm in Sugar Ridge.

He is survived by his wife Ellen and son Wesley.
A public viewing will be held at the Eternal Life
Funeral Home on Friday from 2–4 p.m. Burial will
be private and at the convenience of the family.

My father once had a partner? How had I never known
about this? I looked up at the pictures on the wall and spotted the one of my father at Sappy Ending's ribbon cutting ceremony. A dark-haired man was standing to his left,
smiling broadly for the camera. I gazed at the picture in
the obituary. Yes, it was the same man. I'd never asked my
father about the man's identity before, assuming it was a
friend or prospective customer. To my knowledge, Dennis's
name had never been mentioned in our household. What
had happened to make him leave the farm? The obituary
was from twenty years ago.

The intercom on my phone buzzed and I picked it up.
"Hi, Jessica."

"Leila, we have a couple of customers in the gift shop.
Can you wait on them, or should I call Noah?"

"Yes, of course. I'll be right there." I put the clipping in
my jeans pocket and made a mental note to ask my mother
about it tonight.

CHAPTER FIVE

HEATHER WAS LATE PICKING ME up, so we didn't end up leaving Sappy Endings until six o'clock. We grabbed a quick burger to go and stopped at one of the local dealerships outside of Sugar Ridge. I decided on a hybrid car, and, after some lengthy discussion, they agreed to a one-year lease. What was the point of buying it when I'd be flying back to Florida in twelve months?

It took a while for the dealership to run my credit and approve the loan. We didn't end up leaving until after eight, when they'd officially closed. I would pick up the vehicle tomorrow night after work. I needed to make things as simple as possible.

When Heather dropped me off at my mother's, it was almost nine. The house was dark, except for a light glowing in the front room that I knew came from her *fanoos* on the mantel. The Arabian lantern was a beautiful golden color, shaped like a lighthouse. My mother usually went to bed at nine thirty, but sometimes she turned in earlier to read.

Heather must have guessed my thoughts. "You're in trouble," she teased. "Mama Khoury's already in bed and you're out past curfew."

I smiled at the thought, remembering the countless times she'd grounded me back in high school if I dared stay out past ten o'clock. If I was with a boy, I had to be home by nine. No excuses.

"Well, what else is new, right? Just like old times." I leaned over and gave her a hug. "Thanks for wasting your night on me. Tell Tyler I'm sorry that I stole you away."

She scoffed. "Oh, please, it's fine. This is his night to see patients at the clinic, anyway. It's not like we have to be together twenty-four hours a day. Besides, he knows how happy I am that you're back in town."

"It's only temporary." I wasn't sure if I spoke the words out loud to remind her or myself.

"Hey, I can dream, right?" she grinned. "What time do you want me to pick you up in the morning?"

"Seven fifteen," I told her. "And it's my turn to buy the coffee."

Heather gave a small toss of her head. "Actually, I think I'll wait and grab one of Jessica's famous maple lattes. I have two perms scheduled before noon, so I'll need something sweet to go with all the ammonia."

She laughed, blew me a kiss, and took off. I entered the living room and removed my shoes. There was no sign of my mother. With a sigh I went into the kitchen and grabbed a bottle of water from the fridge. When I flicked on the light switch, I shrieked. Mom was sitting at the table, nursing what looked like a cup of tea in front of her.

"Why are you sitting here in the dark?" I asked. "Is everything okay?"

Mom calmly took a sip of her tea and then shot me a look that could have melted icicles in Antarctica. "Why are you so late?"

Puzzled, I glanced at the wall clock, hanging next to her giant crucifix. "It's not even nine o'clock yet."

She pressed her thin lips tightly together. "I've been worried sick about you."

As usual, she was annoyed with me. "I told you that I was going car shopping with Heather tonight."

"You could have called. I thought something might have happened." Mom rose from the table. She was wearing a black kaftan, also known as a hostess robe. The large, black buttons that ran down the front were surrounded by gold diamond shapes on both sides. Mom had made me a similar one for me for my eighteenth birthday, but I never wore it.

Her dark gaze was pinned on me, waiting for more of an explanation, but I didn't have one. She opened the fridge. "You look hungry. Have some grape leaves."

"Mom, I'm not hungry. I had a burger earlier."

She slammed the fridge as if defeated, the bangle bracelets on her right arm jingling in time as they knocked together. They were solid gold and had been a gift to her from her parents when she'd turned of age. Mom had wanted to pass them on to me, but I'd refused them, protesting that I never wore jewelry. Once again, I'd made the wrong decision. It had only led to another argument between us. There were too many count, and now, here we were, about to start a new one.

Mom folded her arms across her chest. "Leila, I do wish that you would be more considerate of my feelings."

I blinked, not sure I'd heard her right. She was overreacting, but I didn't want to distress her further. This must have to do with my father. "Mom, I'm sorry if you're upset. But I'm twenty-eight years old, and I've been getting my own dinner for the past four years. If you'd rather I lived somewhere else—"

"No, no." She held up a hand. "Of course I want you to stay here. This will always be your home."

Her voice trembled, causing a lump to rise in my throat. I placed an arm around her thin shoulders. "It's okay. I know this must be horrible for you. I miss Dad, too."

Mom patted my hand and then disengaged herself from my grip. "Sit down. How about I make you some tea?"

I'd never seen my mother cry, not even when we'd buried my father. She was as tough as they came, with an exterior more difficult to crack than a macadamia nut. Mom had been brought up to believe that showing her true emotions was a sign of weakness.

"Sit," she ordered. "Or would you rather have *Ahweh* instead?"

The Turkish coffee she made was delicious but so bitter

and strong that it would probably keep me up for the rest of the night. "No, thanks. I'm fine."

She sat down across from me and folded her hands primly in her lap. "Talk to me. How did everything go today at the farm?"

I shrugged. "Okay, I guess. There wasn't much for me to do. I waited on some customers in the gift shop, and then I helped Jessica with the lunch crowd. I went through some of Dad's papers and talked to a few vendors who stopped by. Then I answered some emails on the website. It's seriously in need of an update."

Mom sipped her tea thoughtfully. "That's normal for this time of year. In a couple of weeks, the Christmas rush will begin, and then, soon after the holidays, it will be time to start gathering the sap. That's when you'll long for these quiet days."

"I'd like to start giving tours," I blurted out. "I know that Noah does them, but it's something I'd enjoy."

She looked pleased. "That sounds like it would be perfect for you, dear. I'm sure Noah wouldn't mind."

I had my doubts but didn't particularly care if Noah minded or not.

Mom stirred her tea. "By the way, Chief Crosby said to let you know that he'll be stopping by Sappy Endings tomorrow to talk to you."

I leaned forward. "Does he have a lead on who killed Dad?"

She shook her head sadly. "I don't think so. I believe that Alan is just retracing his steps to find anyone else who might have been at the farm the day your father died. He's convinced that the murder was premeditated."

"I think so, too." My phone buzzed, and I drew it out of my pocket, along with a small piece of paper that fluttered to the floor. The text was from Heather, telling me that I'd forgotten my notepad in her car. I reached down to grab the piece of paper off the floor. It was the obituary for Dennis Browning.

Mom squinted down at the floor. "What's that?"

"An obituary for Dennis Browning that I found in Dad's desk. I never knew that he had a partner when he started Sappy Endings."

"It was a long time ago." My mother stared off into space, her mind obviously focused on something else.

"Why did Dennis leave Sappy Endings?"

Mom blinked, as if coming back to earth. "Leila, that's in the past. It's neither here nor there."

"Yes, but I'm curious. Were he and Dad longtime friends? And why didn't you or Dad ever mention Dennis before?"

My mother made a face. "Dennis was a good friend of your father's, or at least we thought. When your father wanted to buy the farm, he didn't have enough money on his own, so Dennis asked if he could go in on it with him. Your father agreed to a sixty-forty partnership but almost ended up losing it all, thanks to that man." She made the sign of the cross on her chest. "Rest his soul."

"What happened?"

Mom drained her cup. "Dennis had some problems.

Gambling problems. He owed money to unsavory people and asked your father to help him. This was a couple of years after Sappy Endings had opened."

My nose wrinkled. "Then why don't I remember ever seeing him at the farm?"

"Because he was bad news." Mom fiddled with the napkin ring on the table. "He was never around to help with the place when your father needed him. Dennis became more of a silent partner, by his choice. Your father was suspicious that Dennis had gotten in over his head, and, it turns out, he was right. Sappy Endings was doing well, and, one day, Dennis said he wanted to put a second mortgage on the farm. Your father refused, and they had a huge fight. Finally, Dennis confessed that he needed money because he owed thousands to a loan shark. Your father agreed to pay off his debts if Dennis signed his share of the business over to him."

"It sounds like Dad took advantage of him when he was in a bad way," I said honestly.

My mother snorted. "It was nothing of the sort. He was giving Dennis another chance. He told your father that he'd be as good as dead if he didn't pay off his debt." She paused for a long moment. "But some people thought the same thing you did, namely Dennis's son."

"Wesley?"

She nodded. "When your father went to pay his respects at Dennis's wake, Wesley made a scene. He said that your father had ruined Dennis's life. Wesley demanded that he leave immediately."

"That must have been awful for Dad."

Her expression became grave. "It was. Your father refused to talk about it for several days. Do you know that Wesley even had the gall to come and see your father recently? He's got some crazy idea that your father still owes his family money from Sappy Endings. After all these years! He claimed that your father coerced Dennis into signing over his share of the farm. I think he might have been planning to sue him." She looked at me pointedly over the rim of the empty teacup in her hand. "And he still might be."

"That's it, then," I said. "He must have been the one to—"

She interrupted. "I don't think Wesley killed your father. What good would that do if he had planned on suing him?"

"When was Wesley last seen at Sappy Endings?" I asked.

She lowered her teacup to the table. "The day that your father was murdered."

My stomach twisted. "What? Does Chief Crosby know about this?" I picked up my phone and started scrolling the contacts.

"Yes, he knows," Mom replied. "Don't bother him right now, Leila. It's late. Besides, he's coming to see you tomorrow, anyway."

"I think someone should talk to Wesley." *Like me.*

Mom frowned. "I don't want you getting involved in this. Leave it to the police. I told Simon the same thing."

Her reference to my brother forced me to recall my

discussion with Jessica from earlier. "Did you know that Simon asked Dad to borrow money?"

My mother's eyes became as round as dinner plates. "Where did you hear such a thing?"

"Jessica mentioned it to me. She said that Dad and Simon had a terrible argument the day Dad died. Everyone at Sappy Endings heard them."

"That doesn't mean anything. Your brother and father were both well matched in the stubbornness department." Her chest puffed up with pride. "Simon is so much like his father."

Her words hurt like a punch to my stomach. To say that Simon was so much like our father was the highest compliment Mom would ever pay anyone. I quickly pursued another topic. "Have you met Simon's girlfriend yet?"

"Tonya? Oh, yes. She's lovely," Mom gushed. "She was runner-up in the state's beauty pageant a couple of years ago. Her family moved to Vermont when she was in high school. At least, that's what Simon told me."

Tonya was probably a leggy blond. My brother had always pursued the same type in high school—popular, blond, and homecoming queen material. "Why wasn't she at the wake?"

"Tonya was there," my mother said. "That's when I met her. She could only stay for a few minutes. I think you were busy talking to Mr. and Mrs. Ammian when she stopped in. Did you know that she's a real estate agent?"

My mother continued singing Tonya's praises, but I was barely listening. My head was spinning with the new information that I had learned. My father once had a partner by the name of Dennis Browning. His son, Wesley, had gone to see Dad the same day that he died. Was it a mere coincidence? I didn't think so.

But what I found even more troubling was the fact that Simon had also visited our father that day, and that they'd been involved in some type of altercation. I needed to find out more details from my brother, but I had to be careful. If Simon thought for a minute that I was suspicious of him, it might ruin our relationship forever.

CHAPTER SIX

WHENEVER MY FATHER HAD A bad day at work, he would joke with me that things were "a bit sticky at the farm." The memory made me smile as I walked into the office the next morning. I missed him so much that my heart ached from the hole his death had left behind. I tried to tell myself that he wasn't really gone. His spirit would live on forever at Sappy Endings, and hopefully guide me to do the wonderful things he had wanted.

After I placed my purse in the desk drawer, I went outside to the sugar shack in search of Noah. His pickup truck was nowhere to be seen and the door to the shack was locked. We'd gotten off to our own sticky start yesterday, and I was determined to put things right between us—or at least let him think that they were. Despite what my mother had said last night, I wasn't convinced of Noah's innocence. I'd be watching him closely, hoping to catch him in a blunder.

I used my key to let myself inside. There were several maple candles in frosted glass holders at Noah's workstation. They were decorated with red and green curled ribbons for the upcoming holidays. Their sweet smell permeated through the small building, and I had to admit that they looked as good—if not better than the ones I'd seen on a trip to Yankee Candle in Florida. The man was gorgeous *and* talented. I shook myself. He was also an employee, and I had no interest in him romantically. Besides, he probably had half a dozen girlfriends.

A couple of requests had come in for tours yesterday, but Noah must have been keeping a sharp eye on the website, because the emails had disappeared shortly afterward from the inbox. He had to have written the schedule down somewhere, unless he kept a document with the records on his desktop computer, an identical match to the one in my office. I opened the middle drawer of his desk and started rummaging through it. There were tap tubing pieces, supplies for candles, and an instruction booklet about the evaporator, but no appointment book anywhere.

"You're doing a great Nancy Drew imitation."

I spun around. It was like déjà vu of yesterday, except for the fact that Noah was more annoyed this time. His arms were folded over his broad chest, his gaze locked on my face.

My mouth opened in response, but I quickly shut it without comment. What I wanted to say was that this was *my* farm, and I could look anywhere I darn well pleased, then remembered that I shouldn't try to raise his suspicion.

"What are you looking for?" he asked in a stiff tone. Noah made an intimidating and unflinching figure. He was also the only man I'd ever seen who could make coveralls look sexy. It was a chilly fall day, and, when working outside, they were a practical choice on the farm. Noah wore a blue and black flannel shirt over them, like a jacket, and the colors made his eyes appear even bluer.

Quickly, I averted my eyes. Shoot. He was still waiting for an answer. "You look like you're dressed for tapping season."

He shot me a puzzled expression. "Miss Khoury, you know that tapping doesn't start until February or March. I mean, you *should* know that, since you grew up in the business, ma'am."

"Of course I know when tapping season is," I shot back, quickly forgetting my resolve to make a friend of him and gain his trust. "I thought maybe you were repairing some of the tap lines, that's all."

Noah picked up a pail. "Very good. Yes, I do have to replace some of the tubing around the trees. It looks like squirrels chewed holes in them. No need to worry though; it's not a lot of damage, Miss Khoury."

"Could you please drop the *Miss*? It's so formal. Just call me Leila."

"As you wish." An awkward silence filled the room until he spoke again. "Can I ask why you were snooping through my desk?"

"I wasn't snooping," I fumed. "I was looking for a schedule of the daily tours."

Noah frowned. "Why? Did you get a phone call for one?"

"No, it's because I'd like to—" Something furry and warm rubbed against my leg. I jumped about ten feet in the air, as if I'd been electrocuted. The unknown furry creature rushed out of the shack.

Noah burst into laughter while I tried to catch my breath. "What the heck was that?" I asked.

He grinned and beckoned me to the door. I peered out and spotted an orange cat sitting among a group of trees, watching us intently. "He scared me half to death. Where did he come from?"

Noah shrugged. "The little guy's been hanging around here for about a week. I think someone might have dumped him."

"That's awful." How could anyone be so cruel? I stepped out the door past Noah and walked slowly toward the cat. "Here kitty, kitty."

The cat didn't move. He continued to watch me with enormous green eyes.

I dropped to my knees on the grassy area, clicking my tongue against the roof of my mouth to get his attention. "Come on, boy. I won't hurt you."

I was about to give up when he slowly trotted toward me, rubbing his head against my leg. I reached down a hand to pet him. He was a beautiful longhaired cat with orange fur except for the tips of his polydactyl paws, which were snow white. I scratched him behind the ears as he purred and circled around me.

Noah bent down next to me to pet him as well. "He's a

friendly little guy. That's all the more reason I think someone dumped him. If he was feral, he wouldn't come near us. I fed him part of my lunch yesterday. And I'll say this for him, he's quite a mouser." His mouth turned up at the corners. "He left me a couple of presents by the door yesterday."

Ew. I wasn't a fan of rodents. "Well, between his hunting skills and your lunch, it sounds like he's got a sweet deal going for him."

Noah laughed and stared at me thoughtfully. "I bet he'd be a big fan of your mother's cooking, like all the customers. Her baklava and doughnuts are always the first items to go. Do you bake, too?"

I shook my head. "No. I can boil water, and that's about it."

His eyes crinkled at the corners. "I think Jessica is jealous of your mother's cooking."

"Jessica's not like that at all," I insisted. "She's practically a member of the family."

Instead of replying, Noah rose to his feet and went back inside the sugar shack. I wondered if he'd found my comment offensive and trailed after him. The cat followed us, meowing plaintively.

Noah pointed at him. "Why don't you take him home? Unless you already have pets."

"I've never had a pet before," I admitted.

A surprised look registered on Noah's face. "You're kidding."

"Nope. It was never an option. My father was allergic

to cats and dogs, and my apartment in Florida doesn't allow pets."

"Oh, that's right. I remember your dad telling me about his allergies." Noah watched as the cat continued rubbing against me and yowling. "Well, maybe it's time you had one. He sure looks to be fond of you."

"Actually, he looks *hungry*." I crouched down and stroked his soft fur while debating what to do. The cat acted as if I was already his property. And my mother wouldn't object if I took him home. One of the few things we had in common was our love for animals, and she'd always been sorry Simon and I couldn't keep a pet.

"I'll take him to the vet and check to see if he's micro-chipped." I tried to pick the cat up in my arms, but he wriggled free and jumped back onto the ground. He ran ahead in the direction of the main building and then turned around, his huge, jeweled eyes fixed upon me as if waiting to see what I'd do next.

I laughed. "Well, I guess he's decided it's time to eat. I'll take him into my office and give him something. Will you and Jessica be all right without me for an hour or so this afternoon?"

"Hang on a second." Noah took a step toward me. "You never answered my question. Why did you want to see the tour schedule?"

I dusted off the knees of my jeans. It was easier to respond if I didn't have to look at him. "Because I'd like to start giving some and that would free you up to do other things. It would be a bit like teaching in the classroom, and I miss that."

Noah stroked his clean-shaven chin. "I'm afraid that's impossible."

I wasn't sure I'd heard him right. "Why?"

He turned and walked back toward the sugar shack with me following. "You can't be giving any tours until you learn more about the business."

I sucked in some air and reminded myself to count to five, but it didn't help. "Mr. Rivers, I think that I know enough about the business to conduct a tour. I'm used to speaking to a room full of people. The point of the tour is to get people to buy our products, correct? If that's the case, I—"

Noah raised a finely arched eyebrow. "Sorry, but this isn't negotiable. I'm not doing it to be a jerk, Leila. Customers don't come here only for the syrup or to leaf peep. Many of them are interested in the story of how syrup is made. Once you learn the entire process, I will gladly hand the tours over to you. By then it will be sap collecting time, and I'll be too busy for tours." He paused. "I started working here at the end of sap collecting season. Your father said there was no way he could handle it all alone again. And we'll have to hire temporary help this winter because I won't be able to do it all, either."

"I can help with the syrup," I volunteered.

He frowned. "We'll see."

Who did this guy think he was? Noah was not going to tell me what I could and couldn't do. I tried to keep my temper in check. "I'm fully aware that you know more than

I do about the syrup-making process, but I really want to do this. I know enough to get by."

Noah almost smiled. "This isn't about *getting by*. You should know that's not Sappy Endings style." He reached into the pocket of his flannel shirt and withdrew a small, black book. He opened it and pointed at an entry. "We have a busload of people coming in tomorrow at two o'clock. Why don't you come by for the tour? This way you can listen in and see how it's done. You could even hand out the syrup samples."

"You enjoy this, don't you?" I blurted out.

He blinked. "Excuse me?"

"It feels like you're belittling me. But, yes, I can hand out samples and play assistant to you."

Noah placed his hands on his hips. "Okay. Tell me the other two kinds of syrup that we sell at the farm, and I'll let you give the tour."

I laughed. "Oh, please."

A wide grin stretched across his face. "You don't know them, do you?"

My eyes shifted to the drums of syrup on the floor. If there were names printed on the outside, I couldn't see them.

Noah made a tsk-tsk sound. "No cheating."

My face heated with embarrassment. "Well, I know that amber is the most popular kind."

"Correct," he said approvingly. "And the other two kinds are dark and golden. Dark color is robust, with a bit of a stronger taste than usual. Now, will you be here for the tour tomorrow?"

I stared up at him and momentarily lost my train of thought. His gaze met mine, and for a second, neither one of us said anything. My knees weakened, and I became infuriated with myself. Why did he have to be so good looking? No, I wouldn't let myself be swayed by his handsome face. He was an employee, and an arrogant one at that.

Defiantly I stuck my nose out in the air. "I'll try to make it."

A soft feminine voice spoke from behind me. "Oh my. Who's this cutie?"

Heather was standing behind me, and for a brief moment, I worried she was speaking about Noah. Thank goodness I didn't say anything, because she immediately dropped to her knees and started to give the cat chin scratches.

A giggle burst from my mouth, and I quickly turned it into a cough. "What are you doing here? I thought you weren't coming by until lunchtime."

She grinned up at me, her eyes flashing wide with excitement. "I couldn't wait, Lei. My morning appointment canceled, and you just have to see this." She waved a copy of *Brides* magazine at me. "I think I've finally found my wedding dress!"

I gestured toward Noah. "Heather, this is Noah Rivers. Noah, this is my friend Heather Turcot."

She stood and extended her hand. I watched her cheeks turned a dusky pink as he shook it. "I'm pleased to meet you, Noah."

"Likewise. Well, if you ladies will excuse me, I have

work to do." He wasted no time heading out the door with his bucket in hand.

"Oh. My. God." Heather fanned herself with the magazine as she watched him disappear out of sight. "No wonder all the women at Paint and Sip were drooling. He's hotter than a curling crimper."

I rolled my eyes. "Do you always have to compare men to hair equipment?"

Heather giggled and locked her arm through mine. "Sorry. Next time I'll say he's sweeter than a bottle of Sappy Endings's maple syrup."

"There's nothing sweet about him," I fumed. "The man is arrogant and bossy and thinks he knows everything."

She fluttered her eyelashes at me. "Sounds like the start of a great working relationship."

We walked back to the main building with the cat following us. We didn't allow animals inside the building, especially around the café, so we smuggled him under Heather's coat and into my office. Heather stayed with him while I asked Jessica for a breakfast sandwich. She was out of English muffins, so she served it on french toast. I cut the sausage patty up, and the cat gobbled the pieces down.

When I came back into the office with a cup full of water for him, he was chewing on tiny pieces of toast with Heather lovingly stroking his fur.

"He's beautiful," she said, as he snuggled up against her and closed his eyes. "I don't understand how someone could just dump an animal like that. Do you think your mother will let you keep him?"

"Yes, I think so. She loves cats. What should we name him?"

Heather wrinkled her forehead. "Hmm. How about Pancake? It would be appropriate, under the circumstances."

"Here, Pancake," I called. We both waited to see if he responded, but the cat didn't even open his eyes. Now that his belly was full, he continued purring away, his head resting contentedly against Heather's arm.

"Maple?" she said, but he didn't move.

"Wait a second. I've got it. Look at the food he just ate."

Heather wrinkled her nose at the plate. "I've never heard of a cat named Sausage. Then again, you always have to be different."

I scratched the cat behind the ears. "How do you feel about Toast, little guy?"

"Oh!" Heather's eyes widened. "That's so cute."

The cat opened one eye and made a chirping sound, then drifted back off to sleep. The matter was settled.

"Well, that was easy enough. Now, let's have your input on another matter." Heather drew the bridal magazine out of her purse and placed it on the desk next to Toast. "I want you to give me your honest opinion on this dress. It doesn't matter that I'm in love with it already, I need to have your honest opinion."

"No pressure, right?" I teased. "But you've already put a hold on another one."

Heather flipped through the pages at a rapid pace, pretending not to hear me, and then turned the magazine so that the picture was facing in my direction. "Ta-da! What do you think? Is it me or what?"

I sipped my coffee as I studied the dress. The gown was white silk with tulle and stunning crystal beadwork on the bodice and skirt. There was no doubt about it. All Heather needed was a crown to look like a fairytale princess. "Wow. You would look gorgeous in this. How much is it?"

She beamed with satisfaction. "It's perfect, right? And check out the scooped neckline. My grandmother's pearls will go perfect and they're just the right length so that—"

"Heather?"

She looked up to meet my gaze and swallowed hard. "Three thousand dollars."

My mouth dropped open in amazement. "No freaking way. Your father is going to flip!"

Heather's eyes were stricken, as if a client had told her that they hated their new hairstyle. "Yeah, I know. Way more than we budgeted for, but it's so perfect. Do you think it's too extravagant?"

I hated to burst her bubble, but she was my dearest friend and I always tried to be honest. Heather had been planning for this day since she turned thirteen. As a teenager, she'd once even slept with a piece of wedding cake under her pillow, convinced she'd dream about her future husband. Instead, she'd woken up with buttercream frosting all over her hair. Heather made decent money at her job, and she and Tyler were paying for part of their wedding expenses, such as the honeymoon, photographer, and limousine. Sappy Endings was providing the wedding favors, which consisted of sample-sized bottles of syrup with the bride and groom's names and wedding date printed on them. The favors had been a hit at other weddings and also provided my father with future business.

"It's a lot of money," I said, "for a dress that you're never going to wear again."

Heather's lips puckered together, as if she'd eaten a lemon. "Have you been talking to my mother? Seriously, that's exactly what she said."

I picked at the untouched part of the breakfast sandwich. As if on cue, Toast opened one eye and watched as I took a bite. "The wedding is six months away. Aren't you cutting it a bit close?"

She sighed and stuck the magazine back in her bag. "Maybe you're right. I should just go with the one I put a deposit on at the Bridal Boutique. It isn't fair to ask Mom and Dad to fork over any more money. Oh gosh. I'm becoming a bridezilla, aren't I?"

I barely heard her. Pain surrounded my heart as I realized for the first time that my father would never walk me down the aisle. Of course, I wasn't convinced that marriage was in the cards for me, especially after my breakup with Mark. I had no desire to have my heart broken again, and, unlike Heather, I'd never wanted a big wedding. That had been another bone of contention with my mother, who'd wanted to invite the entire state of Vermont to mine. Still, it didn't change the fact that my father was gone forever.

Heather must have realized what was happening. She leaned across the desk and gripped my hand tightly between hers. "Oh, Lei, I'm sorry. That was so selfish of me."

I forced my thoughts away and smiled. "You're not

being selfish. This is your wedding, and you want everything to be perfect. There's nothing wrong with that."

She stared at me sheepishly. "Maybe, but there's more important things to consider right now, especially what your family is going through. You don't really think that Noah could have killed your father, do you? Somehow, I can't picture it."

"Killers don't have to be ugly, Heather." I pulled the newspaper clipping out of my purse and pushed it toward her. "I found this in the desk yesterday. Dennis used to be my father's partner."

Heather raised her eyebrows. "I didn't know that your father once had a partner."

"That makes two of us." I tapped a pencil on the desk's surface, which immediately got Toast's attention. "His son, Wesley, came to see my father the same day he died. Coincidence? I don't think so. I'm going to ask Chief Crosby about it when he stops over today."

Heather read the obituary silently to herself. "Hmm. Browning, huh? I cut his wife's hair a couple of times."

I hadn't been expecting this stroke of luck. Hairdressers did know everyone. "Really? I'd love to talk to her."

"She died a few months ago," Heather said sadly. "I didn't know her that well. Mrs. Browning wasn't a regular customer. She came out to the shop once last year and I did her hair. Then, a few months back, she called and asked if I'd come to her house. You know I don't normally do home visits, especially if they're not nearby, but she mentioned that she'd been sick and didn't have much time left. How could I refuse?"

"That's awful," I said sympathetically.

Heather's face brightened like the sun. "When I finished and she saw herself in the mirror, she became a different person for a second. It made her so happy. That's why I love my job. When people look good, they feel good about themselves. It's not vanity, either."

"I understand."

"She died a week later," Heather went on. "I'm so glad that I went out there and gave her that one happy moment."

Heather was so genuine and sweet that I counted myself lucky to have her for a friend. "You're such a wonderful person. Don't ever forget that."

"Right back at you, love."

I removed the pencil from under Toast's paw. "Do you remember if she mentioned her son Wesley?"

"He was there when I did her hair the last time. I think he lived with her." Heather wrinkled her nose. "Or at least he was staying with her while she was sick. He didn't say one word to me."

"What did he look like?" I pressed.

Heather shrugged. "I don't really remember much about him. He had a large bald spot on the back of his head. I always remember hair details." She paused for a moment. "Wesley was kind of rude, though. His mother introduced us, and then he left the room without speaking to me. His mother said that he'd called in sick because the visiting nurse wasn't coming, and he didn't want her to be alone."

"Did she mention what kind of work he did?" I asked curiously.

Her brow furrowed. "I think he was a dry cleaner—wait,

no. Mrs. Browning said that he worked at a furniture store. I know he wasn't married because she mentioned how much she wanted him to meet a nice girl and give her some grandchildren, but she doubted it would ever happen. She said all he did was play video games when he wasn't working and that he was a loner. Sounds kind of pathetic, if you want to know the truth."

"Hairdressers always get the juicy details," I said.

"Yeah, we're like bartenders," Heather laughed. "Everyone tells us their life story."

I pushed back my chair. "I want to go out and talk to him tonight."

"Not alone," Heather objected. "It might not be safe. I'm going with you. What kind of reason could we give him for going out there at night, though? It's not like we can say we're selling magazines."

Excuse me, Mr. Browning, I wonder if you hated my father enough to kill him. How would Wesley react if I told him that? Not well. I shivered. "Leave it to me. Maybe I'll tell him I'm a real estate agent."

Heather shook her head. "That won't work."

"Why not?"

"You'll understand when you see his house."

CHAPTER SEVEN

BEFORE HEATHER LEFT, THE DEALERSHIP called to say that my car was ready and I could pick it up earlier than scheduled. Since the café and gift shop were slow at the moment, I told Jessica that I needed to step out for a little while. We left Toast sleeping in my office, and when I returned alone less than hour later, he looked like he hadn't even budged.

"You've made yourself at home already, huh?" I laughed and stroked his fur as he yawned and stretched and then helped himself to some water. I called my mother to tell her that I was bringing home a friend for dinner.

She clicked her tongue in disgust. "That's terrible if some-one did dump him, but it's happened before. I don't know why, but people seem to think it's no big imposition for a farm to have one more stray roaming around. Before you bring him home, see if you can schedule him for a vet visit."

My mother sounded excited about the possibility of having a pet, and I selfishly hoped that Toast didn't have an owner frantically looking for him. I'd already fallen in love with the fur ball. Mom gave me the name of a local veterinarian hospital, All Paws on Deck, where my father had brought a couple of strays in the past. It turned out they'd had a cancelation and asked if I could be there in a half an hour. I went over to the café and told Jessica that I needed to run out again, along with my guest in the office. To my surprise, she laughed out loud.

"Aw, shoot, honey. This is your place now," she said. "You could have a giraffe in there, and it wouldn't be any of my business. Take your time. Noah's out in the sugar bush, but it's been so slow all morning that I don't think I'll need his help."

She found me a duffel bag, and I coaxed Toast inside it with another piece of leftover sausage. He wriggled in my arms, but I managed to get him into my vehicle and place the seat belt around him and the bag. He looked adorable with only his head sticking out of it. I was thankful that All Paws on Deck was only a ten-minute drive because Toast yowled the entire time.

The veterinarian office was a gray building with a giant billboard on the front lawn. I laughed out loud when I saw it: *Welcome to All Paws on Deck. Remember, dogs have owners, cats have staff.*

A middle-aged woman with carrot-colored hair looked up from the receptionist counter and smiled brightly as I came in, holding the wriggling cat. "You must be Leila," she said. "I'm Sandy. This is Toast, I presume?"

I nodded. "That's right. I'd like to have him examined and also checked for a microchip. He's been hanging around my farm for the past few days."

Sandy nodded in understanding. "Doctor Horowitz will take care of all that, but let's get a weight on him first."

"Be careful," I warned. "He won't stop wriggling. It's like he knows he's at the vet."

Toast lifted his pink nose in the air and sniffed, as if he found my comment offensive. Sandy picked him up and he immediately began purring, then stared at her with adoring eyes. *Why, you little stinker.* He knew what side his bread was buttered on.

Sandy stepped on the scale with Toast, then placed him on the receptionist counter and weighed herself without him. "Six pounds, two ounces." She made a notation on a clipboard in front of her, while Toast rubbed his head against her pen. Sandy laughed and scratched him behind the ears. "Oh, my goodness. He certainly loves attention. Toast is a bit on the small side, but I'm sure you'll take care of that before long." She placed the clipboard in a holder hanging on a closed door and then disappeared into another room. She returned a minute later with a cardboard carrier. "You can take Toast home in this if you like. They work well for the short term, but you'll probably want to buy a sturdier one."

"Thank you, that will be a huge help. I'll return it as soon as possible," I promised.

Doctor Horowitz called us into the room and gave Toast a complete examination. Toast was on his best behavior, purring contentedly the entire time. He didn't even protest when the thermometer was inserted into a rather delicate place. Instead, I was the one who cringed.

The doctor laughed at my reaction. He looked to be in his sixties, with a head full of dark hair streaked with silver, and a kind smile. "It doesn't hurt him," he assured me. "Toast is healthy, and from what I can tell by his teeth, appears to be about two years old. There's no microchip, and he hasn't been neutered, which I recommend you have done soon, especially if he's going to be an outdoor cat."

"I'd like to keep him indoors, if possible," I said.

He nodded in approval. "Good idea. I'll have Sandy put up a sign about a cat being found, in case you're worried that he does belong to someone. Oh, and I would recommend a distemper and rabies shot for today."

After the shots, Doctor Horowitz placed Toast inside the carrier and asked me if I had any questions for him. "I don't think so," I said. "This is all new to me. I've never had a pet before."

"You're Victor's daughter, aren't you?" Doctor Horowitz asked.

I nodded. "That's right. You knew my dad?"

"Of course. Like everyone else in Sugar Ridge, I love Sappy Endings. I'm quite addicted to the maple syrup. My wife goes in a couple of times a year to purchase it." He smiled. "Your father was a generous contributor to my on-site shelter. He gave us a large donation every year. I was so sorry to hear about his death."

Even though my father couldn't keep pets, he'd done

quite a bit to support them. It shouldn't have surprised me. My father was always giving to someone. "Thank you. He was a wonderful man." My voice shook slightly. "Please send me a donation envelope. Sappy Endings would be honored to continue making donations in his memory."

"Thank you, Leila. I appreciate that." Doctor Horowitz's expression turned grim. "Have the police found out any details about his death?"

"Nothing that I know of." I reached a finger inside the carrier to touch Toast, who looked as if he was sleeping. "How long did you know my father?"

Doctor Horowitz scratched his head. "Let's see. It has to be close to twenty years that he's been making donations. Shortly after my wife and I moved to Sugar Ridge, I stopped at the farm for coffee one day. Your father waited on me, and I told him about our no-kill shelter at the animal hospital. I mentioned that there was a beautiful beagle who would make a great pet for a farm. He told me that he had severe allergies and seemed sad that he couldn't take him. Then he asked me to wait for a moment and came back with a check for the shelter. This world needs more people like him."

"That sounds like something he would have done." I hesitated for a moment. "Do you happen to remember my father's partner back then? His name was Dennis Browning."

Doctor Horowitz stared at me in surprise. "Dennis was your father's partner? I had no idea. He's been gone for several years. Suicide, I believe."

My mouth dropped open. "Yes, they were partners for a brief time. Dennis committed suicide? I had no idea."

"Yes, very tragic," Doctor Horowitz murmured. "He never seemed the type to me."

"How well did you know him?"

"Not well," he admitted. "Dennis had a German Shepherd that he'd bring in for checkups annually. After he died, his son, Wesley, started bringing the dog in, until he passed over the rainbow bridge a few years back." Doctor Horowitz frowned. "I don't think I've seen Wesley since then. He was good with the dog but has trouble interacting with people."

"How do you mean?" I asked.

Doctor Horowitz looked embarrassed. "Forget what I said. I shouldn't be gossiping about a former client. I'm sorry."

"No worries." I tried another tactic. "Wesley blamed my father for Dennis's death. I was hoping to find out a little more about him." And what made him tick.

"I didn't know that." Doctor Horowitz turned apologetic. "Then again, it doesn't surprise me. From what I've heard, Wesley always blames other people for his troubles. He's been fired from several jobs in the past because of his tongue. He's rude to everyone and has always been kind of a loner."

"Do you happen to know where he works now?" I asked.

Doctor Horowitz pinched his nose between his forefinger and thumb. "I don't believe that he *is* working. Since his mother died a few months back, he's disappeared from sight." He reached a hand down into the carrier to pat Toast. "Leila, I have another patient waiting. Bring Toast back in six months or sooner if he's having any problems. When you want to schedule his neutering, give Sandy a call."

Toast meowed, as if voicing his objection.

"I'll do that, in the next week or two. Thank you so much," I said gratefully.

After I paid the bill, Toast and I returned to my car. He started to yowl again, and I couldn't help smiling. My father would have liked Toast—I was certain of that. Then again, my father had liked everyone. He never had an unkind thing to say about anyone.

Tears smarted in my eyes and I quickly wiped them away. "I'm going to find out who did this to you, Dad. I promise."

On the way back to Sappy Endings, I made a quick stop at the pet store, where I bought a bed, cat food, bowls, litter, and a litter box. I hoped that Toast would be content as an indoor cat.

I was only in the store for ten minutes, but Toast was caterwauling at the top of his lungs when I returned, making me feel like an unfit mother. I'd left the window open a crack and the temperature was only in the fifties, but it was evident that he was upset by my sudden departure. As soon as we returned to Sappy Endings, I poured some cat food into a bowl and gave him fresh water. He had just settled down into his new bed on the top of my desk when there was a knock on the door.

"Come on in," I called.

Chief Crosby poked his head around the door and smiled. "Is this a good time, Boss, or should I come back later?"

"Now is fine. Come on in and meet my new assistant."

He looked down at the orange fluffy cat curled up in a ball in his brand-new, paw-printed bed. "Well, it didn't take long for you to break protocol, Leila. I've been in this office hundreds of times, and about the only thing I've never seen is a cat."

I laughed. "Please sit down."

The Chief removed his Stetson and placed it on my desk. He glanced around the office in a somewhat wistful way. "How is everything going?"

I wiggled my hand back and forth. "It's taking me a while to fit in here. Isn't that weird? After all the summers working in the gift shop and helping Jessica in the café, I feel like a stranger."

"Not weird at all," Chief Crosby remarked. "Like any job, it takes time to adjust."

"Have you found out anything new about my father's murder?" Chief Crosby always donned a poker face, which was what helped to make him such a great law enforcement person.

Chief Crosby shook his head. "I came out here to talk to Jessica and Noah again. Both of them have been very cooperative."

I slid Dennis Browning's obituary across the desk to him. "I had no idea that Dennis and my father were once partners. My mother said that he bought Dennis out when Mr. Browning couldn't pay his gambling debts."

Chief Crosby's eyes widened as he glanced at the obituary. "Where did you get this?"

"My father had it in his desk with a pile of other clippings. I'm surprised that no one found it when they searched the office."

"No surprise there." Chief Crosby pushed it back toward me. "Why would anyone who came across this think it was related to your father's murder?"

I twisted a pencil between my fingers. "My mother said that his son, Wesley, came out here the day Dad died."

Chief Crosby nodded. "He did, but like his father, Wesley is all talk and no action. Was he angry with Victor? Sure, but he had no right to be. Wesley's mother coddled him as a child, and he never grew up. He has no siblings, his mother recently died, and as far as I know, he doesn't have any friends. He's looking for someone else to coddle him, I guess."

"You sound like you know him well enough," I murmured.

That drew a smile from him. "I know everyone in this town, Leila. I consider it part of my job. Dennis was a decent guy, but he dug himself into too deep of a hole to climb out of. I have to say it wasn't exactly a shock to me when he killed himself. I saw it coming." He examined my face closely. "I hope you're not thinking about going to see Wesley."

"Of course not." I crossed my fingers behind my back.

"Look, Leila, I know I said that Wesley's all talk, but the guy has a history of making trouble. He's got some serious anger issues and destroyed property in the past. It wouldn't be a good idea to go to his house. In that warped mind of his, he feels that your father cheated him out of an inheritance, but Victor did nothing wrong. Dennis willingly signed his rights away to Sappy Endings. He wasn't coerced into it. This is merely a case of Wesley looking for greener pastures to supplement his lifestyle."

"Was the history on my father's computer searched?"

Chief Crosby nodded. "My men checked the one out in the sugar shack, which Noah uses, right?" He gestured toward the one between us on the desk. "And they checked this one, too." He rose and came to stand behind me. "Why, did you find something of interest?"

"That's the trouble. There isn't any history."

Chief Crosby frowned and grabbed the mouse with his large hand. He moved the cursor into the corner of the screen and clicked on history. The only tabs that appeared were those that I had searched for this week.

He frowned and shook his head. "I don't believe this. Did you delete it by mistake?"

"I know my way around a computer, Chief. I'd never do that."

Chief Crosby shrugged and walked back around the desk to his seat. "It's possible one of my guys might have done it by accident, but I can't see that happening." He cast worried eyes upon me. "Who else has access to the office? Do you keep the door locked all the time?"

"I lock it at the end of the day," I told him. "But during the day—" I stopped, and we exchanged glances. It would be fairly easy for anyone to get in here. The safe was always kept locked, and I was the only one who knew the combination. It had been in my father's will. Noah had been at Sappy Endings the entire week after my father's death. He'd also been the one to find my father's body. Did he shoot him and then rush to the computer to erase any possible history that fingered him for the crime?

"I'll check with my men about this. They better not have screwed up this investigation," Chief Crosby said grimly.

Toast rose and rubbed against him. Chief Crosby absently patted the cat on the head. "Getting back to Wesley, he's been out here before to bother your father. I told your father that he should get a restraining order against the guy, but he wouldn't listen to me." He shook his head ruefully. "In Wesley's mind, maybe he thought if he kept coming back enough, your father would cave and give him money because of a guilty conscience."

Knowing my father and how kind-hearted he'd been, that was a possibility. I decided not to let the chief know of my plans to visit Wesley tonight. He would not take it well. "I have to find out who did this to my father."

"I'll say this for you. You're just as stubborn as him." Chief Crosby's voice turned gruffer than usual.

"Is there something else bothering you, Chief?"

The silence in the room was deafening for a few seconds. "All right, Leila. I hadn't planned on telling you this, but your father had another visitor the day he died— someone besides Wesley." Chief Crosby exhaled sharply. "Your brother."

I tried to remain calm. "So what? Jessica told me he was here. I'm sure Simon came to Sappy Endings plenty of times."

"Yes," Chief Crosby agreed, "but several customers overheard them arguing that day. Your father and I were best friends for a long time, and there wasn't much that he didn't tell me. I know they had their differences, but they were both stubborn as all get-out."

My body went rigid. "What are you trying to say? That Simon killed him?"

"You know me better than that," he scoffed.

"Well, what then? That they argued over money and my brother shot him? That's crazy."

Chief Crosby's face hardened like stone. "Yes, but it's possible that your brother may have gotten himself involved with people who were capable of such a thing. I don't know what Simon's situation is, but I do know that he's asked your father for money before. In the past, Victor gave it to him, but he told me shortly before he died that he was putting his foot down. If Simon owed money to anyone—"

I thought about Dennis and his gambling debts. "Like who? Gangsters? A loan shark?"

Chief Crosby held up a hand. "Let me finish. If Simon

borrowed money from someone unscrupulous and didn't pay it back, maybe they came after your father to collect."

"Simon wouldn't put Dad in any danger." I knew what Chief Crosby was thinking, and I hated myself for thinking the same thing. If a person was desperate enough for money, they'd take it from wherever they could get it. Could Simon have unwittingly caused our father's death?

The chief roused himself from the chair. "I appreciate that you want to help, Leila, but please leave this to the police. Believe me, I'm not going to rest until your father's killer is found."

"None of this makes any sense," I said sadly. "My father didn't have an enemy in the world."

"He was a terrific guy, that's for sure," Chief Crosby agreed. "In fact, Noah said the same thing—everyone who came into Sappy Endings loved your dad."

His statement left a bitter taste in my mouth. Who did Noah Rivers think he was? He works for my father for less than a year and acts like they're best buddies? He wasn't his son; he was an employee. That's all. The man was still a stranger to me, and, even though I had no proof of his guilt, if I had to choose between him or Simon, there was no contest.

"I know what you're thinking." Chief Crosby narrowed his eyes. "But I don't want you going around and causing bad feelings with your employees. You know that your father wouldn't have wanted that. A year is a long time when you're not getting along with someone."

Too late for that. "You're right, I'm sorry."

"As for Jessica, she was almost as distraught as your mother," Chief Crosby said. "In fact, she started crying as soon as I brought up his name."

I couldn't believe that he would mention Jessica in the same breath as Noah. "You're kidding, right? Jessica is like family to us. She's been at Sappy Endings for over ten years. What reason would she have to kill my father? That he didn't give her a raise?"

Chief Crosby raised an eyebrow, and it was plain to see that he wasn't amused by my sarcasm. Instead of responding right away, he picked up his hat, placed it on his head, and touched his thumb and forefinger to the brim. "Like I said, Leila, I'm not leaving any stones unturned."

That goes double for me, Chief.

CHAPTER EIGHT

"I FORGOT HOW DARK AND winding this road was," Heather remarked as I turned onto the street where the Brownings lived.

"And creepy," I added. It had only taken us about twenty minutes to get here but enough time for both of us to start having doubts.

Heather pulled her jacket closer around her and stared out into the night. There was only a sliver of the moon showing, and the street was dimly lighted.

"Everything will be fine." I wasn't sure if I'd spoken the words aloud for Heather's sake or mine. The speedometer said that we were doing twenty miles an hour, but fortunately, no one was behind me. It was deer hunting season, and the animals had a terrible habit of running across the road without warning. I'd narrowly missed one minutes ago. "Is it much further?"

"The next house on the right," Heather said. "Did you figure out what reason we're going to give him for coming by? I think we're a little too old for selling Girl Scout cookies."

"The truth if I have to," I admitted. "I'll ask him why he went to visit my father."

She shivered. "I like the Girl Scout reason better."

I pulled my shiny new hatchback onto a dirt driveway behind a rusted four-door maroon sedan, then quickly shut off the headlights. The house resembled an abandoned shack, and it looked like a bag of trash had exploded all over the lawn. We got out of the car, and upon closer inspection, the house was even more grim. A wire fence was stretched around a shell of a detached garage, and two chickens started bobbing their heads and clucking loudly as we approached. The only outdoor lighting was a bulb attached to the front of the garage, surrounded by cobwebs. A glimmer of light shone from an upstairs window and a shadow appeared inside it. This was the type of house we'd always avoided going to on Halloween.

Heather swallowed hard. "It didn't look this bad when I was here last time. Maybe he's not home."

I pointed at the sedan. "That has to be his car."

Our shoes crunched on the gravel as we walked toward the house. "You said that Chief Crosby doesn't believe Wesley had anything to do with your father's death," Heather said. "If that's true, what do you hope to find out by coming here?"

"He may think the guy's innocent, but I'm not

convinced." I didn't mention Simon and my worry that Chief Crosby was taking a harder look at him. If my mother had an idea what direction the police chief's mind was running in, it would kill her.

"Wesley came to see my father because he wanted money," I said. "What if my father refused and he got so angry that he killed him in the heat of the moment?"

Heather clutched my arm. "A crime of passion," she whispered.

"Exactly. It's too much of a coincidence that he just happened to drop by on the day my father was murdered." If my father had installed a security camera by the back door of Sappy Endings, we might know the person who'd killed him. Instead, his office had been a booming business that day, and I had no idea who the real culprit was.

"Come on, let's get this over with," Heather said. "By the way, I have mace in my purse."

"*What?*"

"Hey, a girl can't be too careful these days."

The front porch steps creaked as we climbed them, and a light over the front door switched on, shining in our faces and blinding us with the sudden glare. Yes, the house had definitely seen better days. The vinyl siding was peeling away, the roof had a blue tarp stretched over it to shield it from rain or snow, and the porch was in danger of crumbling underneath our feet.

The front door creaked and groaned as it opened, and a man appeared in the doorway. He was slightly taller than me and thin to the point of being gaunt. He wore a

Yankees ball cap backward on his head, and his skin was a sickly pallor, but it was his eyes that frightened me. They were dark and cold, like an endless pool of creek water.

"What do you want? There's no soliciting around here." His tone was brisk and impatient.

Heather's fingernails dug into my arm and I held back a yelp. "Are—are you Wesley Browning?"

The man scanned me up and down. "Who wants to know?" Before I could respond, his gaze wandered over to Heather, and I spotted a flicker of recognition. "Hey, I know you. You're the hairdresser who came here to see my mother."

"Yes, that's right." She offered him her hand and after a moment's hesitation, he shook it. "I'm Heather Turcot. I know I'm late with the sentiment, but I'm so sorry about your mother. She was a lovely woman."

Wesley seemed to relax a bit. "Yes, she was. Thank you." He turned his attention back to me, waiting for my explanation.

My resolve was fading fast, so I decided to get it over with. "My name is Leila Khoury. I'm the manager over at—"

"You're Victor's daughter." A muscle ticked in his jaw. "That lowlife swindled my father out of his share of the farm. They were partners, you know."

"Yes, I recently found that out." All the lies I'd been concocting in my head disappeared.

"Why are you here?" Wesley's voice was low and full of suspicion. "You want something."

I drew a deep breath and prayed that he couldn't hear my heart pounding away in my chest. "You came to see my father at Sappy Endings the same day he died." There was no point in beating around the bush anymore. "I'd like to know why you went to see him."

He narrowed his eyes. "I don't owe you any explanation. The police have already questioned me. When's it a crime for a fellow to grab a cup of coffee on the way to work?"

"There's no law against that," Heather piped in.

"I'm not accusing you of anything," I said gently. "All I want to know is why you went to see my father."

Wesley's laugh was bitter. "Victor Khoury owed my father money. He swindled him out of Sappy Endings, and now that place is a gold mine." He stuck his face next to mine. His breath was hot and stank of alcohol. "There were a lot of people who didn't like your old man, honey. Give me my fair share, and then I'll tell you why I went there."

I stepped back, the stale odor of him making me nauseous. "I'm not giving you a dime. So all you wanted from my father was money. And when you didn't get any you—" I broke off in the nick of time, before I said something that I would regret.

Spittle collected in the corner of Wesley's mouth. "You think you know everything, huh, Miss High and Mighty? Well, you don't. I didn't go there for money. Instead, I went to warn your father."

"Warn him about what?" I asked.

He snickered. "I'm not telling you anything else. Get lost before I call the cops and report you for trespassing."

Heather tugged at my arm. "Leila, let's go. We shouldn't have come here."

Wesley tapped the side of his head. "That's right. You should listen to your friend."

"Hang on a second." I wasn't sure that I believed Wesley. Chief Crosby told me he had anger issues, plus the man had been drinking. All he wanted was to get some money out of me. I took a step toward him, pulling Heather along with me.

"You're a liar. What would you have to warn my father about?" Maybe he would admit to shooting my father if I pushed him a little further, but at what risk? This wasn't only about me. I had Heather's welfare to consider as well.

Wesley lit a cigarette and exhaled a puff of smoke into the cool, crisp night air. "I didn't think you'd believe me. A little rich, stuck-up snob like you? I heard that your Daddy left you his entire business. Guess you'll sit back and let everyone else do the work, huh?"

Instead of me doing the pushing, it was Wesley, and he was about to go too far. "You don't know a thing about me or my father," I burst out. "He tried to help your family. He paid off your father's debts and might have saved him from being killed. You have no right to blame him for your father's death."

"Leila!" Heather tried to drag me toward the car. "Come on, honey. Let's leave before this gets out of hand."

She managed to get me off the porch, but then I dug my heels in and refused to budge. I glared at the man, who was leaning against his front door, watching us in the semi-darkness.

"How does it feel, Miss Khoury?" he asked angrily. "Your father's not the only one to have been murdered in cold blood."

Heather and I exchanged puzzled glances. "Wait a minute," I gasped. "Your father wasn't murdered. Chief Crosby told me it was suicide."

"No." Wesley shook his head and blew out a long, ragged breath. "The old codger told me the same thing. But I don't believe it, not for one second."

He started down the steps, but it was obvious that he was too inebriated when he began to sway from side to side. Heather shrieked and pulled at my arm again. "Leila, can we please go?"

She was clearly frightened out of her wits, and I was to blame. "I'm sorry, Heather. Yes, we'll leave." I stared back at Wesley, who was now sitting on the steps, sobbing into his shirt sleeve. Pity stirred within me for the man, and I wasn't sure why. Somehow, I found my voice again. "I'm truly sorry about your father's death, and your mother's as well. But none of it was my father's fault."

Wesley lifted his head and pinned his dark, listless eyes on mine. "Let me give you a little bit of advice," he warned. "Don't get involved in things that don't concern you, unless you want to wind up like your old man."

Heather yanked me away from the man, and we turned and hurried to my car. Wesley remained on his porch watching us while I backed the car out of the darkened driveway, praying I wouldn't hit anything or anyone along the way.

As soon as Wesley and his house were out of sight, Heather started to breathe normally again. "Holy cow. He scared the life out of me. And so did you!"

"Heather, I'm sorry. I shouldn't have brought you with me. This is my problem, not yours."

"Are you nuts?" Heather cried. "I never would have let you come out here alone. That man is clearly unstable. Did you tell Chief Crosby that you were going to talk to him?"

"No."

She shook her head in disbelief. "Uh oh. I'll bet Wesley calls and reports us. And then Chief Crosby will tell your mother, and she'll go off the wall."

There was no doubt about that. "What if Wesley's telling the truth? Could he have really wanted to warn my father about something? Remember what he said—'There were a lot of people who didn't like your old man.' Maybe he does know who killed him, or else he's trying to extort money from me."

"I'm betting that it was all about the money." Heather glanced sideways at me as I stopped for a red light. "Do you think that both of your fathers' deaths could be related?"

"I don't know," I said honestly. "Chief Crosby said that Dennis committed suicide. Doctor Horowitz told me the same thing. Besides, Dennis died many years ago. I'm not sure how they would connect."

We drove in silence for several minutes, both of us lost in our own thoughts until I turned the car onto Heather's road. My mind was racing with different scenarios, but

Heather put a stop to them with her next question. "Lei, did Chief Crosby tell you if anyone besides Wesley came to see your father the day he was killed?"

I gripped the steering wheel tightly and didn't answer.

"Well?" she pressed.

"Maybe." I pulled the car into her driveway and placed it in park.

Confused, she continued to stare at me. "What does that mean?"

I turned to face Heather and exhaled sharply. There was no point in trying to lie to her. We always knew when the other one wasn't telling the truth. Heather wanted to help and could be trusted, but it was so hard to say the words out loud. "Chief Crosby told me that Simon came to see Dad the same day that he died. He asked to borrow money."

Heather wasn't impressed. "So what? I've asked my father for money plenty of times."

"This is different," I said. "You know that Simon and my father have always had a rocky relationship. Apparently, he's been desperate for money, and this isn't the first time he's asked to borrow some."

"Maybe Tonya's bleeding him dry," Heather suggested. "She showed Tyler and me a house a couple of weeks ago. Your mother mentioned that Simon's girlfriend was a real estate agent so when I saw the name Tonya Donnelly on the listing and her picture, I put two and two together. I asked her if she was dating Simon and she said yes."

"I love it when you're nosy. What's she like?"

Heather hesitated for a moment. "She's nice, I guess. To be honest, I thought she was a bit stuck on herself."

"That's what I was afraid of."

Heather studied me in silence for several seconds. "There's something else you're not telling me."

I let out a deep breath. "Chief Crosby said that several customers overheard Dad and Simon arguing in his office. Jessica did, too."

"No way." Heather's face registered alarm. "Simon's not the violent type. I will never believe that he had anything to do with your dad's death. Did the chief actually say that he was a suspect? Does your mother know about this?"

I had to smile. Heather sounded as if she was defending her own brother. "I don't think that Mom knows about it. She would never forgive Chief Crosby for suggesting such a thing. In the chief's defense, he said that he isn't ruling anyone out."

"It would kill your mother if she knew that Simon was considered a suspect."

"Tell me about it." Mom would defend Simon to her dying day. "He's never disappointed her like I have."

"Stop that," Heather scolded. "I know what you're thinking. It's not your fault that Mark backed out of the wedding."

It had been four years since that fateful day, but still seemed like yesterday. Mark had come to the house, and we'd gone out for coffee. As I sat there thinking of white lace and wedding cake and our planned honeymoon to Aruba in thirty days, he'd confided to me that he couldn't go through with the wedding.

Well, at least he hadn't left me at the altar.

"You know that he had his reasons, and I really can't blame him." I was tempted to ask Heather if she'd heard any news about him. His parents still lived nearby, and I couldn't help but wonder if he'd been back for a visit recently. What did it even matter? He hadn't loved me enough to marry me then, and he wouldn't change his mind four years later.

"Look," Heather said calmly. "Everything in this life happens for a reason. I'm convinced that you and Mark weren't meant to be. I know that you loved him, but, maybe, deep down, you were also hoping to gain your mother's favor by marrying him."

She had a point. Mark's parents had been friends with mine for many years. I never knew for certain but suspected that my parents had a dowry put away for me, which had led to Mark's parents arranging for us to meet each other. Despite my objections, I'd fallen hard for him. When he'd broken our engagement, all I'd wanted was to run away and hide from the world. It hadn't taken long to realize that I couldn't run from my problems.

"You may have missed your calling. I think you should have been a psychiatrist."

Heather giggled. "I told you, it comes from everyone telling me their problems daily. I'm getting good at solving them." She leaned over to hug me. "I'll come by Sappy Endings tomorrow at noon. My first appointment isn't until one thirty. We can brainstorm some more ideas and have lunch."

"Sounds good."

CHAPTER NINE

I WAITED IN THE CAR until Heather had gone inside and then drove the short distance to my mother's house. The car's clock read seven thirty, and I was starving. I found my mother on the living room couch watching television with Toast, who was sleeping contentedly.

"Looks like you've made a new friend," I joked.

My mother softly stroked Toast's head. "He's such a good boy. I think I'll give him a bath tomorrow. By the way, he loves the meat and rice I stuffed the grape leaves with."

"You shouldn't feed him food like that," I objected.

She waved a hand in the air dismissively. "A little bit won't hurt him. Did you eat? There's plenty left."

"I'll get them. You relax."

Mom ignored me and rose from the couch. Toast opened one eye, looked at us, and then closed it again, as if exhausted with the effort. Mom set a place at the table and put a plate of grape leaves and a bowl of *ema* in front of me. The hearty soup was prepared with kofta meatballs, vermicelli, and rice and cooked in tomato sauce. It was a favorite of both mine and Simon's.

"Help yourself," she said. "I'll be back in a few minutes. I have to run across the street to check on Mrs. Middleton."

The sumptuous taste of cinnamon lingered on my tongue. "What's wrong with her?"

Mom picked up a Tupperware bowl filled with grape leaves. "She had her appendix out and is all alone. Her daughter's working late tonight, so I said I'd pop in for a little while." She eyed me sharply. "You never told me where you went tonight."

"Oh. Heather wanted me to look at some bridal gowns with her."

She gave me a shrewd look that said I wasn't fooling her but thankfully didn't press. I hated lying to my mother, but if she knew the truth, she'd have a stroke.

I finished eating shortly after she'd left, then rinsed and put my dishes in the dishwasher. Toast jumped off the couch and followed me past the staircase to where my father's study was. He began scratching at the door. Mystified, I opened it, and he ran inside.

It was a small, cozy room tucked away in the corner of the lower level. An Oriental rug in shades of brown and blue that my mother had knotted together lay on the floor. There was also a handsome oak desk with matching book shelves. Toast jumped into a plush easy chair and meowed, claiming it as his own.

Like his office at Sappy Endings, Dad had a desktop computer here as well. I sat down in his chair and wiggled the mouse until the screen brightened, then immediately went to recent history. A list of searches came up on the screen for the past three weeks. There weren't many, and I immediately saw one that stood out from the rest. *Lawsuit.* Had something happened with a customer to make him concerned?

I clicked on the tab but there were only general terms to be found. *How to file a lawsuit. What happens when someone sues you. What does it mean to sue someone.* Maybe he had talked to Theo about it and he'd recommended an attorney who specialized in the field.

The front door slammed, causing me to rise to my feet. When I reached the doorway, Simon appeared before me. He looked surprised. "Hey, sis. What are you doing in here? Where's Mom?"

"She went across the street to see Mrs. Middleton." I managed to avoid the 'what was I doing in the study' question by leading him toward the kitchen. "And what's my handsome brother doing here? Shouldn't you be off writing some award-winning article?"

He shot me a saucy grin and reached into the cupboard for a bowl. "Mom said she made *ema.* I can't work on an empty stomach."

We were true addicts when it came to our mother's cooking. The remaining grape leaves were sitting on the stove in a casserole dish, covered with tin foil. Simon helped himself to several as well as the soup. The kitchen was the favorite room in my mother's well-loved and immaculate home. It was always cozy and warm and heavy with the scents of allspice, cinnamon, and cloves. Mom used the spices in all of her traditional dishes. As for the grape leaves, she usually handpicked the leaves herself from the neighborhood or trees on the farm.

"I've missed Mom's cooking." I helped myself to a cup of *Ahweh*. "There's nothing half as good as it in Florida."

"I'm sure she'd be willing to teach you how to make grape leaves," Simon teased.

"Very funny." Simon knew that cooking was another bone of contention between my mother and me. She loved and excelled at it while I'd never been interested in learning. In fact, she'd once tried to get me to make grape leaves as a teenager. After I'd refused, she'd screamed that I'd never get a husband if I couldn't cook. She probably thought that was why Mark had dumped me.

Simon sat down at the table across from me and started reading something on his phone while I drummed my fingers on the table. "No phones during meal times,"

"Sorry, Mother." He grinned and pushed the phone away. "I was reading through my article for a last time before I turn it in. It's about how the unemployment rate is affecting our local economy. I think it might make front page tomorrow."

"That's fantastic." I stirred some cream into my mug. "Have you ever made front page before?"

Simon refilled his soup bowl. "Once. Remember when I did the story about the flapjack-eating contest at Sappy Endings?"

"Oh, right. I forgot about that." We were both silent for several seconds, thinking of that day. Dad had been so excited to host the contest, and thrilled when the story made front page. I remember him calling me on the phone to say, "Your brother wrote a really nice article about the farm. The kid sure can write, Leila."

"It may have been the only time Dad was ever proud of me."

"That's not true." I reached across the table to cover his hand with mine.

Simon wiped his mouth on a napkin. "All we did was argue, Lei. If it wasn't about my not wanting to work at Sappy Endings, he'd complain that I couldn't do the simplest things he'd asked. Remember the time he asked me to fix the lock on the back door? He yelled at me about it the last day I saw him."

"But that was over a year ago," I protested.

He scraped his bowl. "It doesn't matter. He said I never fixed it right, and I wasn't good for anything, except wanting—"

Simon didn't finish the sentence. I suspected that he was going to say *money* but decided not to press him.

"Let's face it, Lei," Simon continued. "He never forgave me for not wanting to be part of Sappy Endings. And he never understood my passion for writing."

"That doesn't mean he wasn't proud of you." Our father

had had to quit school after the tenth grade to help support his family. He'd been determined that Simon and I have the best education possible. Like any other father, he wanted his children to have more than he did. My heart warmed at the thought.

Simon jumped. "What the—" He stared down at the floor, where Toast was rubbing against his leg. He started to laugh and reached down a hand to pat him on the head. "Where did this little guy come from? Does Mom know he's here?"

"She not only knows that he's here, but I think Toast might be her new favorite male, even over you," I teased, then quickly relayed the story of how he had become a member of the family.

Simon rose to put his bowl in the sink. "Well, she's always loved cats."

"Toast will be great company for her, especially after I move back to Florida next year." Guilt settled around me like a heavy blanket. Sappy Endings would end up being sold eventually and destroying my father's legacy.

Simon leaned against the counter, coffee cup in hand. "So that's it? You're definitely not planning on staying here permanently?"

"I agreed to stay for a year. That's all."

Simon pursed his lips. "Look, Lei, I know that you and Mom have had your share of problems, but don't let that stop you from staying. Sugar Ridge is big enough for the both of you."

"That's not the reason. I have a life in Florida, remember."

He shot me a disbelieving look. "Come on. I know you, remember? You hate your job. You wanted to teach kindergarten, not high school kids. You left Sugar Ridge for the wrong reasons and will be going back to Florida for the wrong ones as well."

"I don't know what you mean," I lied.

Simon rolled his eyes toward the ceiling. "Yeah, you do. You left town after Mark broke up with you. Mom was angry, you were upset, all you two did was fight, and Dad took your side against her, which caused even more problems." A smile tugged at the corners of Simon's mouth. "He never thought that guy was good enough for his little girl."

Simon was right about that part. I remembered Dad saying that I could do better than Mark while I'd cried myself to sleep.

"Okay, that may have been part of it," I admitted. "Mom and I were at each other's throats, and I couldn't deal with the humiliation." The entire town knew my pitiful love story. "But I'm not sorry that I went away. I needed to stand on my own two feet for a change."

Simon patted my cheek lovingly. "I told you to do whatever makes you happy. And I never asked why you were leaving, did I?"

"No, you didn't," I said gratefully.

"Don't you see?" Simon asked. "You and I are a lot alike. We're both trying to figure out where we belong. I want a career in writing." He stared off into space, a dreamy smile on his lips. "I want to walk into the town library one day and see my books decorating the shelves. As for you—you thought you wanted to be a teacher, but now you're starting to wonder if you made a mistake and you belong at Sappy Endings."

"I never said that—"

Simon shook his head and continued. "Dad never liked my writing. Mom wanted you to marry someone that she'd handpicked. She also wanted you to cook and knit and give her lots of grandkids. We both want different things than they planned for us. And that's okay, sis." The light faded from his eyes. "I only wish that Dad had given me a little consideration in his will."

Now we were getting somewhere. It was uncomfortable knowing that I had been left an entire business while Simon had only received personal belongings. "You'll get a share of the farm's profits."

"Not unless Mom decides to cut me in," he said. "Plus, everything has to go through probate, so I probably wouldn't see anything for months. I could really use some money now. Working as a reporter doesn't exactly put me at the top of the food chain."

"You and Dad argued about money the day he died," I blurted out.

He looked startled by my remark. "Who told you that?"

Me and my big mouth. "Jessica overheard, and some of the customers in the café told Chief Crosby about it as well."

A muscle ticked in Simon's jaw. "That guy gets on my nerves. I know he was Dad's closest friend, but I swear he's always had it in for me. He came down to the newspaper office to talk to me today. This was the third time. It's like he's waiting for me to crack and admit I killed Dad."

"That's crazy." I realized that Crosby had to look at everyone, but this was my brother for goodness' sake. "I could lend you five hundred dollars, if that would help."

Simon shoved his hands deep into the pockets of his jeans. "It doesn't, but thanks, sis. Look, it's not a big deal. I've been a little low on cash lately, that's all. If I get that senior reporter job, my problems will be over. I need a few grand to tide me over until then."

The amount he needed was way out of my league. "Maybe Mom can lend it to you,"

"No," he answered sharply. "I don't want Mom to know anything about this. Understand?"

His response both surprised and unnerved me. Our mother would never deny him anything, so why didn't Simon want her to know? I instantly thought of Dennis Browning and his gambling addiction.

"Don't worry, I won't say anything." Since he clearly wanted a change of subject, I decided it was a good time to ask about his new girlfriend. Perhaps she had something to do with his sudden need for money. "Tell me all about Tonya."

"What do you want to know?" he asked.

"Mom said that she was a runner-up in the Miss Vermont pageant."

His face lit up as he smiled. "Yeah, she's a real knockout."

"How long have you two been dating?"

Simon poured himself another cup of *Ahweh* and sat down. "About two months."

It was like pulling teeth to get any information out of him. "And I hear she's a real estate agent, huh?"

Simon folded his arms across his chest and stared up at me. "Okay, Lei, why are you asking so many questions?"

I shrugged. "I just want to know about her."

He narrowed his eyes. "Mom asked me the same questions when I told her that Tonya and I were dating. Are you worried that there's no way a gorgeous, successful woman like Tonya would be interested in me?"

"Oh, stop it," I scoffed. "I think you're a great catch for any woman. You're good looking, smart, and have a great sense of humor."

He leaned back in his chair. "Funny, I happen to think the same things about you. While we're on the topic, why aren't *you* dating anyone? Mom's worried you're never going to give her any grandkids."

Heat crept up my neck. "Did she tell you that?"

Simon shook his head. "No, I overheard her telling Dad a couple of months ago."

Frustrated, I smacked my palm against my forehead. "When is she ever going to stop?"

He gave me a sympathetic smile. "You know she's not going to stop until you're married with a couple of rug rats. Look, I won't meddle in your personal life if you don't meddle in mine, deal?"

Simon had always been willing to talk about his girlfriends in the past, so this was a change of pace for him. I worried that he'd fallen hard for Tonya and might get his heart broken. "Okay," I agreed. "Getting back to Dad and the money, did you—"

"I don't believe it," he grimaced.

"What?" I asked.

Color faded from his face. "My own sister. Do you really think I could have hurt our father?"

"Of course not!" I exclaimed. "Don't put words into my mouth!"

"Then why are you interrogating me?" he demanded. "What, are you working with mighty Chief Crosby now?"

"You know that I love you, and I would never think such a horrible thing. All I want is justice for our father and to find out who ended his life and why." A sob broke from between my lips. "He didn't deserve to die like that, Simon. It's not fair." Tears gushed down my cheeks.

Simon leaped from his chair and put his arms around me. "Hey, don't cry. You know I can't stand that." He kissed the top of my head. "You're right. I need to know, too."

I dried my eyes with a napkin and released my hold on him. "One more question. Did Dad mention if anyone else had come to see him that day, like Wesley Browning?"

Simon wrinkled his nose. "Who's Wesley Browning?"

"A man with an axe to grind. His father was partners with Dad years ago and signed his rights away to the Sappy Endings when he couldn't pay off his gambling debts."

Confusion registered on Simon's face. "Dad had a partner named Wesley?"

"No, I'm talking about his father, Dennis. He committed suicide about twenty years ago."

Simon leaned against the kitchen counter. "I think I remember reading an old article about him in the *Maple Messenger*. I'm actually surprised Dad had a partner. He was such a control freak."

"Don't say that."

He folded his arms. "So, you think that this guy waited twenty years to come and get revenge on Dad for his father's death? Look, sis, if you really want to find out who killed our father, I suggest that you take a closer look at the people right under your nose."

Fear gnawed inside me. "Meaning?"

"I'm talking about Noah Rivers, of course. That guy is hiding something and I don't trust him. He wanted to buy Sappy Endings from Dad, and he still wants it. Whenever I went to see Dad, they were attached at the hip." Simon's mouth formed into a sneer. "Noah wanted the farm so badly that he would have done anything to get it."

CHAPTER TEN

"WHAT ARE YOU SAYING—THAT Noah killed our father?"

"Why are you acting so surprised?" Simon asked. "You're the one who wanted to throw him into jail. Remember when we were in Theo's office for the reading of Dad's will? You came right out and said you thought he'd done it."

"That's true," I admitted, "but I hope I'm wrong." As much as I hated to admit it, Noah was an asset to the place. "He knows how to run the café and gift shop, tap the trees, make the syrup, and do just about everything else." As for myself, I wasn't even close to mastering any job on the farm.

Simon stared at me as if I had two heads. "Wait a second, I get it." He smiled in understanding. "I've even heard Jessica talk about how good looking he is. One day, when I was at Sappy Endings getting coffee, she told Dad that's why so many women were booking tours lately."

I narrowed my eyes. "I'm not interested in Noah. He's an employee. That's all."

"He wants Sappy Endings," Simon repeated. "Maybe Dad refused to sell to him because he wanted the farm to stay in the family, but he liked the guy. That was obvious. He treated Noah like a son." His voice faltered. "More so than he did me."

Sadness overwhelmed me. Simon was right about us being alike. He'd spent his entire life trying to gain Dad's approval while Mom and I had bickered back and forth. It was clear to me why Simon resented Noah. Simon hadn't wanted to work on the farm, but he also didn't want someone else taking his place.

"Noah isn't competition for you," I said gently.

Simon scowled and pulled at his hair. "What's going to happen next year when you leave and the place is sold? He's biding his time, waiting to scoop up the place."

"When you talked to Dad the last time, did you happen to mention Noah?"

"No." Simon opened the fridge, looked inside, and then closed the door. "I didn't have to. Dad always brought him up to me. I swear, it felt like he was deliberately trying to tick me off. 'Noah came up with a great idea for the tours. Did you know that he ran the café the entire day when Jessica was out sick and he took care of the gift shop? Son, it's hard to find a good employee like Noah these days. Heck, it's hard enough to find members of your own family who want to work, either.'" The bitterness in his tone was evident. "'When are you going to get a real job, son?'"

Ouch. Like my father, Simon was proud, and my father's sarcasm must have cut him to pieces. Simon resented it when people didn't take his writing career seriously, and it pained me that he and my father hadn't been able to put their differences aside. "What happened after he refused to lend you the money?"

Simon threw up his hands. "Forget it, Leila. I'm done talking about this."

Before I could respond, we heard the front door open. Seconds later, my mother came into the kitchen. Her face lit up when she saw Simon, and she immediately put her arms around him. "I saw your car in the driveway and told Mrs. Middleton that I had to leave. Did you eat?"

"Hi, Mom." Simon kissed her cheek. "The soup and the grape leaves were delicious, as always."

"Let me wrap some up for you to take back to your apartment," she volunteered.

Simon watched as mom filled a plastic bowl with grape leaves for him. "I met your new roommate," he said teasingly. "Where's he going to be sleeping? In my old room?"

"Of course not." Mom's voice filled with mirth. "That room will always be yours, in case you ever want to come home." She held out the dish to him. "Simon, why don't you save some money and come back here to live? You can have your privacy, and there's certainly plenty of room, even with your sister here."

"Gee, thanks, Mom." She didn't seem to notice the sarcasm in my tone.

Simon smiled at her. "Thanks for the offer, but if Tonya

and I get married, I'd only end up moving out again. I think it's best to keep things as they are."

Mom looked startled, as if someone had insulted her cooking. "I didn't realize things were that serious between you two already."

My brother's smile cast a ray of sunshine across the kitchen. "It won't be long before I pop the question. She's the one for me, Mom. I'm sure of it."

Mom smiled and patted his cheek. "Tonya's a lovely girl. My offer still stands, dear. Perhaps you'd both want to move in—after you're married, of course."

If Simon was shocked, he was careful not to show it. "Thanks, but I'm sure we'll want a place of our own."

"Of course." She wrinkled her nose. "Remember, dear, that a good marriage needs lots of work, time, and patience. Take your father and me, for example."

Simon shot me a look. We'd both heard many times about how our parents' marriage had been arranged, and she hadn't been thrilled by the match at first.

Mom prattled on, oblivious to our exchange. "Of course there are some people who expect that marriage will be a garden of roses from the very first day. Those are the ones who wind up with thorns."

I sucked in some air. That was a shot directed at me and my relationship with Mark. After four years, she still wouldn't let it go.

Simon must have sensed my unspoken agitation, because he was quick to put an arm around our mother's shoulders. "How are you doing Mom? Do you need anything?"

"No, thank you, dear. A visit with my son is all I need right now. Can you stay for a while?" Her eyes held a pleading, almost desperate look.

"Of course I can," Simon assured her.

She looked relieved. "Wonderful. I'm going upstairs to change, but I'll only be a minute."

We watched as Mom left the kitchen, Toast following closely at her heels. With a sigh, I turned away from my brother and started stacking the plates in the dishwasher.

The next morning, as I was cashing out a customer in the gift shop, the front door opened and Chief Crosby stepped in. He nodded to Jessica and then immediately headed in my direction. He did not look happy. I was positive he knew about my visit to see Wesley.

"Have a great day." I smiled and gave the customer her change, then tried to busy myself straightening out dollar bills in the till. Chief Crosby came up to the counter and leaned his arms on it.

"Leila, we have to talk," he said gruffly. "I know what you did last night."

I gave him my best innocent expression. "What are you talking about?" But I already knew my act wouldn't work. Chief Crosby had known me my entire life. He wouldn't be easily fooled.

He shot me a grim look. "I know that you and Heather

went out to the Browning home. Wesley Browning called me this morning and said that you were harassing him."

"I only asked him a couple of questions. It's not like—"

Chief Crosby held up a hand to silence me. "No excuses. I don't want you to have any further contact with that man."

"But I think he killed my father," I whispered, afraid that a customer browsing nearby would hear.

"Look, Leila," Chief Crosby said sternly. "I understand that you need to know what happened, but I also have an obligation to keep you safe. Wesley's had anger issues in the past and he can be dangerous. I'd never forgive myself if anything happened to you."

"Then you do admit that Wesley might have killed my father?"

He glanced around the store, but the customer had gone into the café and we were alone. Chief Crosby leaned in closer. "There's no proof that Wesley was involved in your father's death, but the guy is unstable. Our detectives will continue to handle the investigation, including determining and eliminating suspects. This is an ongoing investigation. Do not—I repeat—do not impede it by going to the Brownings' house again."

I opened my mouth to protest, then quickly shut it without comment. Not only had I put myself in danger last night but my best friend as well. There was no excuse for my behavior.

Chief Crosby drummed his fingers on the countertop. "Do I have your word?"

"All right. I promise that Heather and I will not go out there again." It was only half a lie, I told myself. Heather would not be going to Wesley's again. Since it was my father who had been murdered, I'd have to go it alone.

"Did I hear my name mentioned?" Heather was standing behind me, a maple latte in her hand. She smiled brightly at Chief Crosby. "Hello, Chief. It's so nice to see you."

Heather's smile could melt the toughest of hearts, Chief Crosby's included. He tipped his Stetson at her. "Always a pleasure, Miss Turcot. When's the big day?"

"May fourteenth." Her face was glowing as it always did whenever someone mentioned her upcoming wedding. She and Tyler had dated since college. "I'm so glad we didn't do it earlier in the spring, because Leila's my maid of honor and the sap has to come first."

"Well, congratulations. He's a lucky guy." Chief Crosby turned back to me. "I've got to get back to the station. Please remember what I said, Leila."

"What was that all about?" Heather whispered as he exited the building. "Did he find out about last night?"

"Wesley called and told him he had visitors." I was about to continue but spotted Noah grabbing a coffee at the café. He stared across the walkway and our eyes met. He'd obviously seen Chief Crosby talking to me. Jessica was cleaning off the countertop and looked over in my direction. Great. Nothing was a secret around here.

"Let's go into my office," I suggested. "I've got to reconcile the sales slips from yesterday. Why are you here, anyway? Don't you ever work anymore?"

She suppressed a giggle, and the sweet smell of maple drifted up from her drink to my nose. "We were supposed to do lunch, remember? Maybe we can get takeout from the diner."

"Heather, I can't. I'm sorry. There's a tour this afternoon, and I promised Mr. Perfect I'd sit in."

Heather sipped her latte and stared over at Noah, who was walking toward the back door. "Hmm. He does look pretty perfect to me."

"Oh, stop it." I waited until he'd let himself out the door, then led Heather into my office. "He says that I can't give any tours until I know what I'm talking about. Nice, huh?"

"I'm sure he didn't mean it to be insulting," she said kindly. "You never collected sap with your dad, right? And he probably gets a lot of questions about it." She took another sip of her drink. "Oh, I made an appointment for you at Bridal Boutique next Tuesday night so you can be fitted for your gown."

I tried not to groan. Unlike Heather, I wasn't fond of dresses and preferred jeans and sweaters to anything else. It was another example of how different we were. "You told me that it could wait until December."

She made a face. "Yes, but that was when I originally thought you wouldn't be home until then. Why wait? There could always be a delay with the dress or maybe the wrong size comes in. It's better to get it over with."

"Fine, I'll be there." I reached for the receipts on the desktop and watched as she sipped away at her drink. "Jessica made cinnamon and maple crullers today."

Heather's eyes widened with delight. "Ooh. Be right back." She quickly reached for the doorknob.

"I thought you were giving up desserts until after the wedding."

She paused to consider my question. "Right. I'll start tomorrow." She closed the door behind her while I resumed my work. Thirty seconds later, she threw open the door.

"Boy, that was fast," I joked.

Heather leaned across my desk. "You will never guess who's over at the café."

I sucked in a sharp breath. "Wesley?"

She shook her head. "Simon's girlfriend, Tonya Donnelly. She's grabbing a coffee to go."

The receipts could wait. I jumped up from the chair so fast that I almost knocked it over. We moved into the gift shop, behind the register in the center of the store, where we had a perfect view of the café. A blond woman was standing at the prep station with her back to us. She was adding cinnamon to her coffee. "You said she showed you a house, right?"

Heather nodded. "Yes, she works for Brick Lane Realty. Remember the house I texted you about last month that had the sauna and gym?"

I dragged Heather by the arm toward the café. "Say no more. You can introduce me."

Tonya threw a stirrer into the trash and looked up as we approached. When she spotted Heather, a glimpse of recognition showed in her bright green eyes. "Hello," she greeted us.

"Hi, Tonya," Heather smiled. "It's so nice to see you again."
Tonya furrowed her brow. "Heather, right?"

A pleased look came over my friend's face. "Yes. You have a good memory."

Tonya laughed, displaying a perfect set of white teeth. "It's my job." Her jaw dropped in amazement. "Oh! Did you change your mind about 14 Winter Pond Road? It's still available."

"I wish," Heather said with regret. "We crunched the numbers, and the price is a little too steep for us."

I was grateful for their chit chat, for it gave me a moment to study Tonya. She was more beautiful than I'd anticipated. I could find no flaw with her features—the small turned-up nose, full red lips, and cornflower blue eyes. Her fair complexion was flawless, and she looked to be wearing little or no makeup. Tonya's hair color was a mixture of honey and gold and fell below her shoulders in perfect waves.

Her body was long and slim in a full-length leather coat, and she held her head high with confidence. Real estate agents usually dressed for success, but Tonya was clearly a designer name gal. Her handbag bore the distinct mark of Gucci, and her black leather boots appeared to be Prada. Could Tonya and her expensive clothing habits be the reason Simon suddenly needed money?

"Please forgive my manners." Heather laid a hand on my arm. "This is my friend, Leila Khoury. She's the new owner of Sappy Endings. Leila, this is Tonya Donnelly. She works for Brick Lane Realty."

Tonya's eyebrows rose slightly at the mention of my name. "You're Leila?"

I nodded. "And you're Simon's girlfriend. It's nice to meet you."

Tonya held out her hand to me. A diamond bracelet on her slim wrist glittered in the overhead lighting. "It's lovely to meet you, Leila. Simon thinks the world of you."

"It's nice to meet you, too." She was unfailingly polite, but there was an air of sophistication about her that was the opposite of Simon's down-to-earth nature. It made me wonder what they had in common.

Tonya cocked her head to the side and studied me for a moment. "I'm sorry, did you say that *you* were the new owner?"

"That's right," I nodded.

A flicker of confusion crossed her lovely face. "But I thought that Simon would inherit the business."

Simon and Tonya obviously had a lapse in communication. "He didn't tell you?"

Tonya shook her head.

"Sappy Endings was left to Leila," Heather said proudly. "Simon never wanted to be part of it, anyway."

A shadow crossed Tonya's face. "Oh. I didn't know. Well, that's wonderful. I'm sure you'll make your father proud."

"Thanks, I'm going to try," I said.

Heather started talking very fast. "Simon's such a great guy. He feels like my brother, too, because I spent so much time at Leila's house while I was growing up." She glanced down and noticed Tonya's bracelet. She gasped out loud. "Oh my gosh! What a fabulous bracelet!"

Tonya smiled in genuine pleasure. "Thank you. Simon bought it for me for our two-month anniversary." She fluttered her eyelashes at me like Bambi. "Your brother is very generous."

"Yes, he is." Simon was a true gentleman and had always treated his past girlfriends well, but I didn't remember him buying such elaborate gifts before. He didn't have that kind of money to throw around, and a bracelet like that had to have set him back a few thousand dollars.

Simon had asked my father for a loan and been refused, so how could he afford to buy Tonya such an extravagant gift? He'd be angry if I interfered in his love life.

"My mother's anxious to have you over for dinner," I said.

Tonya's smile faded. "She is?"

"Lucky you," Heather remarked. "Mrs. Khoury is the best cook in town, maybe the entire state."

Tonya pressed her lips together, and I thought I glimpsed a look of panic in her eyes. "That sounds lovely, but I don't usually eat dinner," she said. "I follow a strict diet since I've been doing some work for a modeling agency and need to watch my weight."

"I'm sure she'd be happy to change it to lunch, then," I offered.

Tonya's mouth twitched, but she said nothing. That was when I realized the truth of the situation. Tonya didn't want to socialize with my mother over breakfast, lunch, or dinner. Would she end up as my sister-in-law? Something about this relationship felt off to me.

"Are you giving up real estate for modeling?" Heather asked curiously.

She shook her head. "Not anytime soon. I really enjoy the business and all the people that I meet. Besides, the market is booming, and I've made some great commissions lately." She pushed her hair back and proudly showed Heather and me the diamond earrings she was wearing. They had to be at least a full carat. "I was able to buy these for myself with my last commission. A little birthday present," she said proudly.

"They're beautiful!" Heather oohed and aahed appropriately over the earrings, further adding to Tonya's pleasure.

I'd been mildly curious before, but now I was growing concerned. Tonya could afford to buy her own diamonds while Simon didn't make enough money to supply them. Was she aware that he didn't have the money? Or worse, didn't she even care? I hoped that she truly loved him.

"Tonya, I'm glad we ran into you. Is there a chance you could give us some information on a property?"

She removed her iPhone from her purse. "Of course. What's the address? Did you want to schedule a showing?"

"It's not for us," Heather broke in. "Leila's interested in it as an investment property."

If possible, I would have pinched Heather for that remark, but it was impossible to do without Tonya noticing. With no other choice, I recited the address of the Browning property. When Tonya pulled up photos of Wesley's house, she'd probably burst out laughing. No one would be using that place as an investment property. It looked like it was ready to be bull dozed instead.

Tonya typed some information into her phone then stared at the screen for several seconds. She frowned and looked up at me with a puzzled expression. "This house is in foreclosure. Do you know the owner personally?"

I hadn't been expecting this. "Are you sure?"

Tonya nodded. "Positive. If anyone's living there, rest assured they'll be kicked out soon. Foreclosures do take longer these days because there's so many of them, but it'll occur sooner than later. That's what happens when you decide not to pay your bills." She lifted her delicate nose in the air and sniffed, as if she smelled something putrid.

Her comment shocked me, but I said nothing. Vermont was primarily a rural state. Tonya hadn't been born here, but being in the real estate business, she must be aware that there were many people who had lost their jobs or health and couldn't afford to pay the bills. What did she and my brother talk about? If they even talked, which I was starting to doubt.

Tonya finally put the phone away and stared up at me. She scanned the blue jeans and wool sweater that I was wearing and I saw her nose wrinkle ever so slightly. She simply smiled and said, "I'll keep an eye on it and let you know when the auction comes up."

"I'd appreciate that," I said gratefully.

Her smile brightened. "Well, if you'll both excuse me, I need to get back to the office. Nice meeting you, Leila."

"You, too," I replied, but she was already hurrying toward the door.

Heather waited until the door had closed, and then turned back to me. "Wow. Tonya's totally different when she's showing a house."

We started walking back toward my office. "What do you mean?"

Heather gave me one of her *give me a break* looks. "At the showing she was pleasant and sociable. She had some great ideas for the house and was very approachable. Today she was more self-absorbed. It's only my opinion, but I think she's all wrong for Simon."

"Thank goodness. I'm glad I'm not the only one who thinks so," I said in relief.

"And that bracelet!" Heather exclaimed. "Your brother must have been saving his pennies for a long time."

If only it were that simple. I sat down heavily on my chair and leaned my head against my arms. "Not exactly."

"What do you mean?" Heather asked.

I blew out a breath. "There's no way that Simon could afford that bracelet, Heather. My father refused him a loan when he asked for one. So, who or where did he get the money from?"

CHAPTER ELEVEN

AFTER HEATHER LEFT, I PICKED up my cell phone and dialed Theo's number. He answered in his usual authoritative voice. "Theo Martin."

"Hi, Mr. Martin, it's Leila Khoury."

"Leila!" He sounded delighted to hear from me. "You should know by now that you can call me Theo. Don't be so formal. What's up? How's Selma doing?"

My brain, which had been running in a million different directions, shifted back to my mother. "About as well as can be expected."

"Of course," he said soberly. "I've been meaning to stop by the house this week to see her. Tell her that Laura and I send our love."

"I will. Mr. Martin, er, Theo, did you know Dennis Browning?"

Theo was silent for several seconds. "I know the

name but didn't know him personally. What's this about, Leila?"

"His son Wesley threatened my father, the same day that he was murdered," I said. "I'm wondering if he would have shot him."

Theo's response was again slow in coming. "Anything is possible. Your father told me about his so-called partnership with Dennis. I know it caused Victor a lot of stress."

I clutched the phone tightly between my hands. "Wesley claims that my father took away the farm from his family."

"From what I've heard," Theo said, "Wesley Browning is all talk and no action."

"How did Dennis die? I thought he committed suicide, but Wesley told me that he was murdered."

"You've been in contact with his son?" Theo asked in surprise.

"I went out to his house the other night to talk to him. I also know that his home is in foreclosure. Since his mother died a few months ago, I'm guessing medical bills might have eaten away at any money they had, so he went to my father to ask for—"

"Leila," Theo said sharply. "I understand how badly you want to find the person responsible for your father's death, but you need to be careful. Have you talked to Chief Crosby about this?"

It was no surprise that Theo was siding with Chief Crosby, but I'd still hoped he might give me the information I was seeking. "Yes, and he said the same thing, but now I'm starting to wonder if Dennis's death could be connected to my father."

"I don't see how," Theo mused. "He died many years ago, didn't he? From what your father told me, I believe he was found dead in his vehicle one night. The man had a gun collection and shot himself with one of his own guns." He sighed. "Such a tragedy for his family. You can't get inside a person's head and change their way of thinking. I know your father was terribly sorry for his wife and son."

I mulled this over in my mind. "Does this mean that Wesley will end up living on the street soon?"

"To be honest, I have no idea," Theo admitted. "I don't know if Wesley has any other family." He paused. "I'm surprised you're so concerned about the man, especially since you believe he may have murdered your father."

"I'm not sure what I believe anymore." I wasn't completely convinced that Wesley had killed my father. In my eyes, Noah was still a suspect. As for my brother, I would never believe that he was guilty of such a heinous crime, but what about his new girlfriend? Could she have been involved somehow? She'd seemed disappointed when she discovered that Simon wasn't inheriting Sappy Endings.

I glanced down at my watch. It was five after two. The tour had already started without me. Shoot. Some manager I was. "Sorry, Theo, but I have to run. Maybe we can talk later?"

"Of course," he said. "I'm always here if you need anything. Take care, dear."

I mumbled goodbye and ran out of my office to the back door. An empty Green Mountain bus was parked in front of the sugar shack. I flung open the door to the building and was unprepared for the sight before me.

About twenty people had crowded into the area around Noah's desk and the packing station in the corner. A couple of children were sitting on the smaller sized drums that held syrup. Everyone stopped what they were doing at my noisy and unannounced arrival.

Noah was standing above us on the walkway area, next to the evaporator. It looked as if I'd interrupted him in midsentence. Like everyone else, his gaze came to rest on me, and I thought I saw his mouth turn up at the corners. Oh great. What was he up to?

"Hello, everyone." My voice resembled something in between a mouse's squeak and the shrill cry of an owl.

"Ladies and gentlemen." Noah pointed his finger in my direction. "Please allow me to introduce the new owner of Sappy Endings, Miss Leila Khoury."

Everyone's gaze traveled back to me again. Surprise registered on their faces. "*She* owns it?" an older man said, skepticism obvious in his voice. "I thought you owned it, Mr. Rivers."

Noah folded his arms across his chest and looked pleased. "No, sir. I work for Miss Khoury."

Everyone was still looking at me, as if waiting for me to say something. My breath caught in my throat. "I'm sorry I was late." I felt like a sightless person groping my way around in the dark, and furtively tried to think of something else to say. "I'm so happy you could join us at the farm today."

The silence was so loud that you could have heard a

piece of hay drop. Everyone turned back to Noah while I chided myself for sounding like an idiot.

Noah continued on, not missing a beat. "You may have noticed the taps wrapped around the trees outside when you arrived. We collect sap through those, and it runs from the tap into the evaporator. This is the sugarhouse, or shack, where we make the syrup. Who can tell me what type of trees are on the farm?"

A little girl of about ten raised her hand. "Oak?"

Everyone laughed, including Noah. "Not quite."

A slender redhead in her early twenties smiled adoringly at him. "They're maple trees."

"Very good," Noah said approvingly.

He climbed down from the walkway as he continued talking. I noticed the redhead nudge a blond woman next to her. The blond whispered something in her friend's ear, and they both giggled. It was so obvious that they were more concerned with checking out Noah than how maple syrup was made. My face burned until I could barely see straight. I'd always found the giggling schoolgirl routine so immature.

Noah didn't acknowledge their giggles, but he must have heard them. His voice was calm and confident as he continued his speech. The passion for the farm rang out in his words like bells.

"Sappy Endings has been in business for almost twenty-five years," Noah went on. "When Victor Khoury, Leila's father, purchased the farm, it was being used for dairy and maple syrup production. But the former owners were getting on in age, and Victor saw that they weren't using the place to its full potential. Today, Sappy Endings is one of the top producers of maple syrup in the entire state of Vermont."

He glanced over in my direction, and I prayed that my face wasn't giving me away. My father had always teased me about it. 'Your face is like an open book, *habibi*!' He had never told me the details of how he had come to acquire the farm. Dad had worked with Noah for less than a year, but this man knew more of the farm's history than I did. Hurt ran through me. I never should have left Sugar Ridge. I'd missed out on the last four years of my father's life and would never get them back.

Noah was still watching me. "In late January or early February, when the weather begins to warm, we drill a small hole in each of our 5,000 maple trees and place a sterile spout inside them."

The little girl who had mentioned oak trees earlier raised her hand. "Doesn't it hurt the trees?"

Noah gave her a broad smile. "Not at all. When the sugaring season is over in April, the spout is removed, and the hole in the maple tree begins to heal. After a couple of years, the hole is completely filled with a new growth of wood. Most maple trees live to be over 150 years old."

"What happens then?" asked a fortyish-year-old male with a mustache. "Are you the only one here who makes the syrup?"

Noah stole a glance at me. "At the moment, yes, but that may change eventually. Right, Miss Khoury?"

"Ah, yes." I tried to sound authoritative and failed miserably. "That's correct."

Noah's eyes twinkled at me, and dread filled my body. "Miss Khoury, would you like to tell everyone how many gallons of sap it takes to make one gallon of maple syrup?"

Why, you dirty snake in the grass. He hadn't told me that there was going to be a test. I wanted to shoot him a murderous glare but couldn't risk it with everyone in the room staring at me. I tried to remain calm. I knew this. My father had told me the answer before. *Think, Leila, think!*

I cleared my throat and smiled at everyone, who in turn stared back at me with blank expressions. "Well, Noah, I believe it's about thirty gallons. Give or take a few."

"That's very close." Noah's tone reminded me of the same one I used with students when they came up with an incorrect answer. "But it's actually fifty gallons." He turned back to the crowd. "It's very important that the weather is right for syrup making. Freezing nights and warm days, which usually happen in March, make the maple sap flow from the trees. The sap is then gathered through a modern pipeline system. It flows directly from the trees into the tubing system and straight to our sugarhouse. The sap goes through the tubing into the evaporator where it is boiled down into maple syrup. The evaporator itself weighs over 1,000 pounds."

"That thing is huge!" A woman exclaimed.

Noah continued. "A maple tree will yield about twenty-five gallons of sap in an average season. We have more than seventy miles of tubing in our sugar bush, which is enough to stretch from Sappy Endings to the border of Massachusetts."

His talk was interesting, but I found myself barely listening. I was too busy chiding myself for giving the wrong answer. If my father was looking down at me, I could imagine him shaking his head in disappointment.

The room had gone silent, and all necks had craned toward me. Surprised, I looked up and realized that Noah had asked me a question. *Crap.* "I'm sorry, what was that?"

Noah smiled sweetly at me. "Leila, would you please pass out samples of the syrups to our guests?"

"Oh! Yes, of course." I made my way over to Noah's desk, where there were three different jugs of syrup and tiny paper cups. People started coming up to me and indicating their preference.

"Which is the most popular kind?" one woman asked.

"Amber is the most popular kind, but they're all delicious. The dark syrup has a bit more of a robust flavor."

"Can I sample all three?" An elderly man with a long white beard asked eagerly.

I nodded as I continued to pour. The samples were disappearing faster than I could set them out. "Of course, you can sample whatever you like."

One woman with short gray hair smacked her lips in my ear. "Oh my, this is delicious! I'd like three quarts of the amber syrup, please."

Noah appeared next to me. "If anyone would like to make purchases, please follow Leila into the gift shop." He touched my arm gently and my entire body tingled as he whispered in my ear. "I'll finish up with the samples here. When I'm done, I'll come give you a hand in the gift shop."

I knew that this was Noah's way of offering me a chance to escape from my earlier embarrassment. I should have appreciated the gesture, but my pride had been hurt. Instead, I turned on him with barely controlled anger.

"No, thank you, Mr. Rivers." I spoke the words low so that the customers wouldn't hear. "I can handle it just fine by myself."

CHAPTER TWELVE

I SPENT THE NEXT HALF hour ringing up purchases in the gift shop. The line grew quite long at one point, and I half-expected Noah to ignore my request and show up to assist me, but he never appeared. Jessica was swamped in the café, but we both managed. In fact, I was glad to be so busy. It kept my mind off the earlier embarrassing moments.

After the customers had departed, things quieted down, and I went to relieve Jessica since she needed to leave early for a doctor's appointment. I spent the rest of the afternoon answering phones and serving up pieces of my mother's baklava along with maple lattes. Besides the baklava, my mother had sent in maple doughnuts today, but they'd run out fast this morning. She topped each one with a partial slice of bacon. The maple icing on the doughnuts was creamy and sweet and mixed perfectly with the saltiness of the bacon.

At five o'clock, I was placing the CLOSED sign on the front door when Noah appeared with a box of candles for the gift shop. I went over to empty the till as he arranged the candles on the shelves.

"These have been going fast," he said. "I'll make more tomorrow. We're getting orders for them on the website, too."

I didn't answer.

"Something wrong?" he asked.

"Not at all." I busied myself with sorting receipts in the drawer.

Noah came over and leaned on the counter, facing me. "Did you enjoy the tour?"

"It was all right." I kept my head bent and refused to look at him. To my surprise, he reached over the counter and gently touched my arm. My body reacted as if he'd sent an electric shock through it. I recoiled and stepped back, colliding with the wall.

Noah looked confused. "What's the matter with you?"

"Nothing," I said sharply. "Only that I felt like a total idiot."

"You did fine," he assured me.

"Oh, sure." I emptied the rest of the till and slammed the register drawer shut. "By the way, I didn't appreciate the pop quiz. I suppose you thought it would be fun to make me look even more pathetic."

I picked up the zippered pouch with the money and started for the office, but Noah stepped in front of me, blocking my path.

"Leila," he said firmly. "Do you think that I wanted you there so I could embarrass you? That wasn't my intention. I'm sorry."

The angry retort I had planned died on my lips. His voice was gentle and kind, and his expression concerned, not mocking as I'd thought. I forced myself to look directly into his deep-set eyes, which resembled an endless pool of cool, blue water, easy to lose myself in.

My voice cracked. "I don't belong here. Honestly, I'm not sure where I belong."

Noah gave my arm a little shake. "Yes, you do belong here. Victor wanted you to follow in his footsteps. He had faith in your ability." He hesitated for a moment. "And so do I."

I stared up at him. "Why? I've been a total jerk to you since I came here."

"You've had your reasons," he said quietly. "When you lose someone you love, your entire world changes." His eyes held a sad, faraway look. "Sometimes it takes a long while to find yourself again."

"You sound like you speak from experience."

Noah abruptly changed the subject. "You're not planning to run away again, are you?"

My spine stiffened. "Did my father tell you that?"

"No, Jessica mentioned it once. She said that you and your fiancé broke up and you left Sugar Ridge to take a teaching job in Florida about four years ago."

Great. I sucked in some air. "Did she tell you anything else?"

"Why, is there more?"

I shook my head in disbelief. "Okay, don't get me wrong. I adore Jessica, but she's a bit on the nosy side."

Noah laughed. "Yeah, that happens sometimes when a person works by themselves all day. They crave gossip."

"Well, in that case, I'm sure you know everything about me."

"No, I don't," he admitted. "And I don't need to, either."

His statement made me even more curious about him. Heather had said she didn't think Noah was married, but he'd recently bought a house. "Do you live alone?"

Noah gave me a lopsided smile. "Well, well. Who's being nosy now?"

"I was only making conversation," I lied.

He picked up his jacket from the counter. "In answer to your question, no. I don't live alone."

"Oh, I see." I couldn't help being curious about his girlfriend. She was probably gorgeous like him. In fact, I was certain of it. He could have any woman he wanted. "You seem very at ease with giving tours. That kind of surprised me."

Noah furrowed his brows. "Why?"

I shrugged. "Because you don't—"

"Talk much?" he asked. "Yeah, somehow it's easier in front of people I don't know. And once you've done it, oh, a couple of hundred times or so. You'll find out."

"Maybe."

He looked at me thoughtfully. "I don't mind helping

you, but I do have one golden rule. You need to show up on time. Punctuality is a must in my book."

I realized that he was teasing me, but still had to wonder why he was being so nice all of a sudden. After all, he had wanted to buy the farm from my father. Did he have something up his sleeve? "Thank you."

Noah turned and started down the walkway to the back door, making sure it was locked. "It was pretty obvious that you were Victor's favorite kid. The only time he ever talked about Simon was when he came for a visit."

I stopped at the door to my office. "Did Simon drop by often?"

He considered my question. "I don't know, maybe once a week? Sad to say, all they ever did was argue."

I nodded. "Yeah, it was like that at home, too."

Noah frowned. "I don't think your brother likes me."

Simon's comment about Noah and my father being joined at the hip came to mind. "Oh, I'm sure you're mistaken," I lied. "Simon likes everyone. He's very personable once he gets to know you."

"Well, he's never expressed an interest in getting to know me, which is fine," Noah said shortly. "It was pretty obvious that he felt like I as invading his turf, but that doesn't make sense. From what I understand, Simon never wanted any part of Sappy Endings."

What Noah didn't realize is that the farm wasn't Simon's biggest concern. My brother had been jealous of Noah's close relationship with our father. "Yes, that's right. Simon never liked working here. He's always wanted to be a writer."

"Your Dad told me once that he wished they were closer."

I sat down behind the desk. "He actually said that?" I was discovering many new things about my father today. He'd obviously trusted Noah and was comfortable telling him intimate details about his life. But someone had also betrayed my father's trust. I couldn't lose sight of that fact.

An awkward pause followed before Noah spoke again. "Victor was worried about your brother. He was afraid that Simon owed people money. Money that he couldn't pay back."

It was a statement, but I caught the unspoken question in his words. "That's not true," I insisted.

"Well, it's none of my business." Noah removed his key-ring from his jeans pocket. "Anyhow, time to go. I'll lock up the sugarhouse and see you in the morning."

"Good night, Noah."

"Leila."

I looked up to find Noah's eyes pinned on mine. "I know why you agreed to take this job. You want to find who killed your father, and I respect that. I only hope that I'm not still at the top of your list."

"Noah, I know we got off on the wrong foot, and I'm sorry—"

"Good night, Leila."

He turned and left the gift shop abruptly. Defeated, I put the cash pouch inside the safe and locked the door. A deep sadness settled over me. The fact that it was already pitch black outside thanks to the recent time change didn't improve my mood, either. That was one thing I hadn't missed while in Florida. There was a reason why it was called the Sunshine State. Oh, well. I could handle the shorter days for one more winter.

I shrugged into my jacket, picked up my purse, and set the alarm. As I opened the front door, someone grabbed my arm. Startled, I shrieked and whirled around to find myself staring into Wesley's dark, piercing eyes.

"Let go of me!" I managed to cry.

Instead of letting go, he pushed me up against the side of the building. "I need to talk to you. Alone."

My body was paralyzed with fright. "Wh—what do you want?"

"You have to believe me." Wesley tightened his grip on my arm. "My father didn't commit suicide. Chief Crosby won't listen. No one believes me, but it's true. When I told the chief you were trespassing at my house last night, he got angry with me instead. Can you believe it?"

"Please leave," I whimpered. "You're scaring me."

Wesley's eyes were red rimmed, as if he hadn't slept in days, and he reeked of cigarette smoke and alcohol. I flinched and tried to move away, but he was stronger.

"I'm not gonna hurt you," he said. "I only want justice served. My mother told me on her deathbed that there's no way my father would have killed himself." He grabbed the collar of my coat, tightening it around my throat. "For God's sake, don't you understand?"

"Let me go!" I screamed.

Wesley put a hand over my mouth. "Please don't scream. Listen to me first."

"Get your hands off her!"

Before I realized what was even happening, Noah grabbed Wesley from behind and shoved him away from me. Wesley turned around in anger, his eyes bulging out of their sockets as he charged at Noah like an angry bull. He threw a punch and Noah ducked, then rammed his fist into Wesley's stomach. Wesley doubled over in pain, grunting and swearing under his breath.

"Get out of here," Noah said hoarsely. "And don't come back."

Wesley staggered away from us, holding his stomach with both hands. "You're gonna be sorry," he croaked. "I tried to warn you."

Noah rushed to my side. "Are you all right?"

I managed to nod, still in shock over what had happened. "Where did you come from? I thought you'd left."

He shook his head. "I had a phone call as I was about to leave the sugar shack. My—" He stopped abruptly. "Never mind. We need to call Crosby and report this guy. Do you know who he was?"

"His name is Wesley Browning." I looked around for my keys. They'd fallen onto the cement when Wesley had grabbed me. My hands shook as I tried to insert the key into the door knob.

"Here, let me." Noah took the keyring from my hand. He unlocked the door, ushered me inside, and turned off the beeping alarm. I went into the gift shop and sat down on the stool behind the register.

Noah was already on his cell phone. "Chief Crosby?

Noah Rivers from Sappy Endings. Leila was just attacked. No, she's okay." He stopped to listen and, even from several feet away, I could hear Chief Crosby's voice on the other end. "Yeah, that's the guy. Wesley Browning."

There was another murmur that went on for several seconds until Noah spoke again. "Yes, we'll be here. Thank you."

He clicked off and turned to me. "Crosby's coming right over. He was just leaving the station when I caught him." Noah examined my face closely. "So, who is this Wesley Browning? And what did he want with you?"

"His father, Dennis, was once partners with my dad. He died a long time ago, and Wesley blames my father for his death. In his words, my father ruined his father's life." I paused. "And his as well."

Noah wrinkled his forehead. "Have you talked to this guy before?"

"Yes, I went to his house last night. I needed to ask him some questions. He told Chief Crosby that I was trespassing on his property. When he grabbed me, he started going on about how his father never would have killed himself. He said he tried to tell Chief Crosby, but he didn't believe him."

"Yeah, I've seen Crosby in here plenty of times, talking with your dad. They'd sit in his office and make small talk for ages." Noah smiled. "I remember how one time I had to go in there and drag Victor out to help me collect sap. Crosby ended up coming along with us. They kept up a conversation the entire time." He glanced at me worriedly. "Will you be all right in here for a minute? I want to take a look around the parking lot and make sure that nutcase is gone."

I placed my hands on either side of the register to steady myself. "Noah."

He looked at me questioningly.

I swallowed the lump of fear in my throat. "I wanted to say thank you—for what you did. If you hadn't been here, I'm not sure what would have happened to me."

"There's no need to thank me," Noah said quietly. "I'd have done it for anyone."

CHAPTER THIRTEEN

I DIDN'T SLEEP WELL THAT night. The memory of Wesley's panic-stricken face kept appearing before me in my dreams and caused me to jerk awake with a start. Toast seemed to sense my agitation and came to lie next to me. I stroked his head and listened to his rhythmic purring, which helped to soothe me.

Chief Crosby had come out to Sappy Endings and taken statements from both Noah and me. He'd phoned later in the evening and let me know that Wesley was nowhere to be found. He'd left a police officer to watch over the Browning house, but Wesley had not yet returned. Had he left town? Where would he have gone? The man had demons chasing him, and it was only a matter of time until they caught up.

At about five o'clock, I gave up, rolled out of bed and went to take a long, hot shower. After a breakfast with my mother of herb bread, scrambled eggs, and a steaming mug of *Ahweh*, I'd left for the farm as the sun was breaking through the clouds. Thankfully there was no sign of Wesley's car anywhere. I let myself into the quiet building, determined to busy myself all day with a new filing system in the office.

Jessica called on the intercom at about nine thirty for me to come and help her. Noah had scheduled another tour, and there was a large number of customers who wanted coffee. When I returned to the office at about eleven, the landline rang, and I snatched it up. "Good morning, Sappy Endings." I tried to sound more cheerful than I felt.

Someone breathed heavily into the other end. My chest began to constrict with fear as I listened. "Hello?"

The breathing continued, and I didn't wait to hear anymore. I slammed down the receiver and tried to shake off the dread. Every business received prank calls. *Nothing to worry about.* It was probably a teenager who had nothing better to do.

I was looking over the order sheets Noah had given me when the phone rang again close to quitting time. I'd been so engrossed in reading them that I almost jumped out of my seat. With trepidation, I reached out and lifted the receiver. "Good afternoon, Sappy Endings."

The dreaded breathing came again, but this time there was a voice attached to it. "Leila? It's me. Please don't hang up."

The hairs on the back of my neck rose. Wesley's voice. "What do you want?" I asked sharply.

"Look, I'm sorry about last night." He was panting heavily, as if he'd run a marathon. "I—I didn't mean to scare you. Guess I had too much to drink."

My stomach twisted into a knot. "I'm hanging up now."

"No, wait!" He sounded desperate. "I have to talk to you."

"Please leave me alone. You're scaring me."

"But you should be scared." Wesley's breathing became labored and he started to cough violently. "It's not safe for you. Or me, either. Bad things are going to happen."

A chill traveled down my spine. I'd had enough of this man intimidating me. "Don't call here again." I slammed down the receiver and went out to the walkway area. The gift shop was empty and the café deserted. Jessica emerged from behind the counter when she saw me.

"It's been dead as tombs in here this afternoon," she said. "Honey, would you mind if I left a few minutes early? I'd like to pick up my new glasses before the vision center closes."

"No, of course not. Have a good night and drive safe."

Jessica slung her purse over her shoulder. "Are you okay? You seem a bit out of it today."

"Oh." I waved my hand in the air, as if swatting a bug. "I didn't sleep well last night. That's all."

Apparently, Noah hadn't told her about my confrontation with Wesley, and, for that, I was eternally grateful. I wasn't in the mood for Jessica's twenty-question routine.

She said goodbye and let herself out the main entrance. I locked the door behind her and shut the lights off in the café. I spent a few minutes straightening out the shelves in the gift shop.

"All good to go?"

I shrieked and whirled around. Noah was standing there with his denim jacket draped over his arm. I put a hand to my heart. "You scared me."

"Sorry." His handsome face twisted into a frown. "Are you all right? You look like you've seen a ghost." Recognition dawned in his eyes. "Did Wesley stop by? I was out in the sugarbush this afternoon so—"

"No, but he called. Twice."

A muscle ticked in his jaw. "Leila, this guy is messing with your head. You need to call Crosby and tell him Wesley is stalking you."

He was right, but there was also a tiny doubt in my mind that wondered if Wesley was telling the truth. Did he think that his father's death and mine were related? Still, I couldn't risk another meeting with him. The man was clearly unstable. "You're right. I'll call him as soon as I get home. You can go ahead and leave, if you'd like."

"Forget it," Noah growled. "I'm walking out with you."

"Thanks, but it's not necessary."

Noah took a step toward me and placed a hand on my arm. "It *is* necessary. I'm not leaving you here by yourself. That psycho could be waiting outside for you again. Why are you being so stubborn?"

"I don't mean to be. I realize that you'd do the same thing for anyone."

I put a hand to my mouth, amazed that the words

had tumbled out before I could stop them. It sounded immature and like something one of my students might say instead.

He studied me for a minute. "Look, I didn't mean it the way it sounded. I'm sorry if I offended you."

"You didn't. It's fine." For crying out loud, I sounded like a lovesick school girl. Noah was an employee. That didn't mean that he had to be my bodyguard as well.

Noah exhaled sharply. "In the past year and a half, I've become very good at distancing myself from other people. I don't always say the right thing and, even when I mean to, it sometimes comes out wrong."

"Yeah, I know how that is, trust me."

"Anyway," Noah continued, "the sugar shack is locked up. I'll check the back door while you grab your things. Then I'll walk you to your car. Is that okay, Miss Khoury?" He winked, and I had to laugh.

"Okay," I said. "I appreciate it."

Noah met me by the front door five minutes later. He opened the door and escorted me out, like a gallant gentleman. "Wait, we didn't lock it," I said.

"I'm going back inside after you leave," Noah said. "I need to call for my ride, anyway. I lent my truck out today."

"I could drop you off at your house."

He acted embarrassed by my offer. "Thanks, but I have plans elsewhere."

Ah. Maybe he was going out with friends or, specifically, his girlfriend. I turned and waved at him. "I'll be fine from here. Good night." Before he could say anything further, I hurried toward my car. I beeped it open and quickly slid behind the steering wheel. I turned on the headlights and noticed that Noah was still standing on the porch, watching me.

A strange sense of foreboding came over me and I struggled to shake it off. I turned the key in the ignition and my tire light immediately came on. What the heck? The car was less than a week old and already low on air? Impatiently I shifted the vehicle into drive and tried to move forward. Nothing happened. I pushed my foot down on the gas pedal and accelerated. The car moved at a snail's pace, as if plowing its way through a pile of rocks.

My knowledge about vehicle repairs was limited, but it was obvious to me that something was wrong. I looked over at the porch. Noah was still standing there, so I let myself out of the vehicle and squinted down at the ground. My body froze.

The front left tire was completely flat, and so was the rear one. Fear lodged tightly in my throat as I walked around to the other side of the vehicle. Both of those tires were flat as well.

"What's wrong?" Noah shouted as he ran toward me.

The realization hit me like a slap to the face. Someone had slashed all four of my brand-new tires. Their message to me was abundantly clear.

Bad things are going to happen.

———————

Much to my surprise, Chief Crosby came out himself to check my car. He snapped some pictures with his phone. "I'll file a report," he said. "Do you have roadside assistance? That will at least cover the tow job. It's doubtful your insurance will pay for the tires, since this is an act of vandalism."

"Noah called a tow truck for me. And, yes, I figured it wouldn't be covered." This was going to hurt financially. I'd probably have to dish out close to a thousand dollars for four new tires. Anger bubbled near the surface for me. "It must have been Wesley."

Chief Crosby looked up sharply. "Why do you say that?"

"Because he phoned me this morning and again this afternoon. He said he wanted to meet with me and had something important to tell me."

"You weren't planning to meet with him, were you?" Chief Crosby's eyes practically bulged out of their sockets.

I shook my head. "No, I hung up on him."

"That settles it," he fumed. "I wish I knew where he'd been calling you from. Leila, the best thing for you to do is to go straight home. I'll have a police car cruise by your house a few times tonight. If you see any sign of Wesley, I want you to call me right away. Understood?"

He wasn't making me feel any better about the situation. "Yes, of course."

"I'll stay with Leila until her ride arrives," Noah offered.

Chief Crosby typed something into his tablet and nodded absently. "Great. Thanks, Noah. I have to get back to the station. I have someone waiting to speak with me there." He placed the tablet under his arm and put his hand on my shoulder. "I meant what I said. Call me any time, day or night. That goes for your mother, too. Please give her my best."

"Thank you for coming out and so quickly," I said gratefully.

"Anything for Victor's daughter." He smiled at me and nodded to Noah. "Take good care of her."

A deep flush came into Noah's cheeks, and he didn't reply. Chief Crosby got into his sedan and zoomed out of the parking lot. He hadn't been gone for more than two minutes when the tow truck arrived. I showed them my road assistance card, and they moved the vehicle onto their flatbed. After a few minutes, they were gone as well.

Resigned, I sat down in one of the rockers on the front porch. Noah had turned on the outside light posts and carried a flashlight in one hand, so our view of the parking lot was more visible than before. He jumped the three steps of the porch in one leap and gestured toward the front door. "Are you okay? Would you rather wait inside?"

No, I wasn't okay. The act of vandalism to my car was terrifying, but Noah's presence helped to calm me. For the moment, I felt safe and secure with him. "I'm all right. Besides, I love the smell of the outdoors." The air was crisp and clear, and the woodsy scent delightful.

Noah leaned against one of the white columns and stared up above. A cluster of stars in the inky sky was like miniature lanterns shining down upon us. "Yeah, I know what you mean. This is a beautiful view. How come your mother and father never built a house on the farm? It seems like the perfect place to live and raise a family."

I shrugged. "My father suggested it a couple of times, but Mom wasn't too thrilled about the idea. I think she wanted Simon and me to grow up in a neighborhood with other kids. She also worried that Dad would never be able to separate work from his personal life."

Noah shoved his hands into the pockets of his jeans and smiled. "Yeah, that was your dad. A true workaholic."

If only he had gone home that last night, perhaps he would still be alive today. I exhaled sharply. We'd never know for certain. "Thanks for waiting here with me." If I'd been forced to stay here alone, I would have barricaded myself indoors.

"Is your mother coming for you?" Noah asked. "I'd offer to take you home, but, like I said, I'm waiting on a ride myself."

"That's okay. Heather's on her way. She was just finishing up with a client when I called."

He nodded and we both fell silent. I tried to think of something interesting to say. *Anything.* "Jessica told me that you worked on a farm in New York State before coming here."

"Yes, ma'am. I worked and lived there for three years, before coming to Vermont."

"But you're not originally from there." It was a statement, not a question.

"No, I was born in South Carolina. My parents divorced when I was five, and then Mom moved me and my younger brother to New York, where we went to school."

I'd suspected that he originally came from the south. "What did you do after you graduated?"

Noah walked over and sat down in the rocker next to mine. He seemed more relaxed with me, and it showed in his manner. "After I graduated from high school, I went into the Marines. Six years later, I came home and jumped at the chance to live and work on a farm."

His smile was wistful, and I wondered what direction his mind was running in. Was he thinking about the person he had lost? Who was it?

To my surprise, he continued speaking. "After being in Iraq, I came home to the States looking for answers. Working with nature helped me so much. I needed a different type of lifestyle and found that I really enjoyed creating things with my hands—like the candles, for example."

The lantern's glow reflected off his face and revealed a mixture of grief and pain in his eyes impossible to be masked. Noah's life had been marked with some type of dark tragedy, and my heart went out to him.

Before I could respond, headlights appeared on the road, and Heather's SUV turned into the entrance. Noah smiled and rose slowly from the rocker. "Looks like your ride is here."

I didn't know what else to say. I started toward Heather's vehicle, but to my surprise, she got out and started hurrying in our direction. "What's wrong?"

"Hey, girl. I need to use the restroom," she said. "Can you let me inside?" She waved at Noah, and he nodded in return.

I opened the door and Heather rushed past me. As I was about to tell Noah good night and wait in Heather's vehicle, Noah's truck turned into the parking lot. An older woman was driving. She wore glasses and waved gaily at the both of us.

The confused expression must have shown on my face, and Noah felt the need to explain. "That's my mother. She needed my truck to run some errands today."

"I didn't know you lived with your mother," I said innocently.

"I don't. She's been staying with us while we get settled."

We. He was undoubtedly talking about his girlfriend or wife. I watched his mother climb out of the driver's seat and then help someone else out of the truck. To my surprise, a little girl hopped down and ran toward us. She had a head of curly blond hair and was wearing a red jacket, jeans, and pink sneakers.

"Daddy!" she cried.

Noah swept her up in his arms and kissed her on the cheek. "How's my best girl today?"

"Great!" she grinned happily at him. "Grandma took me out for ice cream. We both had chocolate chip."

"What?" Noah pretended to be upset. "Where's mine? You mean you didn't bring me any back?" He tickled her side until she started giggling and wriggling in his arms simultaneously.

She wrapped her little arms tightly around his neck. "And now we're gonna go get burgers and fries at the diner."

"Well, you'd better not eat mine," Noah warned.

"Yes, I will!" she laughed.

I'd suspected that Noah had another female in his life, but this wasn't what I'd had in mind. The father and daughter were mesmerizing to watch and made such a sweet picture. I stood there in silence, waiting for the wave of shock to subside. I had never thought of Noah as a father. The child's mother must have the same fine golden hair. *The perfect family*. Noah hadn't mentioned that he was married and had a child, but, then again, he didn't owe me an explanation.

Noah shifted the little girl in his arms and turned to face me. "Leila, this is my daughter, Emma. Em, this is Leila. Can you say hello?"

"Hello!" Emma waved happily at me. She was a beautiful child, with her father's deep-set blue eyes and crooked smile.

"Hi, Emma. It's nice to meet you."

"Do you help my daddy make syrup?" she asked. "I love pancake syrup."

I had to smile. "Well, I'm learning. Your daddy knows more about it than I do."

"He'll show you how. My daddy's a real good teacher," she said proudly.

Noah's mother walked over to us and held out her hand to me. "You must be Leila. I'm Dorothy Rivers. Noah told me all about you."

Dorothy's short hair was a salt and pepper color, and she had the same eye color as her son and granddaughter. Her accent had more of a Southern twang than Noah's, and her smile was so genuine that I liked her immediately. I brushed my fingers against hers. "It's a pleasure to meet you, Mrs. Rivers."

"Please call me Dorothy," she insisted.

"I'm getting a puppy," Emma announced proudly.

"Really?" I asked. "Puppies are lots of fun."

Noah playfully tweaked her nose. "I said *maybe*."

Emma was adorable, and I wondered how old she was. I guessed about five or six. "You're very pretty," I told her.

"So are you. Can you come eat dinner with us?" Emma asked hopefully.

Her request caught us all off guard. Noah's face flushed underneath the light and mine must have rivaled his. "No, thank you, Emma. I have to get home. My friend is waiting for me." I pointed at Heather's empty SUV and then the front door. "She's inside."

Noah's mother held out her arms for Emma. "Come on, sweetheart. We'll wait for Daddy in the truck." She smiled warmly at me. "I'm so glad to have met you, Leila."

"It was wonderful meeting you as well," I said.

"Bye!" Emma called out, her megawatt smile lighting up the night. She skipped happily back to the truck with her grandmother, no doubt envisioning burgers and fries in her head.

Noah watched as they got into the truck and stuffed his hands into the pockets of his denim jacket. "You're welcome to come with us. I'm sorry, I should have thought to ask you before." He paused. "We could bring you home afterward."

It was nice of him to offer, but I felt certain that he was only doing so out of obligation. He never would have mentioned it if Emma hadn't opened her mouth. "Thanks for the offer, but Heather's waiting for me, and we're going to have dinner with my mom."

"Oh, right. Sure. Some other time, then."

"I didn't know you had a child. Emma's adorable." I was tempted to ask where his wife was, but it was none of my business. Maybe they were divorced or she was working and meeting them at the restaurant later. Whatever the case, she wouldn't be thrilled to see me accompanying them.

Noah's eyes lit up like a Christmas tree. "She's a great kid. I'm lucky to have her." He stared at the truck, and a sober look came over his face. "She's the reason I get up every morning."

It seemed like an odd thing to say, but there was no time to pursue it further. The front door of the building opened, startling me, and then Heather appeared. I'd almost forgotten about her.

"Ready?" she asked.

"Yes. I'll set the alarm."

Noah held up his hand. "I've got it. You two go on ahead. See you in the morning, Leila. Good night, Heather."

"Bye, Noah," she called as we walked toward her SUV. She slid behind the driver's seat while I settled myself across from her. Heather craned her neck in the direction of the truck. "Who's driving? Is that his girlfriend?"

I laughed. "That's Dorothy. She has to be about my mother's age."

Her jaw dropped in astonishment. "Oh. My. God. He's into older women? Drat. I thought he'd be perfect for you."

I struggled not to roll my eyes. "Wrong on both accounts. That's his mother. And his little girl's sitting in the truck beside her."

Heather started the engine while Noah jumped down from the porch and ran toward the truck. His mother slid over in the seat, and they drove away. A strange sadness settled over me as I watched them disappear into the night.

CHAPTER FOURTEEN

"ARE YOU SURE YOU'RE OKAY?" Heather asked on the way to my mother's. "What did the police say?"

"Chief Crosby took some pictures and filled out a report. He said it's unlikely they'll find out who did this. My car was out of range of the security camera, so it's possible someone might know the setup of the farm." Meaning of course that it might be the same person who had killed my father. The thought made me physically ill.

Heather must have guessed my thoughts. "This is a warning, Leila. Someone doesn't want you checking into your father's murder."

"We don't know that for sure." But she had to be right. Why else would someone have done this? Sugar Ridge had a low crime rate. People came and went from Sappy Endings all day. Someone had been watching the place and waiting for the right moment to do this when they wouldn't be seen. Goose bumps dotted my arms. The vandal had to be someone who knew the place well—like an employee.

It had started to rain, and Heather turned the wipers on. "I know what you're thinking."

"And what's that?"

She shot me a meaningful look. "You're having second thoughts about Noah being the one who killed your father. It's because of the little girl, isn't it?"

I didn't answer.

"You're a big softy when it comes to kids, Leila."

"All right. Maybe," I conceded, "but I still can't give him the benefit of the doubt. He knows Sappy Endings inside and out. The only other person who even has a motive is Wesley Browning."

"There is another person that you're forgetting." Heather's voice shook slightly.

My jaw dropped in amazement. "Heather, you know that Simon didn't do this. He's my brother, for crying out loud!"

Heather turned her vehicle onto my street. "Come on, Lei. You know me better than that." She parked her vehicle in the driveway behind my mother's car and turned to me, her expression grave. "But there is another employee you're not considering."

"Jessica?" I laughed out loud. "Why would Jessica have killed my father? They got along great."

Heather bit into her lower lip and didn't answer.

Uneasiness settled in my stomach. There was something that Heather hadn't told me. "Okay, spill it."

She swallowed nervously. "It's—nothing."

"We're not going inside until you tell me what it is," I said sternly.

Heather twisted her hands in her lap. "A couple of months ago, I went into Sappy Endings for a latte. It was early morning, and no one else was there except for your father and Jessica."

A light switch clicked on in my brain. I had an idea of where this conversation was headed, and desperately wanted a detour. "Go on," I said quietly.

Her mouth trembled. "Your father was behind the café's counter with Jessica. They had their backs to me and didn't see me come in. I caught part of their conversation. Jessica had a hand on your father's arm and was giggling like a teenager. She said something like, 'I hope Selma knows how lucky she is.'"

Bile rose in the back of my throat. "What did my father say?"

Heather let out a long, ragged breath. "To be honest, he looked pretty ticked off. And his voice was angry. He said, 'Jess, let's not go there again.'"

I sucked in some air. "What happened after that?"

She shrugged. "Nothing. Jessica saw me out of the corner of her eye and dropped her hand. Then she put on this big phony smile and asked how I was doing. Your father acted like nothing had happened. He said hello to me and walked off to answer his cell phone."

"Why didn't you tell me about this sooner?" My voice shook.

Heather's eyes filled with unshed tears. "I'm sorry, Lei. I—I didn't want to hurt you. It's impossible—I mean, there's no way your father would have been carrying on with her."

"No. He wasn't." I shook my head vehemently. "He loved my mother. He wouldn't have hurt her for the entire world."

"What do you know about Jessica's background?" Heather asked.

I shrugged. "Not much. She has two grown sons, and she told me that her husband died right after their twentieth wedding anniversary." I paused. "Maybe I should check into it."

Heather let out a loud sniff and reached for a tissue in her purse. "Your father was a wonderful man, Lei. No one would ever dispute that. Jessica's obviously had him in her sights for a while. He was an attractive man, even at his age. If you had seen the way Jessica was looking at him that day—" She broke off and glanced at me in misery.

The writing had been on the wall, but I hadn't managed to decipher it. "I'm glad I wasn't there." Things were starting to make sense. "Come on. I'm going into my father's study to see what dirt I can dig up on her."

Heather's blue eyes gleamed with excitement. "Everyone has that proverbial skeleton in their closet."

My hand grasped the doorknob, and I inserted my key. "Maybe that's the real reason she stuck around all these years."

Heather drew her brows together. "I don't understand."

"Think about it," I said. "Jessica started working at Sappy Endings shortly before her husband died. When he passed away, she didn't need to work anymore because he left her a huge life insurance policy. She was always telling the customers that she loved her job and this was a great way to keep busy. What if it was all a lie and she only wanted to be close to my father?"

We hung our jackets in the coat closet and walked into the living room. The television was turned on to the local news, but no one was watching it. A delicious aroma of spices wafted in from the kitchen.

"Leila, is that you?" my mother called out.

"Yes, it's me, Mom. Heather's here, too. We'll be out in a minute."

She must have been busy with dinner, because she didn't reply or poke her head out under the archway. Heather and I entered the study, and I shut the door softly behind us. She stood behind my father's chair as I typed Jessica's name into the Google search engine. "The only thing that comes up is her husband's obituary."

"Click on it anyway," Heather advised. "It might give us her maiden name."

I did as she asked and quickly scanned the short obituary. "You're right," I exclaimed. "Here it is. 'Carl is survived by his loving wife, Jessica Ryder Fowler, to whom he was married for twenty years...'"

"Ryder," Heather mused as I typed the name into Google. "I don't know of any Ryders. She might not originally be from around here."

"I think she was born in Massachusetts." I scanned the sparse links that popped up. "Shoot. There's nothing here, but that doesn't mean she doesn't have a history." I reached for my cell. "It's time for drastic measures."

"Who are you calling?" Heather asked.

"My brother. He can get me the information that I need."

"It pays to have the right connections," Heather agreed.

Simon picked up instantly, his voice strained and impatient. "Yeah, sis?"

"Sorry, am I calling at a bad time?"

"I'm on deadline. It's going to be a long night." He sighed. "Everything okay with you and mom?"

"We're fine, but I need a favor. Can you do some checking around for me? I need to find out if a certain person might have been in trouble."

His tone turned suspicious. "Who and what sort of trouble?"

I swallowed nervously. "Jessica Ryder. You might also check under Jessica Fowler."

"Lei, what the heck are you doing?" Simon demanded. "Why are you looking into Jessica's history? Do you think that she had something to do with Dad's murder?"

I lowered my voice. "Listen, I don't want Mom to know about this, okay? It's just an angle I want to check out."

"But why?" Simon persisted. "Jessica's always been a great employee. Dad thought the world of her."

And she certainly thought the world of him. "I can't get into this now, but will you please check around and see if you can find out anything? Trust me on this."

"All right," he said wearily. "I'll see what I can do."

"Thanks so much." I clicked off.

"Oh, my Lord." Heather put a hand over her mouth. "What if she and your father had a one-night stand and she refused to give him up? You know, like that old movie *Fatal Attraction*?"

I gaped at her. "Jessica's not a maniac, Heather." At least I hoped not.

She shrugged. "People do crazy things when they're in love. Jessica's been a widow for a long time. She must be lonely. I know there's a lot of people who can't stand their boss, but others fall madly in love with them and have affairs. What if she demanded that he divorce your mother? Then your mother found out, confronted her, and—"

"Stop," I said. "This is crazy."

Heather ignored my plea. "It could have been a crime of passion. You know, the old, 'If I can't have you, no one else can.' Sure, it sounds crazy, Lei, but if you could have seen the way Jessica was looking at him that day, you'd understand what I'm talking about."

"You have to stop watching *General Hospital* while you're working," I told her. "This isn't a soap opera; it's real life. My father would never be unfaithful to my mother." As much as I refused to believe it, a tiny doubt had managed to work its way inside my head. Heather might have a point. Why else would Jessica have stayed working at Sappy Endings for so long? She certainly wasn't making a fortune and didn't need the money, anyway. Was there a chance that she had gone off the deep end, so to speak?

"Leila!" My mother called impatiently. "What are you two doing? Dinner's getting cold."

I shut down the computer. "Please don't breathe a word of this to my mother. She's been through enough."

"Of course not." Heather watched me anxiously. "Are you going to confront Jessica?"

"I have to. Tomorrow morning, after you drop me off at Sappy Endings, Jessica and I will have a little chat."

"Do you want me to come with you?" Heather asked.

I shook my head. "Thanks, but I'd rather talk to her alone." It was a delicate subject for certain. Plus, I needed to be careful. If I accused Jessica of having an affair with my father and nothing had happened, she would most likely end up quitting. Then again, if Heather was right and the woman had been making advances toward my father, how could I possibly let her continue working there? It was a no-win situation for me.

Heather headed for the kitchen in search of my mother, and I followed. She was removing a tray of meat pies from the oven. My stomach's rumbling noise turned into a full-fledged growl. "Oh, those look so good."

Toast was rubbing against Mom's legs and meowing piteously, as if he hadn't eaten in days. I stooped down to pet him. "Don't worry, fellow," I assured him. "You're a shoo-in to get some."

Heather bussed my mother's cheek. "Mrs. Khoury, your kitchen always smells so divine. I wish you could teach my mother to cook. Too bad I take after her."

Mom laughed in delight. Heather always knew the right

thing to say to her. "Any time you want to learn how to cook, dear, come on over. All women should know how to make at least one nice meal. Remember, a man expects that from his new bride."

Heather leaned against the counter. "It's okay. Tyler knows better than to expect anything edible from me."

"Where were you two?" My mother asked. "Up in Leila's room?"

"Yes," Heather said quickly. "I wanted to borrow a sweater. Um, I felt chilly, but the kitchen's so warm that I don't need it now."

My mother stared at her, confused, while I rolled my eyes. Heather was a worse liar than me. "Mom, do you think Toast misses going outside? I could take him to work with me tomorrow."

My mother put tabbouleh on the table. "Oh, no, not at all. Besides, it's dangerous for cats to be outside. There's plenty of things to amuse him around here. Why, he sat in the window seat napping for almost four hours! I also ordered a scratching post and some toys for him online. They'll be here tomorrow."

"Toast knows which side his bread is buttered on." Heather laughed at her pun. "Tyler wants to get a dog when we get back from our honeymoon. I'm not sure if I'm ready for that."

I went to the sink to wash my hands. "Why? You love animals."

"Sure, but it's a big commitment." Heather stooped down to give Toast some chin scratches, which he seemed to appreciate. "At least he's agreed with me that we're going to wait a couple of years to have kids. I want to get my home business started first."

The room fell quiet, and Heather instantly realized her mistake. She looked at me with stricken eyes, but I shook my head, which she knew meant not to worry. Babies were a touchy subject with my mother. And, if I was being completely honest, they were with me as well.

Heather went to wash her hands and, thankfully, decided to try her luck at another subject. "Toast is certainly lapping up the attention around here."

"He is such good company." My mother looked wistful. "I'm so glad you brought him home, Leila. Somehow, he makes the house seem less lonely."

My emotions were getting the better of me today. As much as I missed my father, I knew that my mother was suffering more. Like a pillow, my heart softened for her and the grief she was going through.

I dried my hands on a dish towel and then leaned over to give my mother a kiss on the cheek. She looked surprised but pleased. Our moments of affection toward each other had always been rare, but I couldn't help myself. My mother might have a knack for saying the wrong thing, but I knew that she only wanted to see Simon and me happy.

"Thank you, Leila." Her voice trembled, and she quickly turned toward Heather. "Sit down, dear, before the food gets cold."

After Heather sat down, she pulled another bridal

magazine out of her purse. "Mrs. Khoury, I'd love to know what you think of the gown I put on order."

Heaven help her. I knew that Heather valued my mother's opinion since she was an excellent seamstress, but she should have known better than to bring up the subject. My mother found fault with every designer gown that she saw. She still believed that handmade gowns were the best ones. I prayed that Heather didn't tell her the price of the dress, because she might go into cardiac arrest.

"I can't wait to see it," she exclaimed. "I've always wanted to help pick out a wedding gown but never had the chance."

Here we go again. It had been four years since my broken engagement, and she was still acting like a child who'd gotten their feelings hurt. Was she ever going to let it go?

Mom gestured at the food. "Come on, Heather. Help yourself. I know how much you love my cooking."

"That's the problem," Heather groaned. "I won't fit into my wedding dress at this rate."

"Nonsense," my mother scoffed. "Besides, men don't want women who are too skinny."

Another shot at me. *Thank you, Mom.*

Heather's worried gaze traveled from my mother to me and then back to my mother. "Well, maybe just some salad. Everything is so delicious. I'm a disaster in the kitchen. The only thing I can make is spaghetti."

Heather and I both loved my mother's tabbouleh. It was a bitter Levantine salad made from finely chopped parsley, tomatoes, mint, onion, and bulgur. My mother seasoned it with olive oil, lemon juice, salt, and sweet pepper.

My mother heaped the tabbouleh onto Heather's plate. "You'll do fine, dear. Wanting to learn is the key."

I gritted my teeth together and said nothing. If anyone was keeping score, it was now three to zero in favor of my mother. I quickly stuffed a forkful of food into my mouth before a sarcastic comment could slip out.

"What about your tires, Leila?" Mom asked. "You didn't tell me on the phone what Alan said. Will insurance cover them?"

Puzzled, I stared at her. "None of the tires are covered, Mom."

She made a face. "Well, that isn't right. It's a brand-new car, for goodness' sake."

"It doesn't matter, Mom. That's the way it works."

"Well, don't worry about the slashing," Mom said sensibly. "Those kinds of things happen everywhere, even in small towns like Sugar Ridge. Some people are just downright mean."

"I'm sure you're right. It was a random act." I nudged Heather with my foot under the table, and she understood my intention. I didn't want my mother to know that the incident might be related to my father's murder, or that I was positive Wesley had been the one to commit the deed.

"It was nice of Noah to stay with you until Heather arrived," Mom commented.

"Yes, it was." There was no point in telling her that he'd been waiting for his own ride.

Heather wiped her mouth with a linen napkin. "I didn't know that Noah had a child."

"Oh, yes. Her name is Emily, I believe." Mom reached for another meat pie.

This was a surprise. Mom had known about the little girl and hadn't told me? What else did she know about the mystery man? "Emma," I corrected. "She's adorable, isn't she?"

"I'm sure she is," Mom agreed. "But I've never actually met her."

Heather and I waited for my mother to continue, but she kept on eating, oblivious to our interest. Getting information out of her was akin to watching sap run. "Has Noah brought her to Sappy Endings with him before?" I asked.

Mom shrugged. "I don't think so. From what your father told me, he's a very private person. Noah did mention to your dad that Emma was living with his mother in New York until recently. She came to Sugar Ridge this fall so that she could start the school year here. I assume the grandmother is staying on until Noah finds a babysitter for after school. At least that's what your father told me a few weeks ago." She sighed, as if remembering.

"Where's Emma's mother? Are they divorced?" Heather asked.

"She died in a car accident," my mother said sadly. "Sometime last year, I believe. It was before Noah came to Sugar Ridge. A drunk driver hit her vehicle."

"That poor little girl," Heather lamented. "How awful for all of them."

Guilt washed over me. I had never imagined that Noah was going through such a terrible ordeal. For the past week, I'd thought that the man was cocky, arrogant, and self-absorbed. Instead, he was a recent widower raising a little girl all by himself. I'd been wrong on all accounts.

My father, in all his wisdom, had once told me never to judge a person without knowing their true circumstances. "It is always better to be kind, *habibi*," he'd said. "It will come back to you in ways that you never expect."

"Yes, it's so sad," Mom agreed. She paused for a sip of *limonada*, the Lebanese version of lemonade. It was more refreshing and flavorful than the American drink, thanks to the rose water my mother used. "I guess that's why Noah came here to Sugar Ridge. He told your father that he had to get away from New York after the accident and make a new start. He probably wanted to get settled here first before uprooting his daughter."

Heather wiped at her eyes with a napkin. She was very sentimental and cried easily. I remembered watching *The Notebook* with her when we were teenagers. She must have gone through two boxes of tissues alone. Her caring nature was one of the things that I loved most about her.

My view of Noah had changed drastically since our first meeting. Did I still think he could be responsible for my father's death? When I pictured him with Emma in his arms, the answer that immediately came to mind was no.

Heather sniffed. "I don't know what I'd do without my mother."

"Me either." I smiled at Mom, but she didn't even glance my way as she got up to place her dish in the sink. With a sigh, I turned back to my food. Yes, we still had our work cut out for us.

CHAPTER FIFTEEN

AFTER THEY'D FINISHED EATING, MY mother and Heather sat at the table with the bridal magazine spread out between them. They started discussing fabrics and what type of bouquets the bridesmaids should carry. Heather wanted roses for herself and thought lilies would go well with the bridesmaid dresses, but my mother suggested chrysanthemums since they were cheaper.

Bored with the subject, my thoughts shifted back to Noah and his daughter. His words from earlier this evening came back to me. "She's the reason I get up every morning." At least he had his mother to help with Emma, but they'd suffered such a tragic loss that my heart went out to them. I pictured them at the diner, with Emma happily dunking her french fries in ketchup. The image made me smile.

"What are you smiling at?" Heather asked suddenly.

I forked some salad into my mouth and chewed slowly, deliberately delaying my response. "Was I smiling? Sorry, I won't do it again."

"Smart aleck." Heather's eyes twinkled with mischief. "Just for that, maybe I'll ask the seamstress to put a giant bow on the back of your dress."

My fork clattered when it fell against the plate. "You wouldn't dare! What is this, anyway? The '90s?"

Heather began to laugh as the house phone rang. Mom excused herself and went to the living room to answer it.

"Listen, Lei, I'm sorry for what I did," Heather said sheepishly.

"What are you talking about?" I asked.

"You know, when I mentioned that Tyler and I were going to wait a few years to have a baby. I never should have said the B word around your mother. I know how much she wants grandchildren—"

I pushed my plate away. "No worries. Maybe Simon and Tonya will give her some, and then she'll finally be happy."

Heather poured herself a glass of *limonada* from the pitcher on the table. "I didn't realize they were that serious."

"None of us did," I remarked. "I'm not sure that Tonya realizes it, either."

Heather's face fell. "Oh no. You still think she's using him?"

"You saw that bracelet. I think she cares more about it than him, but I hope I'm wrong." I pressed a finger to my lips. "Let's talk about something else. I don't want my mother to overhear."

"Okay, I'll bite." Heather stretched her long legs out under the table. "I know you're not going to rest until you have an answer about your father. What have you got planned next?"

"I have to talk to Jessica tomorrow morning." Saying her name out loud made me cringe. I was dreading the conversation, but it had to be done. "Even if Simon doesn't find out anything incriminating about her, I'd like to know her true feelings about my father."

"And Noah?" Heather asked. "Do you still think he could have done it?"

I paused to consider. "I know it sounds crazy, but after seeing how he was with his daughter tonight, and hearing about what happened to his wife, I can't picture him as a cold-blooded killer anymore. When I first heard that he'd found my father's body, I'll admit that I was ready to haul him off to prison. But my opinion has changed since then."

"Oh my." Heather's mouth turned up slightly at the corners. "You like him."

I almost dropped my glass. "That's ridiculous."

She straightened up in her chair. "It is *not* ridiculous. And I always know when you're lying, Leila Khoury."

"What are you, my mother now?"

Heather shot me a smug look of satisfaction. "There's nothing wrong with having a crush on the guy. I mean, he is gorgeous."

"I'm not fifteen anymore. I don't have crushes. Besides, my only interest in him is what he can teach me about the business."

Heather winked. "Oh, sure."

"All right," I conceded. "I admit that Noah's good looking, but he isn't interested in me. And I'm not looking for a boyfriend. Let's face it. What happened with Mark is proof that marriage isn't going to happen for me."

A look of horror crossed my friend's delicate features. "Oh. My. God. I pray that your mother never hears you say that. She'd go berserk." Heather snapped her fingers. "Hey! Tyler and I are going dancing at the country club next Friday night. Why don't you come with us?"

I picked up her plate and set it in the sink with mine. "No, thanks. I'm not interested in being a third wheel."

"That's silly," she huffed. "You know that Ty adores you. We'll switch off. He can be your partner for one dance, and then mine for another. Plus, there's going to be plenty of eligible guys that Tyler knows. He'd be glad to introduce you if I—"

"No," I said firmly. "Thanks for the offer, but I'm not interested. Besides, I'll be going back to Florida next year, so there's no sense in starting up a relationship with anyone."

Heather watched me in silence for several seconds as I began to wipe down the table. Her voice was soft and warm. "Why are you punishing yourself, Lei? What happened with Mark wasn't your fault."

I didn't respond.

"You never told your mother the real reason for the breakup, did you?" she asked.

"Let her think what she wants," I said grimly. "For the record, I don't blame Mark for ending our engagement."

It still hurt when I thought about him. Perhaps it always would. I hadn't expected to fall in love with the man, especially since he'd been handpicked by my mother of all people, but it had happened anyway. Heather had mentioned that he'd moved to New York City shortly after our breakup. She hadn't offered any more information, and for that I was grateful. He was probably married by now with a baby or at least one on the way. Children had been very important to him. He'd made that clear when we broke up.

"Maybe you only get one chance in this life to find your true love." I'd thought a great deal about this over the years. "And if that's the case, then I blew it, need to accept things and move on. Perhaps running Sappy Endings is my purpose in this life."

Heather was startled by my statement. "Lei, running a business is great, but you can't let it be your entire world. There's someone out there for everyone."

"My soulmate, right?" I laughed at the thought.

"You're such a skeptic," Heather chided. "He might be right under your nose."

I gave an exaggerated snicker as my mother returned to the kitchen, a pleased looked upon her face. "That was Mrs. Middleton. Remember her son, Terry? She wanted to let me know that he's flying into town next week and will be staying with her for a while." Her face shone with hope. "He's so handsome, and still single. It won't be long before someone snaps him up."

Heather raised her eyebrows at me, and I had a sudden urge to scream. "Mom, we're not having this conversation."

Mom sighed heavily. "Talk to her, Heather. She refuses to listen to me. She's determined to remain a spinster."

Thankfully, my cell phone buzzed at that moment, and Theo's name appeared on the screen. "Excuse me for a second." I practically ran into the living room to get away from my mother. "Hi, Theo."

"Leila, apologies for bothering you. I hope I didn't interrupt your dinner."

"Not at all. We've already finished. What's up?" I asked.

Theo coughed. "I don't know where my head is lately. Too much going on at the office and at home. Somehow, I forgot to tell you that I have a few more papers for you to sign regarding the transfer of the business from your father. Will you be at Sappy Endings tomorrow?"

"Of course. My home away from home," I joked. "What time do you think you'll be by?"

He paused for a long moment. "Hmm, let's shoot for noon. I'm actually in Ithaca, New York, tonight and driving back to Sugar Ridge in the morning. There are a few things I need to take care of at my office first, but I think I could manage to be out there by lunchtime. It also gives me an excuse to have one of Jessica's all-day breakfast sandwiches, too."

I laughed. "That's quite a drive from here. Did you go all the way there on business?"

"No, Laura and I brought Ted out this morning for a college tour to Cornell, and then we met up with some old friends for dinner. We decided it would be easier to spend the night here and drive back in the morning. He loves the campus, so this might be the one. Since he's a straight-A student, I'm hopeful he'll be accepted, and possibly for early admission, too."

"Wow, that's wonderful. It sounds like there's great things in store for him."

"I think so, too." Theo's voice filled with excitement. "I told Laura that he's a chip off the old block. For some strange reason, she thinks she deserves some of the credit." He chuckled and then yawned. "Okay, I'm off to bed. I need to be up by five. I'll see you around twelve."

I made a mental note of the appointment. "See you then. If I'm not in the café or gift shop, come right back to Dad's off—I mean, my office."

"That's the spirit," he said jovially. "Good for you. Spoken like a true business owner. Victor would be very proud of you, Leila."

"Thanks. That means a lot to me."

Heather left at nine o'clock, and my mother retired to her room immediately afterward. I sat down on the couch to read a book I'd started weeks ago but couldn't seem to concentrate.

I'd started to nod off when my phone buzzed, jerking me awake. I glanced down at the screen. Simon. "Hey."

"Hey yourself. Did I wake you?"

I attempted to muffle a giant yawn. "No, I was getting ready to head up to bed. Did you find out anything?"

"I did," Simon said calmly. "But before I go into it, I want to know why you're so suspicious of Jessica. Was she coming on to Dad, by any chance?"

My voice shook. "Why are you asking me this?"

"Just answer the question, Lei."

Simon and I were equally matched in the stubborn department. "Please don't say anything to Mom," I said, "but Heather recently overheard a conversation between Dad and Jessica. It sounded like she was interested in him—you know, romantically."

He swore. "Are you kidding? Dad should have fired her. Maybe he would have, if he'd known about her past track record."

Panic soared through me. "What did you find out?"

"Jessica has a police record," Simon said. "She was arrested back in 1985. I know it's almost forty years ago and might not mean much, but she violated a restraining order. Her ex-boyfriend filed one against her."

"No way," I whispered. "You mean she stalked him?"

"It sounds like it," Simon remarked. "The guy broke up with her and started seeing someone else. Jessica called him at all times of the night and made threats against his new girlfriend. After Jessica violated the restraining order, she was arrested, made bail, then went on probation. I couldn't find out anything else, so I'm guessing her abusive behavior must have stopped then."

"I wish I could believe that," I said with sincerity.

We were both silent for several seconds until Simon spoke again. "Do you think she was in love with Dad?"

"I don't know," I admitted, "but I'm going to find out. Thanks for checking into this."

"Keep me posted, okay?" Simon asked. "And please be careful. If Jessica was responsible for Dad's death—" He didn't finish the sentence. "Lei, I don't want her coming after you or Mom next."

"Don't worry. I'll be careful. Thanks, Si. Love you."

"Love you, too, sis."

I turned out the lights and climbed the stairs to my bedroom with Toast following closely at my heels. He settled next to me in bed, his purrs comforting me in the darkness. Despite my troublesome conversation with Simon, I fell asleep as soon as my head connected with the pillow.

Sometime later, a banging sound awakened me. Floating in and out of consciousness, at first I assumed it was part of my dream. A muffled cry sounded from somewhere in the distance, forcing me to open my eyes into darkness. I laid there waiting for the sound to come again. Nothing.

My eyes began to close again when the noise repeated itself. *Thump, thump, thump.* I shot up in bed, my heart knocking against the wall of my chest. Someone was banging on the front door. I glanced at the clock on my dresser. It was one o'clock in the morning.

My movement disturbed Toast, who had been curled up at the bottom of the bed. He stretched and yawned, then came over to nuzzle my hand, purring away. I patted him absently as the sound came again. Fear settled on my chest like a heavy boulder. Who the heck was at the front door at this ungodly hour? In my experience, the only reason people came to the door this late was if there had been some type of accident. My first thought was of Simon. Dear Lord. My mother would fall apart if something happened to him.

I wrapped my robe around me, grabbed my cell phone, and then padded down the stairs in my bare feet. Holding my breath, I moved the curtain away from the front door, and looked out the window.

Wesley Browning was staring back in at me.

I let out a shriek and let the curtain fall back in place. *Oh my God. He's going to kill me and Mom.* "Go away!" I screamed.

"Leila, please!" he begged. "You've got to listen to me!" He started pounding on the door again. "I swear I'm not here to hurt you."

I moved the curtain back and held up my cell phone. "I'm calling the police."

The porch light shone down on his face. His skin was an ashen color and his eyes bloodshot, filled with terror. "Someone is after me." His voice trembled. "They'll be coming for you, too."

"I don't believe you."

He placed his hands on the door's glass pane. "Please! I think I know who killed your father. The same person who killed my father. You've got to believe me."

My heart raced and my stomach became queasy. I didn't know what to do. Was there a chance he was telling the truth? My head was telling me to call 9-1-1, but my heart would not ignore his desperate cries for help.

"Hold on a minute," I said. "I'm going to get my mother."

Wesley's face convulsed with pain. "I'm telling you the truth, I swear. I should have told you that night you came out to my house, but I think my house is bugged. My life is in danger, and yours, too. Please help me."

The lump in my throat grew until I was afraid it might choke me. "Okay, I'll be right back." I flew up the stairs and barged through my mother's bedroom door, flipping on the light switch. My mother had taken sleeping pills for years so I wasn't surprised when the knocking hadn't awakened her. Sure enough, she was snoring softly into her pillow, a peaceful expression on her face.

I shook her arms vigorously. "Mom, wake up. Please, it's important!"

My mother stared up at me, clearly disoriented. When recognition finally set in, she sat up in bed, her eyes wide and terrified. "What's wrong? Is Simon okay?"

"Wesley Browning is downstairs at the front door. He wants to talk to me. If he tries anything funny, I want you to call the police right away."

"Leila!" She gripped my wrist so tightly that I winced with pain. "Why is that man here? What have you been doing with him?"

"Mom, I don't have time to explain right now, but I want you to stay in the kitchen in case Wesley tries anything. He said he knows who killed Dad—" My voice trembled. "And I think he might be telling the truth."

Her face turned as white as the sheet. She jumped out of

bed and stuffed her feet into pink slippers. "Oh my God. Leila, what are you planning to do? What if he tries to hurt you?"

"I'll be fine," I said with more assurance than I felt. "Nothing's going to happen."

I hurried down the stairs with my mother following. Toast was lying on the couch, watching our movements with interest. My mother caught up with me and grabbed a handful of my robe.

"Please be careful!" Mom begged. "I don't want you to wind up like—"

She stopped in mid-sentence, but I knew what she was going to say. She was afraid I'd be killed like my father. I let out a deep breath and kissed her cheek. "I'll be okay."

With shaking fingers, I undid the chain on the door and stepped out into the night. The air had turned cold and frost had started to gather on the grass. I held up my cell phone in front of me. "I've got 9-1-1 dialed on my phone. If you try anything funny, I'll press Call."

Wesley's narrow face bore a look of intense despera-tion, similar to a man who had run out of luck and knew it. He swallowed nervously. "No matter what you think, my father was a good person. A great husband and father. Then, shortly after he went into business with your dad, he got in with the wrong crowd. He still owed money when he died. When you owe money to loan sharks, it doesn't get crossed off as paid in full when you die. It passes on to the next of kin."

Wesley's situation was far more precarious than I'd thought.

Fearful, he looked over his shoulder, but the street was quiet. "There was no way I could pay my father's debts off. I lost my job, and then my mother got sick. She needed medical care we couldn't afford, so I took out another mortgage on the house. It still wasn't enough, though. That's when I thought that maybe I could run the money up at the track. I'd go to New York sometimes and bet on the ponies. Yeah, I was really good at it. Some people are a natural at that kind of stuff, know what I mean?"

I didn't have an answer for him. It was obvious to me what had happened next.

Wesley turned around, his back to me. "But it all disappeared, practically overnight, and then I owed even more. I did ask your father for money. I thought if he felt guilty enough about my dad that he might give me some, but he refused." He whirled to face me, his eyes silently pleading. "But I swear that I didn't harm him. After your father was murdered, I thought that Sappy Endings would go up for sale."

He wasn't making any sense. "I don't understand. Were you hoping to buy it?" How could he? Wesley didn't have any money.

Rage flashed in his eyes and I backed away a step. "They said it would go up for sale," he whispered. "No one ever thought that you'd be running it. You ruined the plan." His teeth started to chatter violently. "Everyone knows that Sappy Endings is a gold mine."

"Who are you talking about?" I asked. "Is this the same person who killed my father?"

Wesley leaned on the porch railing, gripping the spokes between his two hands. "Yeah. Your father and my father. Look, I didn't mean to scare you that night. I was angry—angry with the hand I got dealt. Sappy Endings should have been my legacy, not yours. If your father hadn't bailed mine out, he would have died sooner." He gave a bitter laugh. "Dad fell into the same old habits, and then I took them over after he was killed."

"Who killed my father?" I demanded.

He grabbed my hand in a tight grip. "Don't you see? My dad's death was made to look like a suicide. And since I know the truth now, I'll be the next one to go. You have to be careful or—"

A car was headed down the street in our direction when suddenly it veered off the road and toward my house, the high intensity headlights blinding us with their rays. The vehicle drove up on the grass while I watched, horrified.

"Get down!" Wesley yelled. He pushed me onto the cement as a loud popping noise filled the night air. A terrified scream broke from between my lips as Wesley fell on top of me. More gunshots were fired and then a car engine roared to life. As it moved farther and farther away, an eerie sense of quiet drifted through the night air.

The front door opened, and my mother ran out. "Leila! Oh my God!" she screamed.

I managed to roll Wesley off me and then with my mother's assistance, rose to my feet. My legs were shaky and I might have fallen if she hadn't helped to support me.

I pressed Call on my phone, and a female voice came on the line. "9-1-1, what is your emergency?"

"Please send an ambulance right away!" I was half crying, half yelling into the phone. The poor woman must have thought I was hysterical.

"What is your address, ma'am?"

"Twelve Mountainview Terrace. Please hurry!"

My mother brought her hands to her mouth. "Dear Lord. Leila, he's not—I mean, he didn't—" She couldn't finish the sentence.

I stared up at her, tears sliding down my cheeks. "Yes, Mom," I whispered. "He's dead."

CHAPTER SIXTEEN

MY MOTHER REFILLED MY COFFEE cup, and I didn't try to stop her. What was the point? There was no way either one of us was going to sleep tonight. Every time I shut my eyes, I saw Wesley's terrified face.

Sitting by the kitchen window, there was no way to miss the flashing lights from the police cars or the rumble of the coroner's van as Wesley's body was driven away. It was hard to believe it had only been an hour since he'd pounded on the front door, wanting to talk to me.

"He was telling the truth," I said softly.

Mom sat down at the kitchen table next to me. "What do you mean?"

"He knew who killed Dad," I said. "Wesley said it was the same person who had killed his father."

My mother was exhausted. There were dark circles of weariness under her eyes, and she looked like she might collapse at any moment. She was bravely trying to hold herself together but I suspected she'd gotten to the breaking point.

She drew her brows together. "I don't understand. If he knew who killed your father, why didn't he come forward sooner? And everyone knows that Dennis committed suicide. He was in a deep depression for a long time."

"Dad's death and Dennis's are connected," I insisted. "But I'm not sure how."

She blinked. "Dennis died many years ago. Isn't it possible that Wesley might have been lying?"

"Anything is possible." A deep, male voice behind me startled us both. We looked up to see Chief Crosby standing under the archway that led to the living room. I hadn't even heard him come inside the house.

My mother rose from the table immediately. "Alan, please sit down. Can I get you some coffee?"

Chief Crosby rubbed his eyes wearily as he pulled out a chair. "That would be nice, Selma. Thank you." He placed his tablet on the table while his eyes studied my face, as if trying to uncover a secret I'd failed to tell him. Uneasiness crept down my spine. He suspected that I was hiding something.

"Leila," he said slowly. "Wesley's death wasn't your fault, so please don't blame yourself."

"It's hard not to," I admitted.

"I realize that, but remember, Wesley had his fair share of enemies. He owed people money, stole from past employers, and was known for starting fights. His death doesn't have anything to do with your father's."

It was as if he'd read my mind. "I'm sorry, Chief Crosby, but I do feel they're all connected. Wesley's, Dennis's, and my father's. Someone must have followed him here tonight." I wrapped my trembling fingers around the hot mug. "Whoever did this figured that Wesley came here to tell me something about my father's death, and they were determined to stop him."

"What exactly did Wesley say to you?" Chief Crosby asked as my mother placed a mug of steaming *Ahweh* in front of him.

I forced myself to think back to our brief conversation. "He said that his father's death was made to look like a suicide. Dennis was murdered, and it had something to do with Sappy Endings. Then he said that whoever had my father killed thought the place would go up for sale when he died."

Chief Crosby swallowed a sip of coffee and made a face, either from the bitter taste or my statement. I was betting on the latter. He set the mug down. "Dennis had no claim to Sappy Endings when he died. The man was in debt and severely depressed. I was called after his body was discovered." He fell silent for a moment, remembering. "It was definitely suicide."

"Poor Wesley." My mother shook her head sadly. "To be killed like that, in cold blood. Just like your father." Her voice shook and she looked over at me. "Leila, you could have been killed as well." She choked back a sob. "I don't think I could live through that again."

I reached over and placed my hand on her arm. Mom rapidly blinked back tears and then wiped her eyes with a tissue. It devastated and shocked me to see her like this. She hadn't even cried at my father's funeral or wake. Her strength was immeasurable, and now I realized how I might have misinterpreted it as uncaring, or unfeeling.

She smiled and patted my hand. "I'm all right now, dear. Thank you."

"I was wrong about Wesley," I confessed. "I don't believe he killed Dad. Wesley saved my life when he pushed me down on the porch." The man hadn't known me, but he'd sacrificed his life to protect mine. If only we'd had more time tonight. "He even suspected someone was following him."

Chief Crosby looked at me gravely. "If that's true, then you're in danger, too, Leila. I won't stand for it. Victor was my closest friend, and I'll do whatever it takes to make sure that his family is protected. I'll have a patrol car stop by here and at Sappy Endings a few times a day until we catch this lunatic."

"We'd appreciate that, Alan," my mother said softly.

He finished the last of his coffee and rose to his feet. "I mean it, Leila. Don't take any unnecessary chances. It's only a matter of time until this person slips up, and then we'll nab them."

The next morning, my mother dropped me off at Sappy Endings at seven o'clock sharp. The building was so quiet and still that I quickly became unnerved. What if Chief

Crosby was right, and someone did want me dead as well? Had I become a marked woman, so to speak? Was it true that my father had been killed for his beloved farm?

I went into the darkened café, flicked on the lights, and helped myself to a bottle of orange juice. I'd had more than my fair share of coffee since last night and as a result, was edgy and jumpy. Of course, it wasn't only the coffee. A dead body falling on me might have had something to do with it.

The front door of the building opened, and Jessica appeared. Her eyes nearly bulged out of their sockets when she noticed me. "My goodness, honey! You're in early this morning."

"Good morning, Jessica." I swallowed a large gulp of juice.

She glanced at me worriedly. "You look all tired out. Didn't you get any sleep last night?"

I shook my head. "Not really. There was a little too much going on." It made no sense to try and hide what had happened from her. Everyone in Sugar Ridge would know about it before long. I relayed my story as quickly as possible.

Jessica's face froze like a statue. "Oh my goodness! The poor man. He was in such bad shape the last time I saw him here." She lowered her eyes to the floor. "It was the same day that your father was killed. Maybe it wasn't a coincidence."

"That's what I'm wondering, too," I said.

Jessica filled a muffin pan with paper liners and the

defrosted dough she'd taken from the freezer earlier. "Leila, it's possible that you might never know what happened that night."

"There's a lot of things I might never know." Heather's remarks about seeing Jessica and my father in the café came back to haunt me. My father always told me that she was the perfect employee.

"What do you mean?" Jessica sounded confused.

"You and my father were very close, weren't you?" I blurted out.

Jessica's smiled faded. "Well, of course we were." Her usual jovial expression had been replaced by a look of apprehension. "Everyone loved your father."

"Did you?" There, I'd finally said it.

She blinked in surprise. "Did I what?"

"Did you love my father?"

The muffin pan slid to the floor before Jessica could stop it. Flustered, she got down on her hands and knees and began to clean up the mess. I stooped down to help her.

"How about a breakfast sandwich?" Jessica asked, refusing to look at me.

"You didn't answer my question. Were you in love with my father?" My voice rose an octave.

Jessica didn't reply. She went into the adjoining room to retrieve another container of dough, her hands shaking as she removed the lid. "Leila, why are you asking me such a thing?"

I folded my arms across my chest. "Because I think it's true."

"Your father was a happily married man. He would never fool around with another woman. Victor was a shining example to us all. She thrust out her chin in defiance. "And I resent your insinuation that I'd try to break up a marriage. Why, that's disgraceful."

"No. What's disgraceful is the way you've been coming on to my father," I said quietly. "And I didn't ask if he was in love with you. I wanted to know if you were in love with him, but I already have my answer."

Defeated, Jessica stared down at the floor for several seconds. "All right. Yes, I was in love with him. Victor knew it, but he was such a sweet man that he never tried to make me feel awkward about it. He pretended that everything was normal."

"But everything was *not* normal. Did you—" I couldn't bring myself to say the words out loud. No, it was a ridiculous thought and would only embarrass us further. My father would never have had an affair with her.

"No," Jessica said quietly. "We were never involved romantically. Victor—I mean your father—didn't love me. He never led me on in any way. I tried my best to persuade him differently, but he never took me up on my offers."

Offers. That meant she'd tried more than once to seduce my father. I couldn't believe that Jessica would have acted in such a manner. Her comment sickened and angered me. This woman had shared Christmas dinner with my family. Dad had always been a generous boss. When her husband died, she'd been gone from Sappy Endings for a month, and he paid her a full salary the entire time. My mother had sent over endless dishes of food for her and her sons. My parents had also made a large donation to Carl's charity of choice. I remembered my mother telling Jessica that they wanted to help in any way possible. How would my mother react when she found out that this woman had been lusting after her husband for years?

My throat tightened. "I can't believe you'd do something like that. And I don't want to believe it."

Jessica took a step in my direction, and I backed away. A tear rolled down her cheek. "Leila. Please don't hate me. I tried not to fall in love with Victor, but it wasn't possible. You see, I've been so lonely since Carl died. He was a wonderful man, much like your father in many ways. When Victor died, it was like losing Carl all over again."

Perhaps she wanted my sympathy, but this only angered me further. "Do you honestly expect me to feel sorry for you? He wasn't your husband, so it's not like losing him all over again. My father was a happily married man, but you couldn't have cared less. All you thought about was yourself. That isn't what loving someone means."

"I did love him, no matter what you say," Jessica insisted. Her hands balled into fists at her sides. "No one loved him more, not even your mother."

In shock, I took a step back from her. Where was this coming from? I thought about Jessica's history of stalking. It sounded to me as if she had never gotten past it. Her boyfriend had broken up with her, and then she had terrified him and his new girlfriend. People did change, but in this case, I wasn't so sure.

"What did you do when my father turned down your—um, invitations?" Nausea rolled through my stomach. I'd told Heather that I would be subtle, but it had proven to be impossible. Jessica's admission had changed my feelings about her forever. Now that I knew the truth, I'd have to tell my mother, which further sickened me.

Jessica looked confused. "I don't know what you mean."

"If you were in love with my father and knew he wasn't interested in you, why did you stay here? Didn't it hurt to see him every day? Weren't you angry that you couldn't have him?" Had she been enraged enough to put a gun to his head? Perhaps Heather's suggestion about a crime of passion hadn't been that far off base after all.

"No, it was just the opposite," Jessica sniffled. "It made me happy to see him every day. I enjoyed being near him."

Dear God. Why hadn't my father fired her? He must have been concerned. A light switch clicked on in my brain, and I remembered my conversation with Chief Crosby the other day. When he had first mentioned questioning Jessica about my father's murder, I'd been outraged by the thought. Jessica was like a member of the family, I'd insisted, and Chief Crosby had acted awkward. Did my father tell him about Jessica's propositions? Heck, Dad had to talk to someone about it, and his family was certainly not an option. The Chief must have known. *Like I said, Leila, I'm leaving no stones unturned.*

Jessica wrung her hands together. "I'm sorry. I shouldn't have done that."

"No, you shouldn't," I agreed. "Then again, you shouldn't have done a lot of things."

"Something wrong, ladies?"

Startled, I turned around to see Noah standing at the counter, watching us. He was dressed in a soft denim shirt that went well with his eyes. His aftershave wafted through the air, its pleasant scent engulfing me. Once again, Noah had caught me off guard. He stood there waiting for either one of us to respond. Finally, I found my voice.

"Please excuse me." My voice trembled. "I have a lot of work to do in the office."

Before Noah or Jessica could say anything further, I walked out of the café and into my office, slamming the door behind me. I stayed in there until ten o'clock, when the garage called to say that my car was ready. They offered me a ride over, and I gratefully accepted. I was relieved not to have to bother my mother to come back out or call Heather. When I returned, I went in through the back door, hoping to avoid the café and Jessica. No one called me to help out in the store or café. I suspected Jessica would rather call someone in off the street first.

At twelve fifteen, there was a knock on my door. I was tempted to yell, "Go away," but instead called out, "It's open."

Theo stuck his head in. "Hi, Leila. Is now a good time?"

"Of course. Come on in." I'd forgotten that Theo was dropping by. He must have gone home to change this morning, as he was dressed in a navy suit with a red tie. I leaned back in the chair and forced myself to be pleasant.

It wasn't Theo's fault that this day had rapidly turned into a disaster. "How was your college visit?"

Theo opened the briefcase on his lap. "Everything was great until I got back to Sugar Ridge this morning and heard the news. How are you holding up?"

I wiggled my hand back and forth. "I've had better days."

His smile was thin. "I can't imagine how awful this is for your family. I can recommend a good criminal attorney if you like."

Puzzled, I stared at him. "What are you talking about? Wesley's dead. Why would he need a lawyer?"

Theo nodded sympathetically. "Oh, yes. Your mother told me. What a tragedy. But I was talking about Simon, of course. I can't believe that he was arrested."

I jumped to my feet. "Is this a joke? Why was he arrested?"

He looked surprised. "For your father's murder."

CHAPTER SEVENTEEN

"YOU CAN'T BE SERIOUS," I sputtered. "My brother would never hurt anyone, especially our father!"

"I don't know much," Theo confessed, "but your mother is beside herself. She looked like she was ready to fall apart when I was at the police station. I thought you knew! Why wouldn't she have called you?"

With trembling fingers, I pulled my cell phone over and touched the screen. It lit up, revealing three missed calls from my mother and a text message that had arrived in the last half hour. I hadn't realized that my phone was on silent. Ugh. Guilt overwhelmed me as I read her message. Leila, please come to the police station right away. Simon is in trouble. I need you.

My mother needed me. When was the last time she'd ever said that? I couldn't remember. Flustered, I picked up my purse and fumbled around inside it for my car keys. "I'm sorry, Theo, but I have to go."

"Leila." He reached out to touch my arm. "Get a hold of yourself, for your mother's sake. Everything will be all right."

"Thanks. And thank you for letting me know."

I started for the door but he stopped me. "I know this is bad timing, but I really need these papers signed. I told you at the reading of the will that you had a few days, but these need to be completed by today. Please, it will only take a second." He handed me a pen. "And while you do that, I'll tell you what I do know."

My hand was shaking so violently I wasn't sure that I could sign anything. Theo pointed out the two separate pages where signatures were required, and I hastily scribbled my name while he talked.

"From what I heard Chief Crosby tell your mother, a gun was found in Simon's car." Theo hesitated before delivering the final blow. "Ballistics confirmed that your father was killed with the same gun."

"It's not true!" I threw open the door to my office. "Theo, I have to go."

"I'll get a copy over to you," he called after me, but I was barely listening.

Jessica was swamped at the café. She stared at me quizzically while I rushed out the front door but I didn't have time to stop and explain. As I was getting into my car, someone yelled my name. I turned to see Noah running in my direction.

"What's wrong?" he asked as he reached me.

"I have to leave for a while." My voice cracked. "My brother is in trouble."

Noah's mouth formed a thin, hard line. "Tell me what I can do to help."

His voice was kind and concerned, and practically my undoing. "You can't do anything. He—" The words stuck in my throat, and that was when I lost it. Like a fountain, tears streamed out of my eyes, and I began to sob.

Noah pulled me toward him and placed his arms around me. I didn't try to resist and clung to him gratefully as I sobbed into his shoulder. His strong arms held me tightly and securely while his hands moved across my back. It had been a long time since a man had held me, and I'd forgotten how much I missed the intimacy. I raised my head from his shoulder and took a step back. His gaze met mine and then traveled to my lips. A warm spark flickered through me and I quickly averted my eyes.

"I'm sorry." I dried my eyes with the back of my hand.

Noah reached into his coat pocket and offered me a handkerchief. I dried my eyes and offered it back but he shook his head. "Keep it."

"Thank you," I said softly. "Thank you for being so kind."

"Tell me what's happened to Simon," he said.

"My brother Simon—" The words came out in a strangled cry. "He's been arrested for my father's murder. My mother's at the police station. I have to go to him."

A vein bulged in Noah's neck. "I'm sorry, Leila." He reached for my hand and closed his around it. "Come on, I'll drive you."

"No," I tried to pull away. "Jessica needs you here."

"I was going on lunch anyway," Noah said. "Jessica will be all right for a while. The lunch rush is just about over. I'll text her when we get to the station and let her know what's happening. You're in no condition to drive yourself."

Noah was already leading me toward his truck, and I didn't have the strength to argue anymore. "All right. Thank you."

Noah opened the passenger side door of his truck for me and helped me up. The truck smelled like him, warm and alluring. There was a Barbie doll wedged into the back of my seat and the sight of it made me smile.

"A friend of yours?" I managed a small laugh.

His face broke into a grin. "Sorry about that. Em's got more of those things than I have room for. Her grand-mother loves spoiling her."

I welcomed the opportunity to talk about his little girl instead of Simon's arrest. "She's beautiful, by the way."

"Thanks. She takes after her mother." His face immediately sobered, and I felt a pang of sympathy for him.

"What was your wife's name?" I asked.

Noah was quiet for several seconds, and I began to wish that I hadn't asked. "Ashley," he finally murmured.

I waited to see if he would elaborate, but he drove on in silence. It was obviously still too painful for him to talk about her, and I decided not to press him further.

"Jessica told me what happened at your house last night." He stopped at a red light and turned to face me. "Are you all right?"

"No," I said honestly. "I'm not all right. I watched someone die, my brother's been arrested, and Jessica's—" I couldn't go on.

Noah turned into the police station's parking lot and shut off the engine. "What about Jessica?"

I waved him off. "We'll talk about it later. I need to see my mother and Simon right now."

Noah got out of the truck and came around to open the door for me, but I didn't wait for his gallant gesture. I ran toward the building's entrance with him following. Once inside, I headed straight for the information desk when I spotted Chief Crosby coming out of a nearby office. I hurried toward him.

"Where's my mother? And Simon? Are they okay?"

Chief Crosby placed his hands on my arms. "Calm down, Leila. They're both fine. Your mother's waiting in my office. Selma's already put up his bail money. The release paperwork is almost done, and then he'll be able to leave."

"But what does this all mean?" I asked. "Simon will have to stand trial?"

Chief Crosby looked over my head and nodded at Noah, who had caught up with me. "I'm afraid so, but it won't be for a while. Anything can happen before then."

"How could you arrest him?" I said angrily. "You were my father's best friend—*you know* that Simon wouldn't do this!"

"I realize that you're upset, but please try to listen to me," Chief Crosby said calmly. "I have to do my job. The murder weapon was found in your brother's car. We can't ignore something like that. I'm sorry."

"Why were you searching his car in the first place!" I wanted to know. "Don't you need a warrant for that?"

For once, Chief Crosby looked embarrassed. "Simon's car was pulled over for speeding early this morning. When Simon went to grab his license out of the glove compartment, the officer spotted a gun. Simon didn't have a permit, so Officer Loudon brought him into the station. We ran some tests and found out that it was the same gun that had shot your father. I'm sorry, Leila."

Tears stung my eyes. What else could go wrong? In a matter of twenty-four hours, I'd seen a man die, had an argument with an employee, and now my brother had been arrested for the murder of our father. Stick a fork in me, I was done.

"Someone is setting him up," I fumed. "Don't you see? That gun must have been planted in his car. The real killer wants Simon to take the fall."

Chief Crosby put a hand on my shoulder, but I shook him off. I knew this wasn't his fault, but it still felt as if he had betrayed my family, especially my father. They were wasting time arresting Simon when the real killer was still on the loose.

"Can you please take me to my mother?" My voice sounded bitter, but I didn't care.

He coughed. "Certainly."

I turned to Noah. "Will you wait for me? If you feel like you need to go back to the farm, I understand—"

"Take as long as you need," Noah assured me. "I just texted Jessica and she said not to worry—it slowed down right after we left. She's sending prayers for your brother."

Her phony expression of sympathy made me sick, but there wasn't time to think about her now. My mother and brother needed my support.

I followed Chief Crosby down the narrow, sterile-like hallway to his office at the end. The room was a mess with piles of paperwork on the desk and filing cabinets. A wilted plant sat in one corner, looking depressed. There was a half-eaten sandwich lying on top of a manilla folder. In front of the desk were two dark blue plush chairs. My mother was sitting in one of them, hands folded in her lap, with her head bowed as if she was praying.

I sat down in the chair next to her. Without thinking my arms went around her. She held back a sob as she hugged me against her.

"Thank goodness you're here, Leila," she said in a shaky voice. "We'll be leaving for home as soon as Simon's papers are in order. He's going to be staying with us for a couple of days."

"That's great." I turned my head to see Chief Crosby standing awkwardly in the doorway, looking as if he didn't know what to do next. "If this goes public, it's going to ruin Simon's career at the newspaper."

"I can't promise anything," Chief Crosby said, "but I'll do my best to keep it under wraps. On the bright side, this may catch the real killer off guard. They've been known to slip up once someone else has been arrested for their crime. It makes them feel safer."

My mother dried her eyes with a tissue. "Simon does not belong in jail," she said. "He's a good man, like his father."

Chief Crosby plopped down in his chair. "Selma, after Victor's murder, we started obtaining court orders to check Simon's bank records. Simon deposited ten thousand dollars into his account the day Victor died. A few days later, he withdrew five thousand dollars. He wouldn't tell me what he used the money for. Do you have any idea?"

A mental picture of Tonya and her diamond bracelet that she'd proudly displayed came to my mind. Tonya told Heather and me that it had been a present from Simon a few days earlier. I didn't know much about jewelry but suspected that's where the five thousand dollars had gone.

I waited for my mother to answer first. She shook her head mutely, and then I spoke up. "He bought a bracelet for his girlfriend. A diamond bracelet."

"What?" My mother's eyes almost bugged out of her head. "Are you sure?"

"Yes, Heather and I both saw it. Tonya was wearing it when she came into Sappy Endings the other day."

My mother groaned and put her head in her hands. "I knew that girl was going to be trouble. She's no good for my son."

Despite the seriousness of the situation, I forced back a smile. No woman would *ever* be good enough for Selma Khoury's only son.

"Simon isn't talking," Chief Crosby remarked. "At least now we have a good idea what the money went toward. But where or whom did he get it from?"

"Simon said that my father refused to give him a loan," I said. "So how else would he have gotten the money?"

Chief Crosby rubbed his chin in a thoughtful manner. "Maybe he did give Simon the money after all. Perhaps Simon didn't want you to know and asked Victor to keep it a secret between the two of them."

My mother stared at Chief Crosby in shock. "My son is not a liar, Alan. I can't believe that you would suggest such a thing."

"Selma, you know me better than that." Chief Crosby sounded as if her words had wounded him, which surprised me. He always had the same neutral cop face and tone, no matter what the circumstances were.

Mom narrowed her eyes at him. "You had my son arrested. If Victor could see this—" She turned away from him and sobbed into my shoulder.

With a sigh, Chief Crosby rose from his seat. "Selma, Leila, I'm not the enemy here. I think the world of your family, but I've got a job to do. The evidence was presented to me, and it can't be disputed. Simon has no prior record. You've paid his bail, and now all you have to do is take him home."

I stared up at him defiantly. "And what happens if you don't find my father's real killer in time?"

He didn't answer me.

CHAPTER EIGHTEEN

"I'LL SEE IF SIMON'S PAPERWORK is finished," Chief Crosby said gruffly. "And then I'll bring him in here."

He left the room, and I was alone with my mother. She leaned back in her chair and closed her eyes. I swallowed nervously. "Mom, I need to tell you something."

She opened one eye and turned her head in my direction. "Leila, I'm not sure if I can handle any more bad news right now."

"It's about Dad," I said bluntly.

My mother's eyelids popped open and she straightened up. "What about your father?"

"I had a talk with Jessica this morning. Mom, I—uh, I'm starting to wonder if she had something to do with Dad's death."

Her mouth dropped open in amazement. "What? That's not possible."

There was no going back now. Besides, my mother had a right to know. "Jessica told me that she had a—" The words wouldn't come out. I drew a deep breath and tried again. "She was—"

"I know what you're going to say," Mom interrupted quietly. "She was in love with your father."

"What?" I gasped. "You mean that you knew?"

"No, but I suspected," she said. "You only had to see the way she looked at him."

My mother was a tough one to figure out at times. When Mark and I had broken up, she'd refused to speak to me. I suspected she would react much the same way this time. Or perhaps she would have driven over to Sappy Endings and had it out with Jessica. But this reaction? No, I hadn't been expecting it.

"I don't understand. Why would you let her stay on at Sappy Endings if you thought that she was in love with Dad?"

Mom gave me a plaintive look. "Because I wasn't positive. Besides, I knew that your father wasn't having an affair with her. Leila, your father loved me, and I loved him. If there's trust in a marriage, you don't worry about such trivial things."

Since I had never been married, I took her word for it. "Every time I look at her, it makes me sick," I confided. "What if she was the one who killed him?"

"Don't you think that would be a little drastic?" Mom asked. "I can't imagine killing someone—especially someone that I loved."

I paused to consider. "I can't either, but things like that have happened before. She couldn't have Dad, so she didn't want you to have him, either. She told me that she'd propositioned him a few times. Plus, an ex-boyfriend of hers had a restraining order against her."

My mother stiffened. "I didn't know about the propositioning."

"I don't want her at Sappy Endings anymore," I declared. "I'll fire her at the end of the day."

"Leila," Mom said quietly. "I don't appreciate the fact that Jessica was trying to tempt your father. It hurts me to know this, and not only for the obvious reason. I thought of Jessica as a friend."

"And that's why I'm firing her," I remarked.

She shook her head. "You're the boss, Leila, and I want you to do as you see fit. But I would suggest waiting a while."

"Why?" I asked, puzzled.

"If she is guilty," Mom said thoughtfully, "this would give her an excuse to disappear. We can't afford that right now."

I stared at my mother in admiration. "Mom, that's impressive thinking."

She began to smile, but it quickly vanished when the office door opened and Simon entered, with Chief Crosby behind him. Mom stood and wrapped her arms around him. "Are you all right, my son? Did they hurt you?"

Simon's face flushed with both embarrassment and anger. He was enraged at being put in this situation, and I didn't blame him.

"I'm fine, Mom." He disengaged himself from her grip as gently as he could. "Thanks for bailing me out."

"I want you to come and stay with Leila and me for a few days," she insisted. "You shouldn't be alone right now."

He sighed. "Mom, I appreciate the offer, but I'll be fine."

Chief Crosby cleared his throat. We'd almost forgotten about him. "You're free to go any time you want, son," he said gruffly.

Simon pinned him with a death glare but said nothing.

"Is there any way I could talk to Simon alone for a minute?" I asked. "Maybe out by the information desk or—"

Chief Crosby held up a hand. "You two can stay in here and talk. Take as long as you need. Selma, would you like some coffee? Or maybe tea?"

"No, thank you, Alan," Mom answered stiffly. She raised her eyes at me in questioning and then patted Simon's hand. "I'll wait for you by the information desk."

Chief Crosby shut the door behind them, and I was left alone with my brother. He sat down in mom's deserted chair and stared at the floor. "How are you holding up?"

He shrugged. "I've had better days."

"Don't shut me out," I implored. "We've always been able to talk about anything."

Simon lifted his eyes until they were level with mine. "What do you want me to say, Leila?"

"I know that you didn't do this. How did that gun wind up in your car?"

He snickered. "Come on. You know as well as I do. I was set up."

There was no doubt about that. "By whom, though? Who had access to your car? Did you see any other vehicles around when you left Sappy Endings the night Dad died?"

Simon shifted uncomfortably in his seat. "I can't remember, Lei. I was angry when I left the farm." He stared at me in misery. "If I had known it was the last time I was ever going to see Dad, I wouldn't have acted like such a jerk to him."

"Don't beat yourself up over it." I covered his hand with mine. "Someone got into your car and planted the gun there. Do you have any idea when it might have happened?"

"No," he said sheepishly. "I never lock my car. There's nothing valuable inside. Honestly, I can't remember the last time I looked in the glove compartment, either." Simon rubbed his eyes wearily. "They're going to make sure I fry."

"That's not going to happen. I won't let it happen," I promised. "How fast were you going when the officer pulled you over today?"

Simon wrinkled his brow. "Thirty-five in a thirty-mile-an-hour zone. Unreal. The guy must have had to make his quota for the month. I haven't had a ticket since I first learned to drive."

"Oh, right." The memory brought a smile to my face. "That was the only time I ever saw Mom angry with you."

"Dad's face was purple," Simon added. "But I think he was more upset about you being in the car with me. He thought I was corrupting you."

"That's silly," I fumed. "Besides, I'm older than you."

He shot me a look of disbelief. "So what? That never mattered to Dad." He started to mimic our father in his deep, stern voice. *"Why can't you be more like your sister? When are you going to learn to stand on your own two feet?"*

"Mom's said the same things to me about you," I reminded him.

Simon chuckled under his breath. "Yeah, you're right. I guess we've got more in common than I thought. And at least Mom's not always asking me when I'm going to give her some grandchildren."

"Well, she will be now," I said. "By the way, I met Tonya the other day."

His face fell. "Where did you see her?"

"She came into Sappy Endings for coffee. Heather introduced us. Tonya showed her a house a couple of weeks ago." I waited for a reaction from him, but he only shrugged. "She's gorgeous."

"Yeah, she is," Simon said scornfully. "And she knows it, too."

He'd done a complete turn-around from our talk the other night. "Are you two having problems? Does she even know that you've been arrested?"

"Tonya dumped me." His voice broke. "She found someone else and told me it was over. I loved her, Lei. How could she do this to me?"

My heart broke into a million pieces for him. "I'm so sorry. I know this is difficult, but it could have been worse. What if you'd married her and then found out that you'd made a terrible mistake?"

Simon put his head in his hands. "Sis, I know you're trying to help, but it's not working. I'm in debt up to my ears. I may lose my job. I've been arrested for murdering my father. I'm not sure how things could get much worse."

I took a deep breath and asked the million-dollar question. "Simon, if Dad didn't lend you any money, where did you get the ten thousand dollars from?"

Simon's body went rigid. "Where did you hear about that?"

"Chief Crosby said that they checked your bank transactions," I said. "What'd you do with the money?"

"It doesn't matter," he said shortly. "I can't get it back."

"You bought Tonya a diamond bracelet. She showed it to me and Heather."

Simon's face suffused with anger as he jumped out of the chair. "What is this, another inquisition? If you already knew the answer, Lei, why'd you even bother to ask? Are you working for the police, too?"

"Get it back from her," I said.

He started to laugh hysterically. "Are you kidding me? Tonya was a user. She got what she wanted out of me and moved on, so why would she give it back?"

I wasn't sure who I was more upset with—Tonya for taking advantage of my brother, or Simon for letting her. I'd always felt protective of my younger brother, but it wasn't for me to judge him. Simon was a grown man and didn't need me to fight his battles. Love could be cruel sometimes. I'd learned that firsthand.

"What did you tell Crosby when he asked how you got the money?"

Simon's jaw locked into place. "It's none of his business. Anyway, a friend loaned it to me."

"But that's not true, I'm guessing?"

A vein bulged in his neck. "If you must know, I went to a loan shark."

"Are you crazy?" I asked in disbelief. "They could kill you if you don't pay the money back!"

"I've borrowed from them before," Simon said calmly. "I can't get a loan from my bank. My credit's in the toilet, so what else was I going to do?"

"Is that why Dad refused to loan you money this time?" I asked.

He glared at me. "No. If you must know, Dad did give me some money that day. He promised me more, but there was a condition attached."

My brow furrowed. "What type of condition?"

Simon's mouth hardened into a fine, thin line. "Dad said that he would lend me the rest of the money if I agreed to come and work at Sappy Endings."

"He was going to make you the owner?" My voice started to quiver, but I couldn't help it. Despite my complaints about inheriting the farm, I was starting to enjoy the work. I felt like I was beginning to accomplish things on my own and that my father had put me in charge for a reason. The thought of letting him down made me try harder. But what if I discovered that I hadn't been Dad's original choice to manage the farm?

Simon must have guessed what direction my mind was running in. "Don't worry, sis. Dad made it perfectly clear that I wouldn't be in charge. To be honest, I figured that it would be Noah."

"Noah's actually a pretty decent guy," I said. "You should give him a chance."

He ignored my remark. "Dad wanted me to help with the sap making. Before Noah came along, he had to hire help during the prime season. It's gotten to be too much for one person."

"Yes, I know." I'd already decided that I would be the one helping with the sap collecting and syrup-making process. If I was going to run Sappy Endings, I needed to know how to do every job associated with the farm.

"Dad tried to go on about other plans he had for the farm, but I stopped him," Simon said. "Even if he had wanted me to be in charge, I still would have told him no. He kept saying that writing was good for a hobby, but it wouldn't pay the bills. We both started yelling at each other, and after a few minutes, I left through the back of the building."

That was why Simon hadn't been caught on the camera. "And this was after hours, right?"

Simon nodded. "About five fifteen, I think. Sis, if I had known that it would be the last time I ever saw Dad, I wouldn't have said the things I did to him." His voice grew heavy with emotion. "But he became so insistent upon it. There was this weird sense of urgency about him that day. I'd never seen him like that before."

That was when it dawned on me. "Because he knew that his life was in danger."

CHAPTER NINETEEN

SIMON AND I WENT OUT to the information desk and found my mother sitting with Noah, talking in hushed voices. They both stood as we approached. Chief Crosby was nowhere to be found.

Simon jerked a finger in Noah's direction. "What's he doing here?"

My mother looked at Simon in surprise. "He gave Leila a ride."

"How thoughtful," Simon muttered. "And how convenient."

"Stop acting ridiculous," I told him. "Noah saw that I was upset and in no condition to drive. That's all."

"Yeah, right." Simon's voice filled with bitterness.

Noah lightly touched my arm. "I'll wait for you in the truck, Leila." He nodded to my mother and started for the door as Simon reached out and roughly grabbed his arm.

"Stop it!" I cried.

Simon thrust Noah up against the wall. "This is all working out the way that you planned, isn't it? My father wouldn't sell you the farm, so you got rid of him, and now you're trying to get cozy with my sister?"

Horrified, I grabbed my brother's arm. "What's the matter with you? It's nothing like that!"

Noah knocked Simon's hand away and gave him a slight shove backward. "Look, I know that you're upset, but I didn't have anything to do with your father's death."

"Right," Simon sneered. "How ironic that the gun that killed my father is found in my car, and you were the last person to see him alive." He reached for Noah again.

"What in tarnation is going on in here?" Chief Crosby demanded in a loud voice. He crossed the room in angry, deliberate strides. "This is a police station, not a boxing ring!"

"It's nothing, Chief," Noah said. "Only a little misunderstanding." He turned to me. "I'll be outside."

Chief Crosby laid a hand on Simon's shoulder. "I don't want to see you wind up in any more trouble. Go home and try to relax, son."

Simon slapped his hand away. "Don't call me son. You're not my father. You could never come close."

Chief Crosby looked startled. "I didn't mean anything. It's just an expression."

"Simon, why are you doing this?" My mother wailed. "That's enough. Alan's been very good to us. I didn't raise you to disrespect the law."

Simon didn't reply. He shot Chief Crosby a hateful glare, turned on his heel and pushed open the door, slamming it shut behind him.

The rest of us were silent, not knowing what else to say. Chief Crosby tipped his hat at my mother. "Selma, I have to get back to work. If you need anything at all, please let me know. I'll check in with you tomorrow to see how Simon's doing." He hesitated. "I feel terrible about what's happened, but I hope you understand that I was only doing my job."

"Thank you, Alan," Mom said curtly. She moved toward the door, and I held it open for her. We walked toward her car where Simon was sitting in the passenger seat, arms folded, and a scowl upon his face.

"Do you want me to come with you? Let me tell Noah that I won't be going back to the farm. I'm sure that he and Jessica can handle things without me," I said.

My mother forced a smile to her lips. "No, dear. You go back to work. Simon and I will be fine until you get home. Dinner's at six."

"He's going to be okay." I stepped forward, intending to hug her, but my mother turned away and got behind the driver's wheel. Confused, I watched as she started the engine and the car pulled away, with neither one of them bothering to acknowledge me.

Noah must have seen our entire exchange but said nothing as I got into the truck. He shifted the vehicle into drive and pulled out of the lot. "You okay?" he asked.

"Not really." I leaned my head back against the seat and closed my eyes. Noah had the radio tuned to a country western song. A woman was singing about regrets. How ironic. "I'm sorry for what Simon said to you."

"Forget it," Noah said. "He feels like the entire world's against him right now. I've been there myself. Some days you want to run away and hide."

I didn't answer.

"How about you?" he asked gently. "You're not thinking about leaving, are you?"

I stared out the window. "No. My father's counting on me to take care of his business. Besides, I already ran away once, when I left Sugar Ridge four years ago." A horrible thought occurred to me. Had my father also told Noah about my broken engagement? "Did my father ever mention why I left here?"

"Jessica told me, remember?"

"But did my father?" I pressed.

He hesitated for a moment. "Victor might have said something about it."

Frustrated, I shut my eyes. Dear old Dad. I adored him so, but how he'd loved to talk. It was apparent who he'd chosen to confide in the last few months of his life.

"He didn't say anything bad," Noah assured me. "Only that you were engaged to be married and things didn't work out. Then he said that you and Selma had argued because you took a teaching job in Florida. That doesn't sound like running away to me."

At least he didn't know the entire story. "Yes, I did. My

mother was disappointed in me because my fiancé broke it off. She and my father arranged our marriage."

His eyebrows rose. "I didn't know those still happened in this day and age."

"Oh yes, in many countries. We still have family and friends in Lebanon. When the Salem family came to Vermont about six years ago, they decided to help plan their son Mark's life—and mine."

Noah took a left turn instead of making a right one to the farm. "Where are we going?" I asked.

He shot me a sideways glance and grinned. "To a place I know that will make you feel better."

"I'm fine, really. We should get back to the farm. Jessica's all alone and—"

"Jessica is fine," Noah interrupted. "She texted me while I was waiting for you. Sappy Endings is quiet for now. There's no tours scheduled for this afternoon, and you need a few minutes to pull yourself together."

We drove up the mountain without speaking until I realized where he was taking me. There was a babbling brook ahead with a lovely pumpkin patch. There was also a corn maze and haunted hayrides held every Halloween. The pumpkin patch looked down upon a valley full of farmland and fall foliage. It was a prime spot for leaf peepers every autumn. The world had turned into vibrant shades of red and fiery oranges, and an immediate sense of calm washed over me as I breathed in the fresh mountain air.

"I haven't been here in years," I said wistfully as we

walked toward the brook. "My father used to bring Simon and me here every year to get pumpkins to carve."

Noah's gaze drifted below to the valley. "It's so peaceful here, isn't it? In a week or so, the rest of the leaves will be gone. But I love coming here any time of year, especially after a rough day. Your father's the one who told me about this place."

"I'm not surprised. He loved it here. Dad brought Simon and me on the haunted hayrides, and he loved them as much as we did. My mother wasn't a fan." I laughed at the memory. "Dad would pretend that he was terrified and beg me not to let go of his hand. He had everyone on the ride laughing hysterically. Then we'd gather around a bonfire and have cider and doughnuts."

"Sounds like a fun time. I can't wait to bring Emma here when she's a little older. When I first came to Sugar Ridge last spring, I came out here nearly every day for the first month or so. It helped me to deal with things—and find the strength to go on."

I studied Noah's handsome profile and glimpsed his private agony. Like his, my life was far from perfect. I had a father who had been murdered and a brother arrested for the crime, plus I was still trying to recover from a broken heart that was four years old. Still, I was filled with pity for him. Unsure of how he'd react if I brought up his wife, I tried another tactic. "Being here makes me feel closer to my father. I miss him so much."

He nodded as if understanding. "I know what you mean. There isn't a day that goes by that I don't miss Ashley, or

Jason, my best friend. He's been gone almost eight years. We grew up together."

"What happened to him?" I asked.

"He was killed while we were in Iraq," Noah said quietly.

"I'm so sorry." I wasn't sure what else to say. "How long were you in the Marines?"

Noah tossed a stone into the brook. "I went in right after graduation from high school and served six years. After Jason died, I came home. The time overseas changed me forever." He let out a ragged breath. "Sorry, I still don't like talking about it. I came home with a case of PTSD. I'm not sure I would have made it if it weren't for Ashley."

"How long were you and Ashley married?" I asked.

"Seven years." Noah shook his head in disbelief. "Funny, isn't it? After I got better, Ashley and I had Emma, and life was pretty perfect for a while. And then, the rug got pulled out from under me." His penetrating blue gaze met mine. "That's why I try never to take anything for granted. You never know what tomorrow will bring."

That was the truth. "When did Ashley—" I couldn't say the word.

Noah stuck his hands in the pockets of his denim jacket. "It'll be a year in December. She was killed a week before Christmas." He gave me a forlorn smile. "Emma cried for her every night the first couple of months. She didn't understand that her mother was gone forever. She kept waiting for her to come back."

My throat was tight with tears. Life could be so cruel at times. Emma shouldn't have to grow up without a mother.

It was bad enough to lose a parent at the age of twenty-eight, but to have her taken away from you at such a young age was unfathomable.

Noah watched as I blinked back tears. "I'm sorry," he said. "I didn't mean to make you upset."

"That's okay," I assured him. "I'm glad that you told me. You've both been through a horrible ordeal."

He frowned. "And so have you. Leila, your father was murdered. You lost someone that you love, like me. Like Emma. It isn't easy for any of us. That's why I never try to make assumptions when I first meet someone. You never know what they might be going through."

Noah had the wisdom of a much older man, and I looked at him with new respect. "I need to remember that. Sometimes I don't stop and think first. I fly off the handle and say things that I end up regretting."

"I was like that, too," Noah admitted. "Being a father has taught me patience."

"You're so lucky to have her. She's a beautiful little girl. And I think you were right to bring her to Sugar Ridge. It's a terrific place to raise kids."

He nodded. "It's been a tough year for both of us, but we'll be okay. My mother is heading back to New York in a couple of weeks. I've got after-school care lined up for Emma, and she seems to be adjusting well." Noah laughed. "I wish I had half her energy some days. She wears me right out."

"I'll bet she does."

"You'll find out what it's like one day," Noah remarked.

"No, I won't," I said shortly.

Noah's smile vanished. "Come on. You're a teacher. You obviously love kids."

"Yes, I do love kids. But it's not in the cards for me," I said.

"I'm sorry to hear that." Noah's voice was soft.

To my relief, he let the subject drop. "I hope you don't mind my asking, but what were you and Jessica talking about this morning—or, rather—arguing about? I've never seen her so upset before."

The mention of her name made me wince. I hesitated for a moment before answering, then reminded myself that I didn't owe Jessica any allegiance. "She—she admitted that she was in love with my father."

"Oh," Noah mumbled. "I wondered about that."

"You knew?"

He shook his head. "No, but I overheard them talking a few weeks ago. I didn't mean to eavesdrop, but I'd come to your father's office to ask him something. I was about to knock when I heard him yell at Jessica to stop it."

I sucked in a sharp breath. "Then what happened?"

Noah seemed uncomfortable with the topic. "Jessica sounded strange—so unlike herself. She said something like, 'You can't ignore me forever. One day you'll realize who really cares about you. I just hope it isn't too late for you then.'"

A chill ran down my spine. Once a stalker, always a stalker. How far had Jessica taken it?

"What are you going to do?" Noah asked suddenly. "I'm

betting that you're not going to turn a blind eye to this. Will you let her go?"

"I'm not sure," I said honestly. "My mother asked me to think it over for a while. Remember what I told you about flying off the handle? I think my mother's right and I shouldn't make any hasty decisions. It would be tough to get by without Jessica, and the customers all love her, but honestly? I'm not sure that I can stand looking at her every day. What would you do if you were in my situation?"

Noah shrugged. "You're the boss, Leila. It's your decision."

"But what if she's the one who killed my father? At least this way I can keep an eye on her."

"Is that what you're doing with me, too?" he wanted to know.

Despite my overwhelming embarrassment, I forced myself to look directly into his eyes. "No. I was wrong to jump to conclusions on the first day, and I'm sorry for how I behaved. I honestly don't believe you had anything to do with my father's death."

"What made you change your mind?" Noah asked. The sun had started to sink lower, and the sky had become a brilliant blaze of golden and orange hues. I shivered, for the air was growing chilly. Without a word, Noah removed his jacket and placed it around my shoulders.

"Thank you." It was then that I noticed a tattoo on his upper left bicep that hadn't been visible to me before—a small rose with a name written in cursive underneath it.

Ashley. He was still patiently waiting for me to answer his question, his gaze focused on my face.

"I'm trying to turn over a new leaf," I quipped.

He barked out a laugh at the pun and extended his hand to me. "Come on. Ready to face the world again?"

I placed my hand in his. "Why not. There's nothing better to do, right?"

CHAPTER TWENTY

TO MY RELIEF, THE REST of the afternoon passed quietly at Sappy Endings. Noah assured me he would assist Jessica if needed, and I was grateful that I didn't have to face her. I was still worried about Simon and called my mother to see how he was doing.

"I dropped him off at his apartment." Her tone was sulky, like a little girl who'd been refused dessert. "He didn't want to come home with me. I swear, I don't know which one of you is more stubborn."

"Maybe I'll stop over to see him before I come home."

"Please do," Mom begged. "If you can bring him here for dinner, he may decide to stay the night. He kept telling me that he wanted to be alone."

This didn't exactly come as a surprise. Simon was a proud man, and to be arrested—for his father's murder of all things—had to be both devastating and humiliating.

I refused to entertain the notion he was guilty. But who was, then?

I absently flicked through the day planner on my father's desk. Some business cards were stuck in between the pages. On the page for October 3, I found one that made me do a double take. *Tonya Donnelly, Real Estate Agent.*

Surprised, I held the card in my palm and continued to stare at it. Could Tonya have had something to do with my father's death? Yes, she had used Simon, but to what extent? I was determined to find out. I picked up my phone and dialed the cell number on the card.

"Tonya Donnelly," she answered pleasantly.

"Hello, Tonya. It's Leila Khoury."

An awkward silence passed between us for several seconds. When Tonya spoke again, her voice was cool and reserved. "Hi, Leila. How are you?"

"Not very well," I admitted. "It's been a rough couple of weeks for my family."

"Yes, I'm sure." Her tone was flat and unsympathetic. "What can I do for you?"

"I'm calling about my brother."

She sighed. "Is he out on bail yet?"

"Excuse me?" How did she know that he'd been arrested? There couldn't be anything in the paper yet. "Did Simon call you?"

"No," she said, sounding annoyed. "And I would think that your family has enough money to bail him out without asking me to help."

"That's not why I'm calling," I snapped. "Simon said

that you broke up a couple of days ago." And probably right after she found out he wasn't going to inherit Sappy Endings was my guess.

"We did," she said, "but I don't think that's any of your business."

"How did you know that Simon had been arrested?"

She hesitated before answering. "The woman at Sappy Endings told me when I came in for coffee this morning."

I muttered a curse word in my head. What was wrong with Jessica? Did she have to go around telling my family's business to everyone? "I found one of your business cards on my father's desk."

"So?" she asked.

Her snobby attitude was starting to get on my nerves. "You never told me that you'd met my father."

"I go into Sappy Endings for my nonfat lattes all the time," she said simply. "Of course I've met him. He was a very nice man."

"Did Simon introduce you to him?"

"No," she snapped. "What's this all about, anyway?"

I took a deep breath. "Did you talk to my father about selling the farm?"

"I might have," she replied. "How do you think I get listings? Do you think that I wave a wand and that sellers magically appear?"

Anger bubbled near the surface for me. "So, you applied for the job of real estate agent. I'm sure the sale of Sappy Endings would make a very nice commission for an agent. Aren't rates up to 8 percent now?"

"I didn't do anything wrong," she huffed. "Besides, your father told me that he had no plans to sell. He said that, when he passed on, the farm would stay in the family."

"And that's why you attached yourself to my brother, because you thought he might wind up with it."

Tonya laughed bitterly. "I don't need to listen to this. And, if you must know, your brother proposed to me this week, and I said no."

"Of course you did, once you found out he wasn't inheriting Sappy Endings. You didn't love him. You were just using him."

"Think what you want, Leila. I have more important things to do." Tonya clicked off, and I was left listening to dead air.

Could Tonya have killed my father for a lousy commission? It sounded insane, but people killed for crazier reasons. Or had she thought in her infinite wisdom that Simon would inherit the farm so she tried to frame him for our father's murder?

I made a mental note of anyone else who might have something to do with my father's murder. Noah? Maybe I was wrong, but, whenever I thought of him with his daughter, I couldn't see him as a heartless killer. Wesley Browning had a motive, but he was dead. Was there a chance that Wesley had killed my father before someone killed him? Plus, there was Jessica to consider. I needed to talk to Chief Crosby about her.

My earlier discussion with Simon had convinced me that our father realized his life was in danger. Dad knew

Simon had been to a loan shark, and someone wanted Sappy Endings at any cost. Wesley mentioned that, after my father's death, it had been expected the farm would go up for sale. By whom? And how did this all connect?

With new determination, I leapt out of my chair and opened the filing cabinet, where my father kept the farm's financial records. I reviewed past checkbooks and online bank statements, searching for any unusual transactions. Nothing. Was there a disgruntled employee I'd over-looked? Besides Jessica and Noah, there was no one, except for occasional temporary help. Wesley said that the same person who killed his father had killed mine. How was he so certain, especially with his life being threatened, too?

The wall clock continued to tick away precious minutes of the day. It was four thirty. If things were still slow, I'd ask Noah to lock up for me. The library was open until seven o'clock. Perhaps they would have the information I needed.

The door to my office opened abruptly. Startled, I looked up to see Heather standing in the doorway, hands perched on her well-rounded hips.

"What's wrong?" I asked before it dawned on me.

Her mouth set in a stubborn line. "You know darn well what's wrong. I've just come from your house. I stopped to see your mother and asked her if she'd be willing to do the alterations on my gown. She's a better seamstress than anyone at the Bridal Boutique."

"I'm sure that made her very happy."

Heather narrowed her eyes until they became tiny slits.

"Yes, but she was half-asleep. She told me what happened last night with Wesley, and about Simon's arrest. Why didn't you call me?"

"I'm sorry, Heather. There was so much going on, and it was the middle of the night."

"So what? I'm your best friend. That means I'm on call twenty-four hours a day." Her voice faltered. "We both signed up for that job in first grade, remember?"

Her voice was heavy with emotion, and guilt surged through me. I fondly remembered the childish pact we'd made in our secret clubhouse in Heather's backyard when we were six years old. We'd promised to always be best friends and tell each other everything. It looked like I'd failed my performance evaluation.

"I couldn't love you any more if you were my own sister. You know that," I told her. "I did mean to call you first thing this morning, but I could barely drag myself into the shower and out the door. Then, after Simon's arrest, everything else slipped my mind. I'm so sorry."

Heather's eyes filled with tears as she wrapped her arms around me. We held each other for several seconds until she managed to choke out a sob. "My God, Leila. You could have been killed. And now Simon—" Her voice broke. "I don't believe it."

"Neither do I. Wesley told me last night that the man who killed my father also killed his."

She shot me a puzzled look. "But I thought Dennis killed himself."

"That's what everyone thinks," I said. "But he was so

insistent that I'd like to find out for sure. I feel my father knew his own life was in danger. Somehow, I need to get to the bottom of this."

Heather's eyebrows drew together. "What do you have in mind?"

I slung my purse over my shoulder. "I want to see if I can find out any information on Dennis Browning. There must have been a newspaper article or something written about him after his death. The *Maple Messenger* devoted an entire page to my father after he was killed. Their deaths must be linked."

Heather puckered her lips together, as if she'd eaten a lemon. "Are you going to ask Simon to help?"

"It's probably not the best time," I said. "I'll start at the library. Want to come?"

She picked up a piece of maple candy that I'd left on my desk and unwrapped it. "Try and stop me. No offense, Lei, but someone has to watch your back. You've had enough close calls lately."

———

Fifteen minutes later, we were standing in the information line at Sugar Ridge's library. I'd always loved the smell of books and the woodsy scent of the building. Being here brought back happy memories for me. As a child, my mother would bring me here every week and let me check out two books. She'd spend an hour happily browsing through ones on cooking or sewing while I'd curl up in one of the antique plush chairs by the fireplace, lost in Nancy Drew or a Little House book. The library was one of the oldest buildings in Sugar Ridge and had been beautifully preserved over the years. My father had served on their board of directors and believed it was the foundation of learning for us all.

"Hello, Leila, Heather. What can I assist you with?"

Paige Turner had been head librarian for as long as I could remember. She was in her early sixties and had a devout love of Gothic literature and clothing, and a very low tolerance level for people who couldn't return books on time.

"I'd like to view the *Maple Messenger* on microfilm if you still have them?"

Paige peered at me through her thick eyeglasses. "Oh, yes. Digitization is too expensive for us at the present time. Perhaps one day it will happen. What year are you looking for?"

"Um, 2002, please."

Paige nodded and held up a finger. "The computer is over by the window. It's the one that overlooks the general store. Wait here while I locate the film for you. I keep them in my office." She disappeared into an adjoining room.

"After all these years, she's still a drill sergeant." Heather couldn't resist a snicker. "I swear, she'd keep every book under lock and key if possible. Remember the time I took out *Wuthering Heights* for a book report and then couldn't find it for three months? She sent my parents a letter every week!"

We started to laugh but quickly sobered when Paige returned with the film and placed it in my hands. "Thank you, Paige."

"The library will be closing soon," she reminded me and then turned to Heather. "What book are you looking for?"

Heather's face was blank. "Huh?"

I nudged her foot with mine. "Didn't you say that you wanted to read *Jane Eyre* again?"

"I did? Oh, that's right, I did!"

Paige beckoned Heather to follow her upstairs while I headed for the other end of the library. After I loaded the film and began to turn the hand crank, Heather appeared with a worn copy of *Jane Eyre* in her hands.

"Make sure you return it on time, Miss Turcot," I teased.

"Jeez. That woman has the memory of an elephant. 'Don't bring it back late, Heather, like you did with *Wuthering Heights*.'" She studied the pages of the *Maple Messenger* over my shoulder as they whizzed by on the screen. "Do you think you'll find anything?"

"I hope so. After this, I'm out of ideas."

When the day of Dennis's death started to approach, I slowed down my cranking. Two days after his death, I spotted a short article about him. It said that Dennis Browning had been found deceased in his car, with a revolver in his hand. His 18-year-old son had found the body.

"Did you get a good look at the vehicle or the person who shot at Wesley last night?" Heather wanted to know.

"No. It all happened so fast. After the first shot, Wesley

pushed me down on the cement, and I couldn't see anything. If he hadn't have done that, I might not be here today."

"If everyone believed that Dennis died by suicide, the family might have tried to keep the details about his death private at first," Heather suggested. "I have a customer whose husband killed himself about ten years ago. It's too painful for the family to talk about even now. If that was the case with Dennis, there might not have been a write-up in the paper."

She had a good point, but I kept turning the crank. "Let me check a few more pages for the heck of it."

Heather glanced at her watch. "It's a quarter to seven. Not to rush you, but the drill sergeant should be making an announcement any minute now."

I blew out a sigh. "Oh, fine." I let go of the crank and was about to remove the film when I spotted a picture of my father. I quietly scanned the headline. "No way. Look at this!"

Heather read the caption out loud. "Local Friends Remember Dennis Browning and His Generosity."

Dennis's death had garnered a half-page spread in the newspaper. The first paragraph talked about how he had tragically died the week before and how shocked his friends and family were when they discovered that he had killed himself. His wife said he had been suffering from depression for a while. The article went on, talking about how he had once been a part owner of Sappy Endings Farm until he'd sold his share to current owner Victor Khoury.

"He was a good friend," Victor Khoury was quoted

as saying. "It was quite a shock for me to hear what had happened. I never would have suspected Dennis of doing such a thing." I pointed my finger at the line. "You see? My father didn't believe it was suicide, either!"

Heather's lips moved silently as she read the rest of the article. "There's nothing useful here, Lei. It only talks about how he volunteered on committees and ran the local Boy Scout troop that his son was in. Sounds like he was a decent guy until he started gambling his life away."

Several pictures accompanied the article, and I stopped to study each one. There was a picture of Dennis and his wife on their wedding day. A black-and-white photo of him as a toddler. I spotted the photo of Dennis taken with my father at the grand opening of Sappy Endings—the same photo hanging on my office wall. The last photo caused my heart to stop beating for a second. My father and Dennis were standing together, flanked by a man on each side. I adjusted the screen for a closer look and shrieked.

Theo was standing next to Dennis, his arm around his shoulders.

"Dennis is with Theo in this picture!" I gasped.

"So what?" Heather asked.

I tried to contain the excitement in my voice, before Paige got the urge to throw us out. "Theo told me that he didn't know Dennis—at all. He didn't start working for my father until after his partnership with Dennis had dissolved."

Heather squinted down at the photo. "What do you think it means?"

"I'm not sure." Uneasiness settled in my bones. The draping of their arms around each other's shoulders signified to me that they were more than casual acquaintances. My father had been good friends with all of these men, including Dennis.

Chief Crosby stood at the opposite end of the line grinning happily for the camera with an arm around my father. It was rare to see him in a good mood. Perhaps the picture had been taken before his ex-wife had run off with another man. Divorce changed people.

There was a brief caption underneath the photo. I increased the size of the article to read it. The byline read, *Good Friends Enjoying a Good Time. Chief of Police Alan Crosby, Sappy Endings partners Victor Khoury and Dennis Browning, and attorney Theo Martin are all smiles as they enjoy Sugar Ridge's annual Chamber of Commerce dinner.*

The photo was dated twenty years ago.

"That proves it," I said. "My father and Dennis were still partners then. Theo lied to me."

CHAPTER TWENTY-ONE

I MADE A QUICK COPY of the photo, and Heather and I left the library before Paige could clear her throat one final time. Heather had followed me over in her SUV, so we exchanged goodbyes in the parking lot, since she was meeting Tyler for a late dinner. After she'd gone, I called Simon's cell, but it went directly to voice mail. I drove to his apartment, which was only five minutes away from the library. I knocked on the door several times, but there was no answer.

My mother must have heard the crunch of the car's wheels on the gravel driveway, because, when I exited the vehicle, she was standing in the doorway. A shadow passed over her face when she realized that I was alone.

"Come, Leila," she said in a strangled voice. "There are grape leaves for dinner, and tabbouleh."

She'd also made *manoush*, a flatbread with herbs and a

favorite of Simon's. It was still warm from the oven. We ate in silence during the meal. Maybe I should have tried to draw her out, but we were both exhausted from the long day and lack of sleep last night.

Mom rose and began to stack the dishes, but I stopped her. "I'll take care of these. Why don't you go up to bed and try to sleep?"

My mother kissed me on the cheek. "Thank you, my dear. Yes, I am tired. Good night." She hurried through the doorway and up the stairs before I could say anything further. I suspected she was afraid to fall apart in front of me.

After I finished cleaning up the kitchen, I sat down on the couch to watch television with Toast. He purred contentedly as I stroked his fur and was such a comfort to me. The house seemed unusually quiet and lonely. It wasn't bad enough that my father had been murdered, but now Simon was also in danger of being ripped away from us.

My thoughts returned to the picture of Dennis with Theo. I went into my father's study and typed Theo's name into the Google search engine on his computer. Martin was a common enough surname, and it took me a while to narrow down the options.

To my surprise, the only references to Theo I could find related to his profession as an attorney in Sugar Ridge. I clicked on the link for his law office page and found a picture of him smiling in a gray suit with a brief description of his background. Most of the details I already knew. He'd graduated from Columbia Law School and earned his degree and Master of Business Administration cum laude.

After that, he'd briefly practiced in Delaware as an associ-
ate, and then gone on to open his own office in Vermont.
His bio went on to mention that he was currently a spon-
sor of the local Little League at Sugar Ridge and had been
a past coach. He was also a member of the Vermont Bar
Association and Sugar Ridge's Chamber of Commerce.

I was so engrossed in reading Theo's bio that I didn't
notice Toast until he jumped up on the desk. He walked
back and forth across the keyboard several times until I
petted him, then finally settled down next to my elbow.

"You're such an attention hog," I laughed, and then
turned back to my search. How strange that there were no
other details to be found. As a last resort, I tried social media.
As I looked Theo up on Facebook, I made a mental note
to update Sappy Endings's page and create an Instagram
account. My father hadn't been a fan of social media but,
if we featured some fun videos of the café and the syrup-
making process, it might help draw more people in.

Theo didn't have a Facebook, Instagram, or Twitter
account. It seemed odd to me that he wasn't present on at
least one form of social media. What was left? On a hunch
I checked LinkedIn and did find him there. Theo listed
himself as an estate planning attorney in Sugar Ridge,
Vermont. The rest of the information was the same as
I'd viewed before, except here his graduation year from
Columbia was listed as 1998. That would make him about
fifty, which sounded right.

Toast watched with interest as I googled the alumni
association for Columbia Law School and reached another

dead end. I needed an account to view it. Well, shoot. I googled the law school's 1998 graduation in every possible way but couldn't find an alumni list. Finally, I hit pay dirt. Someone had posted the commencement program for 1998, with a list of the graduates included. It seemed like forever until I reached the Ms.

Theo's name wasn't listed.

I checked again, in case I'd somehow had missed it, but Theo's name was not in the graduating class. What did this mean, and why would he lie about going there?

Toast tapped his paw on my cell phone. "Good idea," I said and rewarded him with a chin scratch. It was time to come right out and ask Theo about his relationship with Dennis, even if that meant I was reading too much into the situation.

I glanced at the clock. Nine thirty. Theo had been up since dawn and might already be asleep, but I was willing to take my chances. I scrolled through my list of recent calls and pulled up his number. The phone rang twice before he picked up. "Theo Martin."

"Hi, Theo, it's Leila. I'm sorry to call so late."

"Not at all," he said amicably. "I was just lying on the couch reading. How's Simon doing?"

Toast nudged my hand with his nose, and I pulled him close to me. "About as well as you'd expect. He's very upset."

"Try not to worry," Theo assured me. "Simon will come around in a couple of days. And, as soon as your father's killer is found, everything will get back to normal."

"I hope you're right." Silence passed between us as I

tried to decide how to phrase my question. "Theo, you told me that you didn't know Dennis Browning, right?"

"Yes, that's right," he said without hesitation.

Disappointment settled in my chest. Why was he lying to me? "But I found a picture of you with him among my father's things."

"You did?" His tone sounded puzzled. "I don't remember ever taking a picture with him."

"Both of you were at a Chambers of Commerce dinner. My father and Chief Crosby were also in the picture."

"Oh, that!" Theo chuckled. "Dennis was smashed that night. I was taking a picture with your dad and Alan when he photobombed us. We didn't want to be rude in front of everyone, so we let it pass." His laughter became louder, and higher-pitched.

"I see." Yes, it was abundantly clear. Theo had lied about knowing Dennis. My father and Dennis were still partners when the picture had been taken.

"I'm sorry, Leila." Theo's voice was sympathetic. "To set the record straight, I knew Dennis, but we were never friends. I know practically everyone in this town. As for Wesley, I knew of him, but our paths never crossed. I'm sorry that he died last night, but my main concern is for you and your mother. If I'd been home, I would have driven straight over to the house, you know that."

I did know. "Thank you, but there's nothing you could have done."

Theo coughed on the other end. "Leila, can I make a suggestion?"

"Of course."

"Try and get some sleep. You must be exhausted after what happened last night, and now with Simon's arrest—"

I rubbed my eyes wearily. "Simon's concerned that he'll lose his job."

"Well, I hope that doesn't happen," Theo said worriedly. "Your family's been through enough already. Will you let me know if I can do anything to help? Anything at all?"

He sounded sincere and I almost felt guilty for doubting him. *Almost*. Then I remembered what Chief Crosby had said. He wasn't leaving any stones left unturned, and neither was I. "Yes, I will. Good night, Theo."

The next morning, I overslept and arrived at Sappy Endings a few minutes before nine. A man and woman were chatting amicably as they sipped their coffees at a nearby table. Jessica was removing a tray of bagels from the wall oven. The building smelled of warm maple syrup, cozy and inviting on the chilly morning. The farm had become everything that my father wanted it to be.

Jessica's smile faded when I came behind the counter and helped myself to a cup of coffee. "Good morning," I said cordially.

"Hello, Leila." Her voice was barely above a whisper. She turned her back on me to grab another tray of bagels from the oven. Her posture was stiff and rigid, as if expecting a blow from me. For my mother's sake, I was going to hold off on firing Jessica, but I would never feel the same way about her again.

Jessica put the tray of bagels on a trivet and whirled to face me. "Leila, maybe it's best if I leave here."

I stirred a spoonful of maple sugar into my coffee and forced myself to meet her gaze. "That's not necessary." She wasn't going anywhere until I knew if she had murdered my father.

My coffee cup toppled to the floor, spilling hot liquid everywhere. I muttered a curse word and grabbed some napkins. "Sorry, Jessica. I'll clean it up."

"That's all right, I've got it." Jessica went into the back room and returned with a mop. Flustered, I wrung out a sponge and cleaned the cabinet that the coffee had splattered on.

Jessica washed her hands in the sink and then turned to face me. "I believe it *is* necessary. Besides, it's time that I retired. My son and his family are moving to Florida, and he asked me to go with them to watch my grandkids while he and his wife work."

"I see," I murmured, not knowing what else to say.

Jessica removed a jug of maple syrup from the fridge and set it on the counter. "Steve and his family are moving sometime in December, so if you start looking for a replacement now, I'd be able to help train whoever you hire."

Crap. I hadn't even thought about that. I was going to have to interview people to manage the café, and during the Christmas rush, too. I had never interviewed anyone before. Maybe I could ask Noah—no. My father had put me in charge for a reason, and I wouldn't let him down.

"Whatever you think is best."

Jessica twisted her hands together. "I loved your father, Leila. And I would have done anything to make him love me back."

Her words left me shocked and breathless. It was a good thing I wasn't holding coffee, because I would have dropped my cup again. "What exactly are you saying?"

Jessica's face turned crimson. "Um, nothing. I was only being honest with you."

A customer approached the café counter, and I took this as an opportunity to leave. Noah was out in the sugarbush this morning making more repairs to the tap lines, so I'd talk to him about Jessica later this afternoon. I still had a few weeks before she left, but I needed to act quickly. Her comments had scared me.

I tried to call Chief Crosby, but the phone went directly to his voice mail. Afterward, I spent the rest of the morning in the office doing paperwork, then met with a vendor concerning a new type of coffee for the café that he promised would bring rave reviews. After I had replied to some inquiries on the website, my stomach started to rumble, and I noticed that it was one o'clock. The entire morning had flown by. I kept thinking about Theo's lie. I didn't believe his excuse that he didn't remember taking a picture with Dennis. Could he have been involved in the man's death—or my father's, for that matter? If so, I needed some concrete proof that he couldn't dispute. I dialed the number for his office and asked if he was in.

"Yes, but Mr. Martin is in a meeting right now," his secretary said. "Would you like to leave a message?"

"No, thank you." I hung up without identifying myself. There was no time like the present, so I grabbed my purse and headed out the back door. I sent off a quick text to Noah, letting him know that I had an errand to run and would be back within the hour. I glimpsed him among the sugarbush with a small group of people.

I hadn't been to Theo's new house yet, but I was familiar with the location. When I came home earlier this year, my father had told me in passing that Theo's family had moved into a larger home. He'd joked about how much money attorneys made.

"I should have been a lawyer, *habibi,*" he'd laughed. "They make all the money and don't have to get their hands dirty. Then your mother could have had the house she truly deserves, like Theo's wife."

"Mom doesn't care about that," I'd said, and it was the truth. "All she needs is you."

My father had kissed the top of my head, said how proud he was of me, and how happy I'd made him by coming home. A tear trickled down my cheek and I wiped it away. It was still so difficult to believe that he was gone.

"We're getting close, Dad," I whispered. "I can feel it."

My jaw dropped when I spotted the new Martin home. Theo had moved his family into a Victorian mansion three times the size of my parents' house. The facade was ornate stone, with stained glass windows, a gabled roof, and a tower. The Martins had gotten a head start on their Christmas decorating as well. We still had Halloween goodies in the window of Sappy Endings, but I planned to start the holiday changeover next week.

There were two large spruce trees on each side of the driveway that already had Christmas lights in the shapes of icicles hanging from the branches. A balsam wreath with a large red bow hung from the front door and a Victorian red Santa sleigh trimmed in silver sat parked in the middle of the lawn. The decorations were lovely without being over-done. Laura had excellent taste.

Estate planning must be going very well.

I pulled into the driveway next to a sharp-looking red Corvette convertible, wondering if the vehicle belonged to Laura. If she was at home, Theo would be certain to learn of my visit. As I crossed the sidewalk to the steps of the porch, I thought up a quick excuse for dropping by. I drew a deep breath and then pushed my finger against the door-bell and waited.

After a few seconds, a young man opened the door and stared at me in surprise. He was tall and slender, wearing jeans and a striped blue and white polo shirt. Teddy Martin was the spitting image of his father, with sandy-colored hair, hazel eyes, and broad shoulders that belonged on a quarterback. His white teeth gleamed as he smiled. "Hey, Leila, how are you?"

I'd last seen Teddy and his younger brother, Randy, at my father's wake. Typical teenagers, they'd acted awkward and uncomfortable. I hadn't had a chance to talk to them and catch up. "It's nice to see you, Teddy. I can't believe how much you've grown."

He laughed. "It seems like only yesterday when you babysat my brother and me on New Year's Eve. Remember?"

I groaned. "How could I forget? You guys locked me in the bathroom. Such little monsters."

"Yeah, Dad was furious when he found out. Of course, it was all Randy's idea." His eyes twinkled happily.

I barked out a laugh. "Oh, sure. Blame your little brother. Typical."

"Sorry, please forgive my manners. Come on in." He held the door open. "Are you looking for my dad?" Teddy asked.

I stepped into the foyer, admiring the intricate woodwork and the crystal chandelier suspended from the high-rise ceiling. "Is he at home?" I hoped my question sounded sincere.

Teddy shook his head. "He's at work. I can give him a message, though."

"Oh, there's no need. I wanted to ask him about some legal papers he had me sign yesterday. I thought he said he was going to leave a copy for me here, but maybe I was mistaken."

Teddy drew his brows together in confusion, so I decided to explain further. "Your father told me some bad news about my brother, and I was so upset that I may have forgotten where he said the papers would be."

Teddy's expression changed to one of sympathy. "Oh,

right. Yeah, I heard him telling my mother about Simon's arrest. I'm really sorry."

My body twinged with pain whenever I thought about my brother. "Thank you. I had to run an errand nearby, so I thought I'd stop and see if he'd left my copy here. Do you think you could find them?"

"We could take a look in his study," Teddy suggested.

I knew there was a reason I'd always liked this kid. "That would be great."

Teddy led the way down a sterile hallway, our shoes tapping against the travertine flooring. We entered a room done with dark paneling, velvet-lined armchairs, a fireplace, and built-in bookcases. A large marble desk faced the window and a lovely view of a greenhouse out back. Teddy glanced at the surface of the meticulous desk. "I don't see anything here."

I snapped my fingers. "You know what? Maybe he left it up in his bedroom. When I talked to him last night, he mentioned that he was getting ready for work. Would you mind checking there?"

"Not at all," Teddy smiled. "If you want, I can call my father and ask—"

"Oh, no," I said quickly. "I already called his office and his secretary said he was in a meeting. I can wait down here for you."

"Sure. No problem." Teddy's phone chimed with ringtones from a rock band that I was dimly familiar with. I watched as he pulled it out of his jeans pocket and glanced at the screen before moving it to his ear. "Hey."

He listened for a few seconds and then said, "Hang on a minute."

I didn't dare breathe. *Please, please don't let that be Theo on the other end.*

Teddy put his hand over the phone. "I need to take this call. It's my girlfriend. I'll look upstairs for the papers while I'm talking to her."

"That's fine." The air rushed back into my lungs. "I'll wait here. Take all the time you need."

Teddy walked out of the room while speaking on the phone. Wow, that had worked out even better than I hoped for. As the sound of his footsteps started to fade, I leaped into action. Quickly, I went behind Theo's desk and opened the main drawer, shuffling through papers, invoices, and several pads filled with legal terms. From the looks of things, Theo was quite the notetaker.

I opened the side drawer and began rummaging through it. I wasn't even sure what I was hoping to find—maybe another incriminating picture of Theo with Dennis? A newspaper article describing his death in more detail? Or maybe notes about my father's will? I knew that Theo had lied about knowing Dennis but still had no proof he'd committed a crime.

At the bottom of the drawer were several sheets of copy paper. They all looked to be blank, but I shifted through them anyway. Near the bottom of the pile, I found a diploma from the State University of New York at Brockport. This was a surprise. SUNY schools were good institutions, but they weren't Ivy League. I thought back to my online search from last night. Had Theo lied about going to Columbia Law School? I glanced at the diploma, then did a double take, bringing it closer to my face, and stared at the name before me.

This Bachelors of Arts degree is awarded to Theodosius Edward Martini.

A chill ran down my spine. Theo had another name! Yes, it was similar to his own, but what did this mean?

Footsteps sounded in the hallway and began to grow louder. I shoved the diploma back into the drawer and slammed it shut. I had just enough time to jump back in the chair before Teddy came through the doorway.

Teddy shook his head. "Sorry, Leila. I couldn't find anything."

I waved a hand in the air, as if swatting at a fly. "Oh, it's no big deal. I'll give your dad a call later and find out where they are. I apologize for troubling you."

Teddy's mouth stretched into a wide grin. "No worries."

As we walked toward the front door together, I decided to change the subject. "How did your visit to Cornell go?"

Teddy's eyes lit up. "It was awesome! I definitely want to go there, but Mom wants me to look at a few more colleges before I make my final decision."

"That sounds like a wise move. It's nice to have choices."

A worry line creased his forehead. "Yeah, but I think she said that because Cornell is so expensive. Dad's got a lot on his plate with the new house, and my brother's only a year behind me. Having two kids in college isn't cheap."

It was a serious and honest statement, but I almost

smiled. Teddy sounded like an old soul, wise beyond his years. Simon and I were only two years apart, and college expenses had been rough on my parents as well, especially during times when the farm wasn't pulling in a lot of money. We'd also worked jobs on campus to help with our room and board costs.

"All parents want their kids to have more than they did," I remarked. "There's nothing wrong with that. And I'm sure you'll get in since you have perfect grades."

Teddy cocked his head to the side and studied me. "Where'd you hear that? From my dad?"

"Yes. He told my family how proud he was of you."

"Dad's always bragging on me," Teddy sighed. "I'm not a straight-A student. Trig dragged my average down last year, and I never got it back up. I'm more like a B-plus student. But Dad thinks he can get pull some strings and get me into Cornell because he has friends working there. He's got such big plans for me and wants to see me end up at Columbia Law School like him. I'm worried that I'll disappoint him."

I understood how Teddy felt. "Have you decided on your major yet?"

He shook his head. "Dad wants me to go into estate planning like him. If I do go into law, I'm more interested in criminal. Seven years of school still ahead of me. That's a long time."

"It goes by faster than you think," I advised. "And I'm sure your father must be thrilled about you studying criminal law."

Teddy wiggled his hand back and forth. "Not as much as I'd thought. He said he wanted me to be a doctor, but that's not for me. I hate the sight of blood."

I laughed at his statement while my heart raced with excitement about the information I'd found. I would have recalled a Martini on the list of graduates online last night, but there hadn't been any. The change in names would also explain why I hadn't found anything online about Theo before he came to Sugar Ridge. I was convinced that he was hiding something, and it had to do with my father's murder.

CHAPTER TWENTY-TWO

WHEN I ARRIVED BACK AT Sappy Endings, I noticed that my mother had sent me a text asking me to bring home a bottle of syrup. She was making baklava tonight and hadn't realized that she was out. My mother's kitchen was like a well-oiled piece of machinery—efficient and plentiful. She didn't run out of things, and this proved how distracted she'd become about Simon's situation.

I walked out to the sugar shack and found Noah inside making candles. The scent of crispy pine needles, fir, and winter citrus made me think of the upcoming holidays. "It smells just like a Christmas tree in here."

Noah looked pleased as he stuck wicks into several glass jars and then carefully poured the hot wax around them. "That was my plan. I figured you were right, and we needed a few other varieties besides cinnamon and maple for the holidays. I'm calling this one 'O Christmas Tree.'"

"Thought of that all by yourself, huh?" I teased.

A smile ticked at the corners of his mouth. "What can I say? I'm talented." His eyes, which had held such profound sadness yesterday, resembled the bright blue sky today. Noah was living proof that, despite the terrible blows life dealt us, we had to carry on and be strong for others, like he was doing for Emma. They would be okay eventually and he would find another woman to fall in love with. As for myself, I wouldn't be able to get on with my own life until I found justice for my father.

"Did you hear me, Leila?"

I blinked, slowly coming back to earth. "Sorry, what was that?"

Noah examined my face closely. "I asked if you had other ideas for Christmas candle scents."

"Oh, right. How about gingerbread?"

Noah nodded in approval. "That's a great idea. My mom makes the best gingerbread cookies in the entire state of New York. I'll ask her for some suggestions."

I noticed that several of the stainless-steel drums near his workstation were gone. "Did one of the distributors come for a pickup while I was out?"

"Yes, they picked up fourteen drums. I placed the check on your desk."

"That's great." There were a couple of glass bottles of syrup sitting in Noah's work area, and I picked one up. "My mother asked me to bring home a bottle of syrup tonight."

Noah raised an eyebrow questioningly. "You don't owe me any explanation. It's your syrup, Leila."

My mind was a million miles away, remembering Sunday mornings with my father making pancakes. It was the only day of the week that my mother allowed him to cook in her kitchen. He was such a thoughtful man, wanting her to have a day to sleep in. He'd lavish the syrup over the hot cakes, and I'd always ask for more, which delighted him.

"Are you all right?" Noah asked.

"Fine," I said hurriedly.

"How are things with Jessica today?" he asked. "She didn't need any help while you were out, so I haven't had a chance to talk to her."

I swallowed hard. "She gave her notice this morning."

"Wait a second. She left willingly, or did you ask her to leave?" His handsome face turned a bright shade of crimson. "Sorry. It isn't any of my business."

"It is your business," I insisted. "You work here, too, and I need your help. I have no idea what to do next. Jessica runs the café effortlessly. How am I ever going to replace her?"

He stroked his clean-shaven chin thoughtfully. "Well, we can always take out an ad in the *Maple Messenger,* but they're expensive. We could also put a sign on the front door, advertising HELP WANTED, and place some ads online. And then we can do a lot of praying. How'd you say your cooking skills were?"

I made a face. "Nonexistent. I'll ask Simon about the ad prices. It's an excuse to talk to him, anyway."

"How's he doing?"

"Not very well, but that's to be expected, I guess. He finally called my mother last night but didn't say much, except that he wanted to be left alone." She'd been close to tears when she told me about it this morning.

"Well, I can't say that I blame him," Noah said. "I'd be angry, too, if I was in his position. To be honest, I thought that I'd be the one arrested. You were ready to hang me the first day you met me."

I couldn't argue with that fact. "I'm sorry. I have a terrible habit of jumping to conclusions."

"It's understandable," he said. "You took your grief out on the first person you saw. You never did tell me yesterday what made you change your mind about me."

I set the bottle of syrup down on his desk. Noah's body was close to mine, and the smell of his aftershave drifted pleasantly in the air and successfully distracted me. His voice was gentle, and his eyes kind and caring. A vaguely familiar emotion without a name stirred inside me. Confused, I took a step back. "Emma."

Noah shot me a puzzled look. "I don't understand."

"It was the way you were with her," I explained. "It's plain to see how much you love her, and vice versa. I've spent a lot of time working with children, and it's obvious that you have a very special relationship with your daughter. You'd never do anything to hurt her—" I stopped for a moment. "Or anyone else."

The room was silent and my heart pounded so violently that I was afraid he might hear it.

"She has to come first in my life," Noah said quietly.

"Yes, of course."

"What I mean is—" Noah blew out a breath. "Whenever I do something that might have consequences, I need to think of my daughter first. For example, if your father wanted me to make a delivery overnight to a vendor. I'd have to get my mother to stay with her, and if she couldn't do it, I'd have to tell your father no, even if it meant losing my job."

"My father would never have put you in that position—"

He held up a hand. "I know. My point is that her needs are more important than mine. Say that I was arrested for a crime and sent up the river. What would that do to her life? It's been turned upside down enough already at the age of five. I'd have to be a pretty heartless father to do that to my child. A child·that I love more than anything else in this world."

My eyes started to cloud over with tears. I tried to speak, but the words wouldn't come. Thankfully the intercom buzzed at that moment. Noah picked it up and listened while I wiped at my eyes. "Okay, we'll be right there." He turned to me. "Jessica's getting slammed in the café. She wants to know if we can both help out."

———

The rush didn't die down until almost five o'clock. A bus on the way back from a sightseeing trip had stopped, and all forty passengers had descended upon us, wanting coffee or sweets. Some had also purchased syrup. It had been a bit of a tight squeeze with all three of us behind the café counter, but we'd managed, and it had netted a nice profit for the day.

"You go ahead and leave. I'll finish cleaning back here," I told Jessica.

She seemed confused by my remark. "Are you sure? I don't mind staying a few extra minutes."

I picked up the broom. "No, it's fine. I'll see you on Monday. Have a good day off." It had been easier to work with her while waiting on customers. I didn't care to make idle chit chat with her.

She hesitated for a moment, and then picked up her purse. "Good night, Leila. Bye, Noah."

"Take it easy, Jessica," Noah's deep voice replied. He was wiping down the tables in the café. When he finished, he walked over to the counter and faced me. "I hate to leave you with the extra work, but I promised Emma that I'd be home on time tonight. She's helping her grandmother make dinner for me."

"It's fine. I'm almost done here, anyway. I'm going to lock the doors and do a little work in my office."

"Are you sure you'll be okay?" he asked worriedly. "I don't like leaving you here alone, especially after everything that's happened."

No, I wasn't sure. There was a killer on the loose traveling the roads of Sugar Ridge, and I was his roadblock. But that wasn't Noah's problem. "My car's by the front door, and it's locked. The building's also locked. Don't worry about me."

Concern was etched into his features. It was difficult to drag my gaze away from those gorgeous blue eyes but I managed. *Jeez, Leila. Get a hold of yourself. You're acting like one of your students.* Okay, he was good looking and nice, but he was also an employee. Maybe a future friend. That's all. He had no interest in me, and I didn't have any in him, except for the quality of his work.

"The sugar shack is all locked up. Have a good night," he said quietly. "I'll see you Monday."

After he was gone, I double-checked the doors to make sure they were locked. Despite my brave intentions, I didn't like being alone, but I wanted to do more checking on Theo and it was difficult at home with my mother there.

When the café was clean, I switched off the lights and went into my office. I had to try Chief Crosby again and tell him my theory about Theo and Jessica, but I wasn't looking forward to it. I wiggled the mouse for the computer and again looked at the nonexistent history. Did I think it would just appear out of thin air?

I glanced idly through all the document files my father had stored. There were so many that it would take me days to go through them, and they were all associated with the farm. I remembered the lawsuit tab I'd found at home, but it really hadn't told me much.

My father was not a computer whiz, but then again, neither was I. Still, if he knew his life was in danger, would he have left a clue for me somewhere?

I clicked on Pictures. They were all labeled accordingly.

While his office was a mess, Dad always took the time to label everything. *Simon's Graduation, Leila's Graduation. Pancake Eating Contest, Leila's Dance Recital, Selma's Surprise 50th Birthday Party…*

Wait a second. I'd never been in a recital or taken a dance lesson in my entire life. When I clicked on the file, an article came up instead of a picture of me in a tutu. It was dated May 12, 2000, and read:

ESTATE PLANNER DISBARRED FOR EMBEZZLING CHARGES

Theodosius Martini of Wilmington, Delaware, pled guilty today to money laundering and stealing approximately $500,000 from the estate of Frederick Wilber, for whom he served as an attorney and fiduciary.

Everything was finally starting to add up. This was why I couldn't find Theo Martin listed anywhere. He'd altered his original name just enough to stay out of the limelight. He'd been disbarred from one state, so he'd taken his dirty laundry—or laundering—to another. How my father had found out about Theo's real identity I didn't know, but he must have had proof that he was embezzling from him, and goodness knows who else.

The one thing my father had hated more than anything else was dishonesty. If he'd known about Theo's background to start with, he never would have hired him. A disturbing thought entered my mind. Did my father confront Theo with this information the day he died? I positioned the mouse over the file folder. My mouth went dry when the date came up. The same day as my father's death.

My fingers shook as I punched Chief Crosby's number into the phone. He answered on the second ring. "Everything okay, Leila?"

"Not really." I paused, forming the words carefully as I spoke. "I'm wondering about something and really hate myself for thinking it, but did my father ever say anything negative to you about Theo in confidence?"

A deafening silence fell over the line. "Are we talking about the same Theo here? Your father's attorney?"

"Yes. Is there any chance we could meet and talk about this further?" I asked. "It's a lot to explain over the phone, but there's a good chance that Theo was embezzling from my father. And perhaps he's the one who—"

"Whoa, hang on a minute," Chief Crosby interrupted. "Do you have any proof he was doing this?"

"Not yet," I admitted, "but I found an article saying that he'd been disbarred from Delaware and—"

Chief Crosby broke in again. "If you don't have any evidence, there's nothing I can do."

His attitude was starting to frustrate me. "Did my father ever say anything to you about suspecting Theo of stealing from him?"

"No," Chief Crosby said flatly. "Your father was always pleased with his work. Leila, where are you? Are you home?"

I picked up the copies of the article I'd printed. "No, I'm still at Sappy Endings."

"Look, I know you're upset. How about I stop over

at the house and I'll fill you in on the investigation so far?" he asked. "Will you and your mother be home tomorrow?"

I folded the copies of the article and placed them inside my purse. "Yes, I think so. Mom will probably go to church in the morning, but I don't have any plans."

"Okay, I'll call first." Chief Crosby's voice had taken on its usual stern tone. "Now get some sleep, Leila. It sounds like you need it."

He clicked off, and his abrupt manner wounded me a bit, but I reminded myself that had always been Chief Crosby's style. It was obvious that he didn't like what I'd implied, but I knew he'd look into it.

My phone beeped with a text message from my mother. **Are you still at work? I need that syrup!**

I glanced at my watch and was startled to see that it was after six o'clock. No wonder my mother was annoyed. She'd wanted to make the baklava before she went to bed. Even worse, I had forgotten the bottle of syrup in the sugar shack. Where was my head today?

Sorry Mom. I got held up. Leaving shortly. I sent the text, locked the safe and desk, and placed my key ring in my jeans pocket. Since it was after dark, I didn't want to risk going out to the sugar shack by myself. I'd grab a bottle off the shelves in the store and remind myself to adjust the inventory tomorrow.

A creaking noise startled me. I pressed my ear against the door to listen, but the sound didn't come again. The hair rose on the back of my neck and an eerie sensation swept over me. I was probably working myself up over nothing. With a sigh, I opened the office door to find Theo standing there, his left hand posed in the air as if to knock. In his other hand was a shiny revolver, pointed straight at me.

"Hi, Leila," he greeted me. "I thought we should have a talk."

CHAPTER TWENTY-THREE

"YOU KILLED MY FATHER."

The words broke from my lips before I could stop them, and I silently cursed myself. My impetuousness had caught up with me once again. There was no way to play dumb now.

Theo advanced, forcing me back inside the office. He shut the door quietly behind him. His eyes had grown dark and unfamiliar as they scanned me up and down. "It's too bad you had to interfere, Leila. Now I don't have any choice but to kill you, too."

"Why?" Tears sprang to my eyes before I could stop them. "You were supposed to be my father's friend, and that's how you repaid him?"

"I had no choice," he said simply. "He knew too much, and now so do you. After you called me last night, I started to worry. But when I spotted you snooping through my desk from the security camera in my office, I knew I'd have to do something right away. I'm guessing Simon told you about our relationship."

That was when it dawned on me. Not only was Theo a thief but also a loan shark. "Yes," I lied. "And you were stealing money from my father's estate."

To my surprise, he shook his head. "No, I wasn't, but somehow your father found out about my past. He figured out that I was the one who had loaned Simon money. Simon never said a word to your dad about it. Victor was smart, Leila, and you're just like him. Too bad."

Fear coursed through my veins. Theo was going to kill me, the same way he'd killed my father. Sappy Endings was closed, and no one would be looking for me until it was too late. I had to stall for time—somehow. "Tell me what happened that night," I said hoarsely.

Theo rubbed the barrel of the gun against his chin. "It was late in the day when your father asked me to stop by Sappy Endings. I got here right after closing, and no one else was around." He narrowed his eyes. "I didn't plan on killing him, but somehow I knew it wasn't a social call."

I could barely contain the anger in my tone. "Then what happened?"

"Your father had been acting strange for the last couple of weeks and avoiding my calls. I knew something was up. Victor lit into me as soon as I arrived. He started yelling, saying he wanted to sever all ties with me and find himself a new estate planner. He also said he knew I'd loaned Simon money and wanted me to stay away from his son.

Turns out your father hired a private investigator to follow me around."

A vein throbbed in Theo's neck. "He also told me that he'd made another will, without my assistance, and only Selma knew where it was. He didn't tell her his suspicions about me though."

If he had, my mother might not be alive, either. "My father knew you were going to kill him that night."

Theo wouldn't look at me. "I don't know. Maybe. Like I said, *I* didn't even know that I was going to kill him. And I didn't realize he'd changed his mind about selling Sappy Endings and retiring. If so, he could have saved me a lot of trouble."

"What's that supposed to mean?" I asked.

"In his original will, Sappy Endings was to be sold if he died, and his wife and children would equally split the profits." Theo pushed the hair off his sweating forehead. "But after you left for Florida, I guess Victor thought this would be a good way to bring you back to Sugar Ridge. That's why he changed the will and left the place to you. I'm guessing he left Simon out because he figured he'd sell it." Theo sneered at me. "But he knew his precious Leila would stay and run the farm."

His words left me speechless. Theo continued his rant. "You can't imagine how shocked I was when I read the new will. Your mother gave it to me the morning of the official reading. At least I had a little time to pull myself together." He muttered a curse word. "Your father ruined all my plans."

"And that's why you killed him? Because you couldn't have the farm?"

"No, you stupid little twit," he said coldly. "That night when I came to see him, he told me he was going straight to Laura and tell her about my past charges and my loan shark business." Theo shook his head vehemently. "She would have left me. My kids would have disowned me. There's no way I was going to lose my family because of your father's high morals. He told me to get out and then turned his back on me."

Bile rose in the back of my throat. "And that's when you pulled the trigger? When his back was to you?" I couldn't believe my ears. "You're a spineless coward. You didn't even have the guts to face him when you killed him."

"Careful, Leila," Theo warned. He clicked the hammer on the gun. "After I killed your father, I erased all the history on his computer, in case he had any information on me." He smiled. "Funny, Victor was looking up lawsuits. Apparently, he was thinking about suing me. Go figure."

Too bad that Theo hadn't thought to erase Dad's picture files. "What about Dennis Browning? You killed him as well. He didn't commit suicide."

Theo chuckled. "Dennis double-crossed me. He should have sold me his share of the farm instead of giving it back to your father. We had a deal. But that doesn't matter anymore. Remember those papers that you signed for me? You were all upset about Simon's arrest and didn't take the time to read them. The papers in fact turn the farm over to *me*."

My mouth went dry, making it difficult to speak. "You

really are scum. It won't work, though. Don't you realize that, if my body's found here and you suddenly take over the farm, people will realize you killed me? My mother and Simon will know."

Theo barked out a laugh. "But there won't be a body found. It will look like you decided to slink back to Florida with your tail between your legs. And I'm not worried about Simon or your mother. Simon will be going to prison soon. A friend who owed me a favor planted the gun in his car. The gun that I unfortunately had to shoot your father with."

Anger surged through me like an electric shock. "My mother will know that I didn't leave willingly. She's not stupid."

Theo rambled on, as if he hadn't heard me. "Yes, you and your car will disappear into a lake near the border of New York State. It's all arranged. You'll write a goodbye note before I get rid of you, saying that you knew Simon killed your father, and were so distraught you had to leave." He tossed a pad of paper at me. "Sit down, and I'll tell you what to write."

I didn't move. Theo took a step toward me, but there wasn't enough space to move past him and out the door. Besides, he had the gun pointed at my chest. If I was going to die, I certainly wasn't going to make it easier for him. "No. I won't do it."

Theo's face turned a fire engine red. "Don't be an idiot, Leila."

"Why? You're going to kill me either way."

He chuckled, but his expression was not pleased. Theo had always seemed like such an affable guy, but, at the moment, he resembled an angry bull with his nostrils flaring and his eyes bulging out of their sockets.

"Let's try this again. Sit down, Leila."

He reached for a pen and I took that split second to throw my purse at him. The gun discharged as it fell out of Theo's hand, missing me by mere inches. There was no time to stop and try to retrieve the gun. I pulled open the door and ran out to the corridor.

"Leila!" Theo screamed as I unlocked the back door and ran into the darkness. My sneakers rustled through the grass as I sprinted in the direction of the sugar shack, guided only by lights from the front of the building. I stumbled into the side of the sugar shack, pausing for breath, and searched for the correct key on my ring to unlock it.

The sound of panting and coughing grew louder and I panicked. Theo was gaining on me. My hands shook as I tried to fit the right key into the lock. I'd left my cell back in my purse, but there was a landline in here that I could use to call for help. As I unlocked the door, Theo grabbed me from behind. I screamed and fell against the door, which opened into the shack. The sudden movement must have made Theo lose his balance. I rushed inside, my eyes straining into the darkness, until my thigh connected with the edge of Noah's work table. Pain seared through my body, but somehow, I managed not to cry out.

My hands moved quickly over the surface of the table, searching for anything that I could use as a weapon. My fingers connected with some kind of bottle. Theo's heavy breathing was only a couple of feet away. I picked up the bottle and hurled it as hard as I could in his direction. Glass shattered and Theo screamed in agony. He fell to the floor with a thud, and the world went still.

Still shaking, I ran my hand along the wall until it connected with the light switch. The sudden brightness caused me to shield my eyes and blink rapidly. I stared at the floor. Theo was out cold, lying on his back, with maple syrup all over his face.

I lifted the receiver and punched three numbers into the phone pad. A female voice immediately came on the line. "9-1-1, what is your emergency?"

"Please send someone out to Sappy Endings Farm right away," I panted. "Someone just tried to kill me. He's unconscious but I don't know for how long."

"I'm sorry, but did you say that someone was trying to kill you?" Disbelief was evident in her tone.

I snatched up a roll of twine from Noah's workstation and started to tie Theo's wrists together. Thankfully he was still motionless, an ugly large gash on his forehead where the bottle must have connected. All I could smell was maple syrup. "Yes, he's a killer," I spoke into the phone. "He was chasing me, but I managed to knock him out."

The operator was furiously clacking a keyboard on the other end. "Can you please provide more details, ma'am."

"Well," I began. "It's kind of a sticky situation."

CHAPTER TWENTY-FOUR

"ARE YOU SURE YOU DON'T want me to go with you?" I asked my mother.

She shook her head. "No, dear. You stay home and rest. You've been through quite an ordeal."

It was Sunday morning, and my mother was leaving for church services. Before my father's funeral, I hadn't been to church since last Christmas, but there was no need to tell her that.

I forked another bite of pancake into my mouth. "I'm fine, Mom. It's probably better if you don't go alone."

"Leila, I'm all right," she said gently. "It will give me some time to think about everything that's happened."

That was when I understood that she wanted to be alone. It was no reflection on me. I also had a sneaking suspicion that she was going to stop and visit with my father at his grave. Her life had been an emotional roller coaster for the last few weeks. Now she had to deal with the fact that my father had been murdered by someone they had both trusted and considered a close friend. It was going to take a while before things became normal again. "I'm sorry."

She shot me a puzzled look. "For what?"

"I'm sorry about signing those papers without looking at them. It was really stupid of me."

My mother reached down and cupped my face between her slim hands. "Leila, that doesn't matter. I'm just thankful that you weren't hurt." She smiled brightly. "Besides, I phoned the attorney that drew your father's new will up earlier today. He told me that, since you signed the papers under duress, they most likely won't hold up in court."

"That's a relief," I sighed.

Mom shrugged into her jacket. "I left Simon a voice mail, telling him to come for dinner. He's working at the *Maple Messenger*'s office today."

"On a Sunday?" I asked.

She nodded. "Oh yes. He said it's the only day that the office is quiet." She blew me a kiss. "I'm making all your favorites for dinner tonight. Your father would be so proud of you, Leila." She paused for a second, then smiled. "And so am I."

Before I could reply, she hurried out of the kitchen, and the front door slammed a few seconds later. My mother was proud of me. She probably wouldn't stop hassling me about getting married or giving her grandchildren, but she was proud of me. I'd craved her approval for years and had finally received it. It was difficult for my mother to express her feelings, especially to her daughter, but I was glad that she'd done it. Our relationship had come a long way in a short time.

I went upstairs to take a shower. After I was dressed, I flopped down on the couch with a cup of *Ahweh*, Toast sitting beside me. I finally had an entire day off and no idea what to do with myself. I picked up the Sunday paper and thumbed through it, unable to concentrate. I turned on the television but my attention kept wandering. An uneasy sensation washed over me. There was a detail missing to my father's murder, but I wasn't sure what.

After Theo had regained consciousness and been taken to jail last night, he'd confessed to the murders of my father and Dennis Browning. I'd been at the police station when Theo's family arrived. It was obvious that none of them had any idea what he'd been capable of. Teddy had glanced in my direction but said nothing. Like me, he'd lost his father, but at least he could still visit his.

Wesley had been right. A small consolation for a man who was no longer living. *Heaven help me.* That was it. Wesley was the detail that had been missing. Theo had been out of town the night that Wesley was murdered. Someone had followed Wesley to my house and shot him in cold blood, but there was no way Theo could have done it. Had he hired someone to do the job for him?

On an impulse, I picked up my cell and called Simon, but got his voice mail. I stuffed my feet into sneakers, grabbed my jacket and purse, and headed out the door.

Five minutes later I pulled into the almost-empty lot of the *Maple Messenger*. I tried Simon's cell again, but he didn't answer. His car was the only one in the lot. I went to the double glass doors and started pounding my fists against them. After a minute, I spotted Simon running down a flight of stairs. His eyes widened in amazement when he saw me. He pushed the door open and let me inside.

"What's wrong? Is Mom okay?" His face was pinched with worry.

"She's fine, but I need a favor."

"I should have known this was coming," he said, and put an arm around my shoulders. "Well, you did save me from a life of prison, so I guess I owe you something."

We climbed the stairs to the newsroom on the second floor. Simon had a cubicle in one corner. All of the desks were cluttered with files and news clippings. To my surprise, Simon led me to a small office at the back of the room. "My new digs," he said proudly. "I've been promoted to head reporter."

I threw my arms around him. "That's wonderful! Does Mom know?"

He shook his head. "Not yet. I'll tell her tonight, when I come over for dinner. It only happened this morning. My boss called me when he heard the news about Theo. He apologized for ever doubting me and said that they'd been planning to promote me before this entire mess began. There's a raise involved, but it's going to take a long time until I'm out of debt."

"Mom will help you."

"No," he said sternly. "I got myself into this mess, and I'm going to get myself out of it. Now, tell me what I can do to help my favorite sister."

"Do you keep police reports on file here for murder cases?"

He looked surprised by my question. "Sometimes. It depends on the case. You're not talking about Dad's, right? I've already seen it and—"

"No," I interrupted. "I was wondering if you could get me a copy of the police report from Dennis Browning's so-called suicide."

His jaw hardened. "Why would you want that? Theo already confessed to killing him last night."

"Because we still don't know who killed his son, Wesley. He was gunned down right in front of me, and Theo was out of town that night."

Simon's mouth dropped open. "No freaking way. Some reporter I am, huh? I didn't even think about that."

"Can you please find it for me?" I pleaded. "I'm not sure if it will help, but there's something I need to check on."

He nodded. "Wait here. I'll have to search through the older records downstairs."

Simon was gone for several minutes, and I began pacing the floor. My mother was probably home by now and wondering where I'd taken off to. I sent her a quick text, saying I'd be home soon. After I pressed *Send*, my phone pinged with an incoming text. To my surprise, it was a message from Noah.

Hey Leila. I wanted to see how you were doing. It's all over town what happened last night. Do you feel up to some company this afternoon?

A warm tingle ran through me. Maybe I was reading too much into his message but I did want to see him. My fingers flew over the keyboard. Yes, I'd like that.

Simon's voice startled me out of my thoughts. He handed me a photocopy of the police report from Dennis's death. "Here you go, sis. It took a while, but I finally found it."

I scanned the details. Date of death—June 12, 2002. Approximate time of death—between 4:00 and 7:00 pm. There was a certain signature that I was looking for, and sure enough, I found it. I sucked in a sharp breath. *Pay dirt.*

"Thanks, Simon." I kissed him on the cheek. "Gotta run."

"Wait a second!" he called after me. "What's going on?"

I was already flying down the stairs. "I'll tell you tonight. Love you!"

Less than a minute later, I was pulling my car out of the lot and calling my mother with my hands-free. She answered on the third ring. "Hello?"

"Hi, Mom, it's me."

"Leila, where are you?" She sounded angry, and I wondered what I'd done now.

"I just stopped to see Simon. He gave me a copy of Dennis Browning's death report. I know who killed Wesley."

My mother sounded puzzled. "Who?"

"I'll tell you when I get home. I need to ask you a couple of questions, too."

She didn't answer. "Are you okay?" I asked worriedly. "Did I do something?" Disappointment settled in my chest. I'd thought that we were on our way to a good relationship, but instead, maybe things were back to normal.

"Leila," she said quietly. "Please come home right away. We need to talk."

She clicked off without another word. Dread settled in the bottom of my stomach. Great. I could feel another lecture coming on. For a moment, I debated about going to Heather's instead. That was something I'd done in the past when I knew my mother was angry with me. No, I was too old for that. I couldn't keep running away.

I pulled my car into the driveway behind my mother's. She wasn't in the doorway, so maybe that was a good sign. With a sigh, I inserted my key in the lock and walked into the living room.

Toast was the first one to greet me. He rubbed against my legs, purring and seeking attention until I reached down a hand to pet him. "Hi, big fella. Have you been taking care of things while I've been gone?"

He meowed once in response. "Mom?" I called. "Where are you?"

"I'm in the kitchen, Leila."

Mom appeared under the archway, her eyes large and dark in her slender face. She didn't look well, and, for a second, I worried that she might be ill. "Are you sick? What's happened?"

Chief Crosby appeared behind her and gave me a cordial nod. "Hello, Leila. We've been waiting for you."

His left hand held a revolver that was resting against the small of my mother's back.

CHAPTER TWENTY-FIVE

"ALAN," MY MOTHER WHISPERED. "PLEASE don't do this."

Chief Crosby reached into his shirt pocket for a handkerchief and wiped his forehead with it. "Both of you, into the living room. I'm sorry, Selma. I never thought it would turn out like this."

I clutched the police report against my chest. "You killed Wesley Browning."

Chief Crosby reached out a hand and grabbed the report from me. "Sorry, Leila. It won't look good if that's found with your body."

My mother whimpered out loud while I continued to stare in shock at the man I'd known my entire life. "You signed off on the police report for Dennis Browning's death. You swore that Dennis took his own life when you knew that Theo killed him."

Chief Crosby didn't respond, and my mother's eyes pleaded silently for me to shut up. She was probably more afraid that Chief Crosby would turn the gun on me instead of her. I thought back to all the times that my father had called Crosby a loyal friend. Had he known about his deception? Probably not.

"Is that why Wesley kept coming to see you about his father?" I asked. "Did he know Theo was the one to kill him? Or did he suspect that you were in on it, too?"

Chief Crosby snickered. "Wesley Browning was grasping at straws. The guy was a mental case. He didn't start becoming a pest until his mother died. When she was on her deathbed, she begged him to check into his father's death. She never believed that Dennis killed himself. That was when Wesley started calling me and stopping by the police station unannounced. He was like a whiny mosquito that kept hovering around me. I tried to put him off, but then he told me that he was going over my head to the mayor. He wanted the investigation of his father's death reopened, after all these years."

"And that was when you realized you had to get rid of him." The words fell from my lips.

Chief Crosby shot me a look of contempt. "Theo called me from New York that night and asked me to get the job done. It would have worked out well if you'd been killed, too, Leila, but Wesley had to go be the hero, sacrificing his life for yours. Very touching."

"Dear Lord," my mother whimpered.

"Dennis was supposed to sell his share of Sappy Endings

to Theo all those years ago," Chief Crosby continued. "But he sold it back to your father instead, and Theo was furious. He was always crazy about the farm. He saw endless opportunity for the place and said your father didn't know how to run it. Theo confronted Dennis and shot him in a fit of rage. Then he called me in a panic. I was already indebted to him so I had no choice but to help him cover up the murder up and make it look like a suicide."

"Why were you indebted to Theo?" I asked.

Chief Crosby shifted from one foot to the other. "Theo bailed me out years ago when I needed money. My wife ran up a stack of bills, and then, one day, she just up and left me for another man. I was in debt and needed money. My credit was bad, and I went to Theo out of desperation. He was so happy to help me out that he told me I didn't even need to pay him back, on one condition."

"That's when he put you on *his* retainer," I put in. "And the condition was signing off on the police report, saying it was a suicide."

"Say what you want, but I don't like being compromised in that manner." Chief Crosby ran a hand through his silver hair and refused to look at me. "My job means everything to me. It's all I have. Theo had me right where he wanted, and there wasn't a darn thing I could do about it. He wasn't asking for much—only that I looked the other way when one of his clients got into trouble. But at least I wasn't the one to pull the trigger on Dennis or your father. I loved Victor like a brother. I never could have hurt him."

"What a joke," I fumed. "As far as I'm concerned, you were an accessory to Dennis's murder, and my father's as well. *You* were the friend who did Theo a favor." Theo had mentioned it to me last night, but I never dreamed at the time that he'd meant Chief Crosby. "You planted the gun that killed my father in Simon's car."

"It had to be done," he said. "Everyone heard them arguing that day. He was the most likely person to frame. I was the one who slashed your tires. You were supposed to think that Wesley had done it."

My mother turned on him with a vengeance. "You piece of filth!" she shrieked. "How dare you do that to my son. Victor thought of you as his best friend, but that meant nothing to you. You're not fit to walk this earth."

In one sudden and vicious moment, Chief Crosby backhanded her across the face, and she sank to the floor.

"Mom!" I screamed and tried to rush toward her, but Crosby waved the gun at me.

"Stay where you are, Leila," he said quietly. "I told you to leave your father's investigation to the police, but you wouldn't listen. You're as stubborn as your father. I would have turned Theo in eventually, but you had to go and ruin everything. There's nothing left now but for me to kill you and your mother."

My mother sat up on the floor, her hand pressed against her bruised cheek. My eyes filled with tears as I watched her sitting there, so frail and defenseless. My grief turned to anger when I looked into Chief Crosby's eyes with defiance. "How will you explain our deaths?"

He shrugged. "Home invasion. Someone read about your father's death and knew that there were two women living alone here, with several valuables." He stuffed the police report into his pocket. "Even in a small town like Sugar Ridge, those things happen."

It was hopeless. We'd never get out of this alive, not the both of us, anyway. Simon wouldn't be here until dinner time. Crosby must have stashed his car within walking distance, and he'd managed to cover his tracks nicely. I wouldn't have expected anything less from Sugar Ridge's chief of police.

"Get down on your knees," Crosby ordered. "Both of you. Face the wall."

My mother reached for my hand and clasped it against her heart. Tears shone in her eyes. "I'm sorry, Leila. Not for me, but for you. You haven't even had a chance to live your life yet. Please, Alan. Let her go."

A clinking sound came from the kitchen. Crosby turned around with the gun in his hand, as Toast scampered across the top of the stove, knocking my mother's plate of kibbe onto the floor. I jumped to my feet and shoved the chief as hard as I could. To my surprise, he stumbled and fell on his back. My mother screamed and rushed toward me. At that moment, the door to the kitchen opened and Noah rushed in. He spotted the gun and dove for it at the same time that Chief Crosby did. He grabbed Noah by the shirt, but Noah drove his fist into the man's face. Chief Crosby went down in a heap while Noah waved the gun over him.

Noah glanced at my mother and me. "Are you ladies okay?"

My mother nodded weakly as I helped her to her feet. "Thanks to you," I said gratefully.

He smiled. "I don't know. You seemed to be doing fine by yourself."

"Call 9-1-1, Mom," I said.

My mother rushed to the phone and made the call while I grabbed some duct tape from a cabinet and secured Crosby's hands behind his back. He avoided my eyes.

"How did you get in?" I asked Noah.

"I was coming up the driveway when I heard your mother scream and ran to the kitchen door. I remember your father once complaining about Simon not fixing the lock correctly and was able to force my way in. Lucky for us that your brother hates home repairs, huh?"

The statement made me laugh. "Well, this is one arrest that the Sugar Ridge Police Department will never forget."

———————

"The party was a great idea, Mom." I cut the pieces of kibbe into triangles, its spicy smell making my mouth water. "Dad would have been pleased."

My mother's smile was wistful. "It's hard to believe that your father has already been gone three weeks. But I feel that he is still with us. He will watch over us in the days to come, my dear. And we are both very proud of the woman you've become."

She leaned in and put her arms around me. The gesture was so unexpected and sudden that I had to blink back tears. "Thanks, Mom. That means a lot to me."

Mom smiled warmly. "Leila, I know that you've only been home a few weeks, but I do hope that you will decide to stay, and longer than for the year that you promised your father. Of course, I understand if you would like to get your own apartment, as Simon did."

"Maybe someday," I said, "but, for now, I'm happy staying here. Besides, if I moved, who would get custody of Toast?"

Toast jumped onto a kitchen chair and meowed, as if voicing his opinion.

My mother laughed out loud. "Wonderful. I'm so glad you are staying."

"Only on one condition. That you don't make me take cooking lessons," I teased.

"Well, I can dream, right?" she laughed merrily.

Heather's voice drifted in from the living room. "There's no question about it. Leila has to stay. Now, what can I do to help that doesn't require any actual cooking?"

My mother handed her a tureen of spinach soup to bring into the dining room.

"Are we ready to start?" Heather asked. "I'm starving."

As if on cue, the doorbell rang. I wiped my hands on a dish towel. "I'll grab it."

Simon and Tyler were watching a football game in the living room, booing a recent referee call. As soon as I opened the front door, Emma bounded in with a big smile on her face. She handed me a bouquet of flowers. "Hi, Leila! My daddy said that you invited us for dinner."

"That's right." I stooped down to help her take off her jacket. "These are beautiful—thank you. I'm so glad that you could come."

Noah's mother stood in the doorway a bit awkwardly but smiled graciously. "Thanks for inviting us, Leila. You have a lovely home. Noah's parking the truck. He'll be here shortly."

"Please, come in," I said as she handed me a bottle of wine.

"I thought this might go well with the meal," she said. "I do love Mediterranean food."

"Hello." My mother whizzed past us with the plate of kibbe for the table and then held out her hands to Dorothy. "I'm Selma Khoury. It's very nice to meet you, Dorothy."

Dorothy smiled and squeezed her hand in return. "It's wonderful to meet you as well. Noah has said such lovely things about you and your late husband. I'm so sorry for your loss."

My mother's smile faded, as it always did whenever someone mentioned my father. "Thank you, Dorothy. He is with us today, I'm sure of it. Let me take your coat."

I went out onto the front porch to wait for Noah, who was walking up the driveway. He caught sight of me and smiled. He was dressed in navy dress slacks, a white Oxford, and navy blazer. The jacket brought out the blue in his eyes.

"You look beautiful," he said.

"Thanks," I smiled. "So do you. We're glad that you could come."

"I wouldn't have missed it," he said. "Your mom is a great cook. Is anyone else coming?"

I knew he meant Jessica and shook my head. "No. This is only for close friends and—" I caught myself in time, before saying *employees*. Noah was more than an employee. He'd become a friend and had helped to save my mother's life and mine. I felt indebted to him.

"Come on inside. Everything's ready." I shut the door behind us and led him toward the dining room, but he stopped me.

"I never told you why I was by your house last Sunday."

His tone was serious, and I realized that I'd forgotten about the reason as well. "I'm listening."

He smiled shyly. "I was wondering if you'd like to go to dinner with me some night after work, or maybe next Sunday. My mother's not going back to New York until after Thanksgiving, so I thought it would be a great time. I've heard that Medium Rare has great steaks."

My heart began to pound against the wall of my chest. "Is this a date?"

Noah's eyes lit up. "Yes, it's a date. Unless you have rules about not dating the hired help."

"Let's get one thing straight," I said. "I don't consider you the help. You're a huge part of Sappy Endings. If it wasn't for you, I might not have made it through my first week there. And not to mention that my mother and I are grateful you were at our house at the right time last week."

"Does that mean a yes?" he grinned.

"Yes, I'd love to."

He wrapped his hand around mine. "Great. I know we got off to a rocky start, but I'm really looking forward to getting to know you better."

"Me too." I led Noah into the dining room, where everyone was taking their seats. Heather shot me an inquisitive look, and then exchanged a smile with my mother. They'd obviously noticed that Noah and I had been in the other room for a while. I expected to get interrogated by both of them later.

"Mom, what else do you need me to do?" I asked.

"Nothing, dear. Everything's on the table, so sit down before it gets cold." She patted the vacant chair on her right side. "Sit next to me, Leila, and then Noah can sit on your other side, next to his daughter." She beamed at Emma and then winked at me.

Oh, great. My mother the matchmaker was back.

Noah pulled out my chair for me. To my surprise, Simon pushed back his and came over to us. He extended a hand to Noah.

"I never got a chance to thank you for what you did for my mother and sister the other day. And I'm sorry for misjudging you," he said sheepishly. "I hope that you'll be staying on at Sappy Endings for a long time to come."

Noah pumped Simon's hand in return. "There's no need to apologize. I'm only glad that everything worked out and your mom and sister are okay."

"It's still so hard to believe," Heather commented as

she passed the platter of kibbe to Tyler. "Two men with the most respected jobs in town—a chief of police and an attorney."

Noah placed some baked macaroni and cheese on Emma's plate. He'd told me that it was her favorite, so my mother had made the dish especially for her. "It just goes to show that anyone is capable of murder," he said grimly.

"Will you and your mother both have to testify?" Heather asked.

"I suppose so." I wasn't looking forward to it, and from the shadow that passed over my mother's face, neither was she. I knew how difficult this must be for her and reached over to squeeze her hand under the table. She patted mine in return, which meant that she would be okay.

"Leila, have you told Noah about Jessica's position?" Mom asked, and I knew this was her way of changing the subject.

"Selma, this kibbe is fantastic," Dorothy exclaimed. "It's made from lamb, right? You'll have to give me your recipe."

My mother's face flushed with pride. "I'd be glad to."

"When exactly is Jessica leaving?" Noah asked.

"Actually, her last day is Friday. Her son and daughter-in-law decided that they wanted to be settled in before the holidays." I shook my head at the wine that Simon offered me and poured myself a glass of *limonada* instead.

"What?" Noah looked thunderstruck. "There's no way that we can hire and train someone by Friday."

"It's already taken care of," I said. "We have our new employee."

Everyone turned their heads toward me. "You didn't tell me you'd hired someone," Heather said. "Who is it? Do I know them?"

"You certainly do," I laughed. "My mother is going to fill in for as long as we need her."

Simon's fork clattered to the floor. He bent down to retrieve it and accepted a new one from my mother. "I don't believe it. Mom, you said that you were happy staying home. What changed your mind?"

My mother forked a bite of tabbouleh into her mouth and chewed slowly, making Simon wait for her response. "I decided that, if Leila could put her teaching career on hold to run the farm, I should do my share as well."

"Will there be more Lebanese fare?" Simon asked.

Mom shook her head. "No, we will leave the menu the same. This is Leila's business to run as she sees fit."

A pleased expression came over Noah's face. "Wow. That's great. Is it going to be permanent?" He addressed the question to my mother, but his eyes were pinned on me.

Like the leaves outside, things would change forever. I would always miss my father but was grateful to him for this amazing opportunity, and I didn't mean only the farm. I was referring to the opportunity to get to know my mother better.

Mom smiled and shrugged. "We'll see what happens." She turned her head and gave me a sly wink. "Like my daughter, I've decided to take life one day at a time."

RECIPES

BAKLAVA

- 1½ pounds walnuts (You can substitute your favorite nuts or a mixture of nuts, including cashews, pistachios, almonds, or hazelnuts.)
- ½ cup granulated white sugar
- ½ teaspoon ground cinnamon
- ⅛ teaspoon ground cloves
- 40 sheets phyllo dough (9" x 14" thawed, store-bought)
- 1 cup melted unsalted butter

Preheat the oven to 350°F. Add the nuts to a food processor and pulse to chop finely. In a large mixing bowl, combine the walnuts (or other nuts), sugar, cinnamon, and cloves. Mix thoroughly. Grease a 9 x 13-inch baking pan with butter and layer 20 sheets of phyllo dough on top, using a pastry brush to brush each layer with melted butter. Add half the nut mixture and spread evenly. Layer 5 more sheets of phyllo dough and brush melted butter on each sheet. Add the remaining nut mixture and spread evenly. Add the remaining 15 sheets of phyllo dough, brushing evenly with melted butter between each sheet. Using a sharp knife, cut through the phyllo dough in a diamond or square pattern, making

30 to 40 pieces that are about 1½ inches wide. Bake for 45 minutes to 1 hour.

Maple Syrup Topping
(You can make this while the baklava is baking)

- 2 cups granulated white sugar
- 2 cups of water or rose water
- ½ cup pure maple syrup

In a medium saucepan, add all the ingredients and whisk together. Bring to a boil, and let simmer for 10 minutes. When the baklava is done, pour the maple syrup topping evenly over the cooked baklava. Allow the baklava to cool completely to absorb the syrup. The syrup will thicken as it cools.

Makes 30 to 40 pieces. Serve baklava cold, warm, or reheated.

MAPLE
SHORTBREAD COOKIES

For cookies:
- 1 cup unsalted butter, room temperature
- ½ cup pure maple sugar
- ¼ cup light brown sugar
- 1 teaspoon salt
- ½ teaspoon vanilla extract
- ¼ teaspoon maple extract
- 2½ cups all-purpose flour

For topping (optional):
- 3 tablespoons pure maple sugar

For maple icing (optional):
- 1 cup confectioners' sugar
- 4–5 tablespoons pure maple syrup
- Optional sprinkles or decorate with
  your favorite royal icing recipe

Beat the butter until light and creamy, and then beat in the
maple sugar, brown sugar, salt, vanilla, and maple flavoring

until well combined. Mix in the flour until the dough no longer looks dry and crumbly. Wrap the dough in plastic wrap and refrigerate for 2 hours or overnight. Preheat the oven to 350°F and line at least two baking sheets with parchment paper. Lightly flour a work surface and rolling pin. Divide the dough in half and roll out each portion between ⅛- to ¼-inch thick, depending on your preference. Using your favorite cookie cutters, cut into desired shapes and place on prepared baking sheets. Refrigerate for 10 minutes. If using maple sugar for topping, sprinkle the tops of the cutouts with the sugar. Bake for 10 to 12 minutes, until the edges are lightly golden. (Bake 9 to 11 minutes for thinner cookies and 11 to 13 minutes for thicker cookies.) Cool on the baking sheet for 5 minutes, then remove to a wire rack to cool completely. Makes between 20 and 30 cookies.

Maple Icing

If using maple icing instead of maple sugar for topping, whisk the confectioners' sugar and 4 tablespoons maple syrup together. If needed, add additional maple syrup until the icing is spreadable and smooth. Spread over the completely cooled cookies. Decorate with sprinkles if desired.

MAPLE SYRUP BAGELS

- 1⅓ cups lukewarm water, divided
- 1 tablespoon maple sugar
- 1 packet instant or active dry yeast
- 4 cups flour
- 1 teaspoon salt
- 2 tablespoons olive oil
- Maple syrup (optional)

Combine ⅓ cup of the lukewarm water, the sugar, and the yeast, and let sit 5 to 10 minutes until it foams. In another bowl, mix the flour and salt, and form a well in the middle. Pour the yeast mix and oil into the well, then cover with the surrounding flour. Add the remaining 1 cup water and mix until combined. Knead until the dough is smooth, around 10 minutes. Oil a large bowl, place the dough inside, and cover with a towel. Let it rise in a warm place until it doubles in size, 45 to 60 minutes. Split the dough into 8 pieces and roll into balls. Set on a baking tray and cover for 15 minutes. While waiting, bring a pot of water to a boil and preheat the oven to

425°F. (Tip: Add a small amount of maple syrup to the pot to give it a golden color.)

Using the end of a spoon, poke a hole in the middle of each ball and stretch the hole to 1.5 to 2 inches wide. Put the bagel into the boiling water and cook each side for 1 minute, then drain the excess water by placing the bagel on a wire rack. Next, line a baking sheet with parchment paper and place the bagels on top. Bake for 25 to 30 minutes until lightly golden brown. Makes about 8 bagels.

GLAZED MAPLE DOUGHNUTS

- 1 cup all-purpose flour
- 1 teaspoon baking powder
- 1 teaspoon ground cinnamon
- ¼ teaspoon baking soda
- ¼ teaspoon ground nutmeg
- ¼ teaspoon salt
- ⅛ teaspoon ground cloves
- 1 large egg, room temperature
- ⅓ cup packed light brown sugar
- ¼ cup milk, room temperature
- ¼ cup yogurt or sour cream, room temperature
- 2 tablespoons unsalted butter,
  melted and slightly cooled
- 1 teaspoon pure vanilla extract

For maple icing:
- ⅓ cup pure maple syrup
- 2 tablespoons unsalted butter
- 1 cup sifted confectioners' sugar
- ¼ teaspoon maple extract (optional, but recommended)

- Pinch of salt (optional)
- Bacon bits or pieces for topping (optional)

Preheat the oven to 350°F. Spray a doughnut pan with nonstick spray. Set aside. Whisk the flour, baking powder, cinnamon, baking soda, nutmeg, salt, and cloves together in a large bowl. Set aside. In a separate bowl, whisk the egg, brown sugar, milk, yogurt, melted butter, and vanilla together until completely combined. Pour the wet ingredients into the dry ingredients and whisk until just combined. Do not overmix. The batter will be thick. Spoon the batter into a large zip-top bag for ease. Cut a corner off the bottom of the bag and pipe the batter into each doughnut cup, filling about halfway. If you are short on pans, keep any remaining batter in the bowl at room temperature until you can bake the next batch. Bake for 10 to 11 minutes or until the edges and tops are lightly browned. Gently poke a doughnut with your finger. If it bounces back, the doughnuts are done. Allow the doughnuts to cool for a few minutes in the pan, then transfer to a wire rack.

Maple Icing

In a small saucepan over low heat, melt the maple syrup and butter together, whisking occasionally. Once the butter has melted, remove from the heat and whisk in the sifted confectioners' sugar, maple extract (optional), and salt (optional). Cool for 2 to 3 minutes, then dip each doughnut into the icing. The icing will quickly thicken, so feel free to place it back over heat as you dip. Place the dipped doughnuts back onto the cooling rack as excess icing drips down. Top with bits or pieces of cooked bacon, if desired. Doughnuts are best served immediately. Tightly cover leftovers and keep at room temperature or in the refrigerator for 2 days. Makes about 8 doughnuts.

MAPLE PORK CHOPS

- 4 pork chops
- 2 tablespoons butter
- Salt to taste
- ¼ cup minced onion
- ¼ cup maple syrup
- 1 to 2 tablespoons Worcestershire sauce
- 1 tablespoon apple cider or white vinegar
- 1 teaspoon chili powder
- ½ teaspoon pepper
- Sliced onions (optional)
- About 1 tablespoon flour to thicken the gravy

Preheat the oven to 400°F. Heat the butter in a large sauté pan over medium-high heat. Pat the chops dry with paper towels, sprinkle both sides of the pork chops with a little salt, and place in the sauté pan. Cook until brown, then flip over and brown the other side, about five minutes per side. Remove the chops from the pan and place into a high-sided baking dish or roasting pan. (If your pork chops are very thin and have cooked through at this point,

skip the oven step and tent them loosely with aluminum foil while making the sauce.)

Add the minced onion to the sauté pan in which you browned the pork and sauté for 2 to 3 minutes, until the onion begins to brown. Add the maple syrup, ¼ cup water, Worcestershire sauce, vinegar, chili powder, and pepper to the pan and bring to a boil. Pour the sauce over the pork chops in the baking dish.

Lower the heat to 350°F and bake, uncovered, for 10 to 15 minutes for thick (1-inch) chops, 5 to 10 minutes for thin (½-inch) chops, or until the interior temperature of the pork reaches 145°F.

Brown sliced onions (optional). In the same sauté pan that you used to make the sauce, add a little oil and heat to medium-high. Cook the sliced onions in the pan, allowing the onions to pick up any sauce remaining in the pan. Cook until lightly browned while the pork chops are baking, 3 to 4 minutes.

Place the pork chops on a serving platter and loosely tent with foil. Pour the excess sauce from the baking dish into the saucepan you seared the chops in and whisk in the flour to thicken the gravy. Salt to taste and serve the gravy over the chops and (optional) onions. Makes 4 servings.

Read on for an excerpt of
PENNE DREADFUL,
first in the Italian Chef Mystery series.

THE RICH AROMA OF TOMATOES and onion mixed and wafted through the air, hitting my nose with their distinct perfume. It was a soothing smell that blanketed me in its warm hold. If I were alone, I would have been content to stand in front of my stove all day.

I stirred the sauce and listened as my cousin Gino Mancusi flipped through the sports section of the newspaper at my breakfast counter and grumbled about his beloved Giants losing again.

"The season is pretty much over. I actually thought they might get another ring this time." He sighed and pushed the paper aside. "You shouldn't have gone to any trouble, Tessa. A sandwich would have been fine."

"It's never any trouble." I enjoyed watching others sample my creations and had vowed years ago that no one would ever leave my home hungry. Part of this obsession came from my love of cooking, but I attributed the rest to my Italian heritage. Italians are passionate about almost everything in the world, and food is at the top of the list.

"It's rare for you to go out for lunch," I said. Gino was a police detective in our hometown of Harvest Park. "Did Lucy tell you to come over and check up on me? Is it your day? Oh wait, let me grab the calendar."

"Stop being a smart aleck." He left the counter and came into the kitchen to grab ice out of the freezer for his soda. On his way back, he stopped and planted an affectionate kiss on the top of my head. "That's what family is for, Tess. We're all worried about you."

I squeezed his arm and turned off the burner. "Grab the Parmesan cheese out of the fridge, will you? I just grated it this morning."

Gino nodded without another word. I appreciated all that he and the rest of the family were doing, but I was determined not to start crying again today.

It was still difficult to talk about my husband's death, even with loved ones. I'd spent the last five weeks in a trance—or perhaps shock was a better term. Thanks to my mother, cousins, and my friend Justin, I had finally started to come around. Whenever I thought I'd fully recovered though, a kind word or a nice gesture from anyone would dissolve me into a puddle of tears again.

Last night, my elderly neighbor Stacia from across the street had brought me a fresh baked apple pie. "I know how much you love them, dear." She'd beamed at me from underneath a mass of pink foam hair curlers. Apple pie—anything apple, actually—had been Dylan's favorite, but I didn't have the heart to tell her so. Instead, I'd cried after she left and then devoured a huge slice.

Gino placed the cheese on the breakfast counter. He had classic Italian good looks complemented by dark hair, an olive complexion, and brown eyes that could either be sympathetic or suspicious. I suspected that the latter one was a cop thing.

"Right here at the bar is fine, Tess," he said. "Don't bother setting the table. I have to get back to work in a little while anyway."

"Okay, it's all ready." I ladled the ruby red sauce onto his plate of penne, inhaling the rich savory smell. It was a little bit like summer, with the sweet fragrance of vine ripe tomatoes complimented by the minty smell of fresh basil from my garden.

"It smells great," Gino said as he sat down. "Then again, I've never eaten anything of yours that wasn't top notch. You need to give Lucy some pointers."

"Lucy's a good cook. She's too busy taking care of those devilish twins of yours to do much else. I've got a little bit of extra sauce if you want to take some home to her."

Gino's eyes widened. "A *little*? Come on Tess, I saw your extra sauce." He wiped his mouth on a starched white linen napkin. "When I opened the freezer, there were at least 20 Ziploc bags in there. Maybe you're a bit obsessed with making sauce, huh?"

Like the rest of my family, Gino's focus was strictly on how the food tasted. For me, there was more to it than that. I loved the aromas, the spice, the way preparing food made me feel—relaxed, confident and in control. I'd been cooking for 20 years now, since the tender age of 10. My grandmother, a fabulous cook herself, and I had shared a special bond. Whenever we went to her house, I'd head straight to the kitchen to watch her make dinner and we'd chat the afternoon away. My love of cooking had come from her, and on my 13th birthday, she'd given me a special present—her secret tomato sauce recipe. She'd passed away when I was sixteen, and I'd taken the recipe and made it my own over the years, with the help of a few secret ingredients. Although I could make just about anything, tomato sauce was my passion and specialty, always bringing to mind wonderful memories of our time together.

"No, I'm not obsessed." There was silence in the room, except for the clink of Gino's fork hitting the china plate. He didn't understand. No one did. My love of cooking also helped soothe the grief of losing my husband, at least temporarily. Dylan had passed away a little over a month ago in a tragic and senseless car accident that would probably give me nightmares for the rest of my life.

This wasn't supposed to happen to us. We'd been young, in love, and trying to have a baby. Dylan and I were married for almost six wonderful years. Although by no means rich, we'd lived comfortably enough. Dylan had been employed as an accountant for a large health care firm, We Care, in Albany. As a certified CPA, he'd prepared taxes privately for several clients outside the firm as well. To add to our modest income, a couple of months before Dylan's death I'd begun working as a cook for The Sunnyside Up Café. Back then, my main goal in life—besides starting a family—had been to run my own restaurant someday.

Dylan had been extremely supportive of my passion. He'd always teased that he couldn't wait to quit his job and call me "boss," serving as my maître d'. Kidding aside, I knew he'd been just as excited about the venture as I was. Still, we didn't have anywhere near the funds necessary to make it happen. Since we'd bought the house only two years ago we'd been trying to put money away every month, but there were times when real life intervened. A new roof and hot water tank had helped derail the savings process for a few months. But we remained hopeful that it would happen within the next four or five years.

Five weeks ago, my dream had been replaced by a nightmare. My new goal in life was to simply make it through a day without crying, and my restaurant ownership dreams had been put aside indefinitely.

After the accident, I'd asked my mother to call Sunnyside and tell them I wouldn't be returning. I'd only been there for a few months and it wasn't fair to keep them hanging, although they'd been very supportive of my situation.

Even selling the house had crossed my mind a few times in the last couple of weeks. The first time the realtor had shown us the light blue Cape Cod, Dylan and I had both instantly fallen in love with its charm. Although only about 1400 square feet, it was perfect for us with its large bay window and hardwood floors. I especially loved the stee-pled roof and the window boxes built into the white shut-ters where I planted annuals every spring.

Now, however, it was difficult to stay here alone. There were memories of Dylan everywhere I looked. I missed so many things about him—his deep throated chuckle, the way he held me in his strong arms on lazy Sunday morn-ings in bed, and the long walks we'd take, hand in hand, after dinner on picturesque autumn days, much like this one. Early November in Harvest Park, although chilly, was the perfect time of year to watch multi-colored leaves fall from the trees.

The house was an ideal home for a young married couple and even had the classic white picket fence in the back yard. The only things missing were the standard 2.5 kids and dog, which I'd mistakenly thought we had plenty of time for.

Luigi squawked from the floor and stared up at me expectantly. A spoiled tuxedo kitty, he was looking for his share of lunch too. I cut up a small piece of sausage and set it on a paper plate in front of him.

"That cat eats better than most people do," Gino com-mented. He took another bite of the pasta and groaned with pleasure. "Amazing as always."

This was just the therapy I needed. "Thanks."

He watched me closely as I stood on the other side of the counter. "Aren't you going to eat?"

I shrugged and fiddled with the newspaper. "I'm not hungry."

"Tess." His voice was gentle. "Maybe it's time you went back to work. I'm sure you could get another job as a cook easily enough."

I stared down at my hands. "I don't know. I guess I'm afraid that I might break down in front of someone." My voice trembled. No, I wasn't going to do this now. I could—and would—make it through one day without bursting into tears. Dylan wouldn't have wanted me to carry on like this.

Gino put down his fork and walked around the counter to me. He took my hand and led me out of the kitchen and into my combination living and dining room. "Come on. I need to talk to you about something."

I dropped down on the navy loveseat and Luigi jumped in my lap, curling up into a ball on my knees. Gino sat across from me in the matching arm chair, a line creasing his broad forehead. "You're probably going to hate me for telling you this."

"What? The sauce was too spicy?" I joked.

He didn't laugh. "I should have told you sooner, but you've been so upset I was afraid it might send you over the edge."

Now he had my full attention. My stomach twisted at his words. "What's wrong? Is someone in the family sick? Lucy or one of the twins?" I didn't think I could handle any more bad news.

Gino shook his head. "It's nothing like that." He exhaled a deep breath. "It's about Dylan."

"What about him?" I asked sharply. "Just say it."

He reached forward to cover my hand with his. "We have reason to believe that Dylan's death wasn't an accident."

My body went rigid. There was no sound in the room except for my heavy breathing and Luigi's purring as he snuggled against me. A laugh bubbled to the surface. "Are you saying that someone intentionally killed my husband?"

Gino's mouth formed a thin, hard line. "It looks that way. We believe that somebody tampered with his vehicle."

Anger quickly replaced shock. "You said before that it was a car malfunction. How long have you known about this?"

"A few weeks."

"Meaning, since his death." I hated Gino at that moment. For God's sake, he was family. If you couldn't depend on your own family to tell you the truth, who could you trust? "So why am I only hearing about this now?"

"Look, Tess," he said quietly. "It's an ongoing investigation. We don't have all the details, and nothing has been released to the public yet."

Furious, I rose to my feet, forcing Luigi to jump down and scamper out of the room. "Who cares about the public? I'm his wife and you're my cousin! How could you keep this from me?"

Gino's face flushed and he put a hand on my arm. "You were so out of it those first couple of weeks. I was afraid if I told you then maybe you'd do something crazy, like—"

"Like what? Take my own life? Join my husband in the hereafter?" Angrily I shook his hand off and moved to stand in front of the bay window, looking out at my lawn covered with its gold and orange-colored leaves. "Please leave."

But Gino didn't leave. Instead, he came up behind me and put his hands on my shoulders. As a result, I crumbled. My shoulders started to sag, and the tears I was holding back finally broke free. So much for my new determination.

He held me in his arms while I cried. "I'm so sorry. I wasn't at liberty to tell you anything at first and then as time wore on, I was afraid. That's the real reason I came over today. Gabby said you seemed almost like your old self yesterday. She mentioned that you stopped by her store last night for the first time since Dylan died."

I straightened up and wiped my eyes. "I brought cookies for her club." Gabby was Gino's younger sister and owned a small bookstore, Once Upon a Book, that was only three streets over from where I lived in the center of town. She was my dearest friend, the sister I'd never had.

"Like I said, nothing has been released to the public, but details may have already started to leak." He looked faintly embarrassed. "I've been questioning some people around town, and so has another officer. Unfortunately, he let it slip to someone that the car was tampered with, so it probably won't be long before the news starts to spread."

"I see. In other words, you wanted to make sure you told me before someone else did." Anger surged through my body, mixing with the grief, and I almost wanted to slap him.

Gino wrapped an arm around my waist and led me back to the couch. "That's not it. I swear that I was going to tell you, but you're right, I shouldn't have waited so long. To his credit, his face was full of misery. "Should I go on?"

I inhaled a large gulp of air. "Yes. Tell me everything."

He hesitated for a second. "I don't *know* everything. As we told you from the beginning, a fuel leak was the cause. But it looks like someone tampered with his engine by loosening a fitting, which caused the car to catch fire. Passersby reported seeing flames shoot out from under the vehicle right before Dylan crashed."

"Okay, stop." I had lied, I didn't want to hear that part again—not about how my husband had been trapped in a burning car before crashing into a tree. He'd already been dead when the EMTs had pulled him from the wreckage, but I would always wonder what suffering he might have endured in those final moments.

Gino held fast to my hand. "I did some checking around. Dylan always brought his vehicle to The Car Doctor, right? Matt Smitty wasn't around the day before when Dylan brought the car in, but his mechanic Earl said they only did a tire rotation. He swore he didn't touch the engine." Gino paused, weighing his words before continuing. "You know that Smitty's not one of my favorite people."

I didn't want to get into this now. Matt had been my high school boyfriend. I'd broken up with him after he became too possessive, and Gino had never liked him. "But—" The words refused to fall from my mouth. I paused for a second and tried to gather my bearings. "That can't be right. Why would someone want Dylan dead?" The thought was incomprehensible.

Gino replied to my question with one of his own. "Did Dylan have any enemies?"

I gave him what I hoped was an incredulous look. "How can you ask me such a thing? Everybody loved him."

"Are you sure about that?" Gino's tone was suspicious. His "cop voice," as Gabby called it. "Maybe he screwed up someone's taxes? Reported someone to the IRS for doing something illegal? Did a coworker have it in for him?"

"No. No one I can think of." But Gino had planted a seed of doubt in my head. Maybe there was a disgruntled client Dylan hadn't told me about. "Did someone tamper with his car while he was at We Care? Have you checked out his office?"

"I thought he parked in the garage adjacent to their building. Isn't that for employees only? Plus, there are cameras on every floor."

I nodded, wracking my brain. "He had just eaten lunch before it happened. You were the one who told me his car was parked in the alley behind Slice before he… died." It still hurt to say the word. There was such finality attached, and I suddenly felt as if I was reliving that day once again.

Gino had been the one to come to my house to deliver the news. I was grateful it hadn't come from a stranger, but had immediately gone into shock. Slowly the memories returned, and then I recalled Gino mentioning Slice Pizzeria, the restaurant that Dylan constantly frequented.

A lightbulb switched on in my head. "Do you think that someone at Slice would know anything?"

Slice was a small restaurant situated at the end of the main street in Harvest Park and owned by New York City native Anthony Falducci. I'd met him a couple of times when Dylan had brought me there for pizza. The building was a bit of an eyesore from the outside. It needed a new roof and the brown paint was peeling in various spots. The surface of the blacktop in the adjacent parking lot was cracked in several places. Regardless, it was still a staple in the community and served mouthwatering pizza with a variety of delicious toppings.

"It's possible." Gino was silent for a second. "Actually, that's another reason why I wanted to come talk to you. I had a chat with Anthony, but he didn't have much to offer. I've been trying to get a line on his restaurant but can't find anything. I'm suspicious though. Slice may be the only place where someone could have had access to Dylan's vehicle that day. You guys have a two-car garage, and it would be difficult for someone to tamper with the vehicle at his office building."

I nodded but kept my thoughts to myself. If I could track all of Dylan's activities in his last few days, maybe it would lead me to whoever had killed him.

Gino went on. "Anthony seems golden. He got a speeding ticket a couple of years back but other than that, he's clean. The guy's been a pillar in the community for the last two decades. His brother Vince just started working at Slice and his daughter helps out when needed."

It was well known in Harvest Park that Anthony donated to several organizations every year. On Christmas day, the restaurant was open to anyone in need of a free meal, no questions asked. When word spread of Dylan's accident, Anthony had taken the news hard. I vividly remembered the tears in his eyes during Dylan's wake. "Dylan spent a lot of time there."

"He did," Gino agreed. "Especially lately," he said raising his eyebrows pointedly.

I bristled inwardly. "What does that mean? Why is it a big deal that he liked to go there for lunch? Dylan did Anthony's monthly taxes, so obviously they were close."

"It's just another angle to check out," Gino replied. "All I'm saying is maybe there's a connection."

I swallowed hard and locked eyes with my cousin. "Tell me one thing. Are you positive Dylan's death was no accident?"

I could always tell when Gino was lying. I remembered one especially frigid winter day when he and Tommy Harper were about twelve and they pelted Gabby and me with snowballs while we waited for the school bus, and then tried to pin it on someone else. His mother had seen through his lie as well. Policemen were trained to have unreadable faces, but this was my cousin. I could always see through the mask he wore.

His voice was sober. "No, it wasn't an accident, Tess. I'm so sorry."

I bit into my lower lip as tears flooded my eyes. "Then I want to know who did this." Someone had ended

Dylan's life and destroyed mine in the process. They needed to pay.

Gino stroked his clean-shaven chin in a pensive manner. "I knew you would feel this way." He hesitated for a minute. "If you really want to find who did it, you may be able to help us."

"Anything. What'd you have in mind?"

"There's a help wanted sign on the front window of Slice." He took a deep breath before continuing. "They need a cook."

If Gino had wanted to light a fire under my butt, he'd succeeded. I squared my shoulders, prepared to do battle. "Well, it looks like I'm going on a job interview today."

Acknowledgments

Special thanks to Baird Farm in North Chittenden, Vermont, for the personal tour of your amazing maple syrup farm and answering my endless questions. Jenna and Jacob, I owe you both a debt of gratitude!

As always, a huge thank you to my amazing agent, Nikki Terpilowski, for believing in me and my story. Thank you to my publisher, Sourcebooks/Poisoned Pen Press; editor, Margaret Johnston, who is always a joy to work with; and Findlay McCarthy.

Kudos to retired police captain Terrance Buchanan for taking time to answer my questions. Beta readers Constance Atwater and Kathy Kennedy always come through for me, no matter what the timetable is! Thank you to Kim Davis and Baird Farm for sharing their amazing recipes with me. To my husband, Frank, and sons, Phillip, Jacob, and Jared: thank you for putting up with me and all my weird little writing habits.

Last but not least, much love and appreciation to my cousins Betty Ann Stavola and Ellen Giannini for helping me brush up on our family history. Although I never had the honor to meet my maternal grandfather, I'm confident that he must have been a lot like Leila's dad.

About the Author

USA Today bestselling author Catherine Bruns lives in upstate New York with an all-male household that consists of her very patient husband, three sons, and several spoiled pets. Catherine has a BA in both English and performing arts, and is a former newspaper reporter and press release writer. In her spare time, she loves to bake, read, and attend live theater performances. She's published more than twenty mystery novels and has many more stories waiting to be told. Readers are invited to visit her website at catherinebruns.net.

PENNE DREADFUL

First in the Italian Chef Mystery series—tomato sauce isn't the only thing that runs red!

Local Italian chef Tessa Esposito is struggling to get back on her feet following her husband's fatal accident. And when the police knock on Tessa's door, things just get worse. They've discovered Dylan's death wasn't an accident after all, and they need Tessa to start filling in the blanks. Who would want her beloved husband dead, and why?

With the investigation running cold, Tessa decides it's time to save her sanity by reconnecting with her first love—cooking. And maybe the best way back into the kitchen is to infiltrate Dylan's favorite local pizza parlor, which also happens to be the last place he was seen before he died. Tessa has never been a fan of detective novels, but even she can see that the anchovies aren't the only thing that stink inside the small family business. And with suspects around every corner, Tessa finds that her husband's many secrets might land her in hot water.

IT CANNOLI BE MURDER

Teresa's biscotti have always been killer, but not like this

Six months after her husband's death, Tessa Esposito is hoping to drum up reservations for her restaurant's grand opening. And since a signing with bestselling author Preston Rigotta is sure to draw a crowd, Tessa agrees to cater her cousin's bookstore event, whipping up some of her famous Italian desserts. But the event soon takes a sour turn when Preston's publicist, an old high school rival, arrives and begins to whisk up their old grudges.

That night, a fight breaks out in front of the crowd, and it becomes clear there's bad blood in Harvest Park. And when the publicist is found dead on the bookstore floor the next morning, a stray cannolo at her side, Tessa knows who will be framed as the prime suspect.

To clear both her cousin's and her own name, Tessa must investigate the murder. But Preston's publicist has many secrets to hide, and in the end, the truth is bittersweet…

THE ENEMY YOU GNOCCHI

It's the deadliest thyme of year for the Italian chef

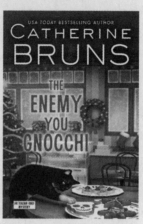

With snow dusting the ground and sauce sizzling on the stove, local chef Tessa Esposito is ready to serve up some holiday cheer. And with the annual Festival of Lights underway, it seems nothing can dim her spirits. Not even Mario Russo, the newest scrooge in town whose espresso bar has been quickly disrupting businesses and stealing customers from Harvest Park's favorite coffeehouse.

But when Mario is discovered at the festival's opening, face-down in a Santa suit, Tessa realizes the bah humbug runs deeper than she could have imagined. And when one of her dearest friends is implicated in the crime, she must make a list of Mario's enemies, check them twice, and discover the cold-blooded killer. Especially before they can sleigh again.